Smoked BY SCOTCH

Bohemia Bartenders Mysteries
Book Eight

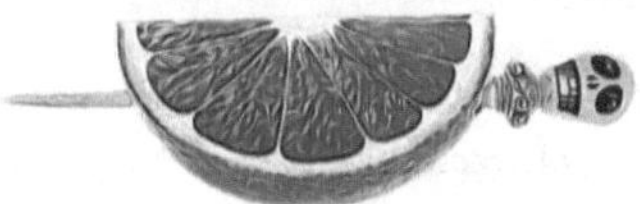

LUCY LAKESTONE

Velvet Petal Press
Florida

Cover design: Sky Diary Productions

First edition

Paperback ISBN: 978-1-943134-51-9

Velvet Petal Press, P.O. Box 922, Cocoa, Florida 32923

Learn more about the author at LucyLakestone.com

About the Book

Hijinks in the heather ...

Mixologist Pepper Revelle is excited about the latest Bohemia Bartenders gig, but she's even more thrilled about where it is—Scotland! She and fellow bartender Neil are finally a thing, they and their friends (and frenemies) are traveling in style, and making cocktails for an iconoclastic scotch distiller's big launch is the glitzy garnish.

Bonus: She gets to work with the sizzling hot Scottish celebrity and TV star who's the front man for the brand—at least until a shocking incident puts her on alert that there's trouble under all that plaid. Could their adorable spokesman's stalkers have leveled up to violence?

The team's job gets thornier than a thistle when they realize the Bartenders' clients have a lot more enemies than they've let on. From the enchanting streets of Edinburgh to the mystical vistas of the Orkney Islands, Pepper finds so many suspects, she's starting to wish a stone circle would whisk her back to Bohemia. As tensions mount, who will get kilt next? And can Pepper and her friends figure out the mystery before they're burned like a chunk of Scottish peat?

Smoked by Scotch is the eighth book in the Bohemia

Bartenders Mysteries, funny whodunits with a dash of romance set in a convivial collective of cocktail lovers, eccentrics and mixologists. These quasi-cozy culinary comedies contain a hint of heat, a splash of cursing and shots of laughter, served over hand-carved ice.

*For the people of Orkney
who made our visit so memorable, especially Magnus*,
who set the record for the most Americans squeezed into a compact car
as he uncomplainingly hauled us through history.*

*Not the Magnus in the book,
but I thought he wouldn't mind
if I stole his name.

A Note to the Reader

While (or whilst) I use American spellings that reflect my American heroine's voice, when it comes to scotch, Pepper and I have dropped the "e" in whiskey (whisky). That said, there are also Scottish words that may look odd to the uninitiated. Just go with it, baby.

And with apologies to the Orcadians, I have made stuff up. As always, there are more details in the Acknowledgments, which you should *not* read first.

- Lucy Lakestone

Chapter One

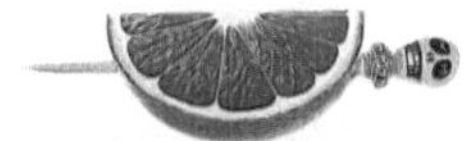

I loved the idea of elevating myself to superstar level in my career, but moments like this made me wonder if the top was all it was cracked up to be. Especially since getting to my Bohemia Bartenders gig involved a soaring staircase more suited to mountain climbers than mixologists.

Old Town, the part of Edinburgh with the castle and some of its most stunning historical buildings, sat atop a cliff that loomed over the rest of the city. Or so it seemed as I climbed approximately a thousand steep steps on my way to one of the most thrilling jobs of my life.

I almost didn't mind the stairs. Almost. I was in Scotland! Honestly, I wouldn't have minded making crappy vodka tonics in exchange for a location this magical. Apart from the stairs, that is. But the joy of this job was not just that I was here with my fellow mixologists and friends. We were also making scotch cocktails for an upstart distillery that dared to conceive of the tradition-rich whisky as something other than smoky sensuality in a glass. Though of course it was that, too, and to underscore just how sexy scotch could be, they'd partnered with a hot Scottish celebrity whose TV show I adored. I couldn't wait to meet him.

Arch Halliday was a big part of why we were here. His obsessed fans, dubbed the Archies by some snarky entertainment scribe, constantly followed the actor. With all the love came a lot of letters, including creepy correspondence that seemed linked to his scotch gig. The head of the distillery wanted us to identify the poison pens with the idea of stopping the harassment. He didn't want the stalkers to scare off his pet celebrity—or worse.

That much he'd confided to fellow distiller Mark Fairman, a friend we'd helped in the past. Mark had hooked us up with this job. We weren't exactly bodyguards, but Mark seemed to think I had a knack for solving mysteries, and who was I to turn down a trip to Scotland?

Especially when I got to share a room with Neil, handsome cocktail nerd, lead bartender and, finally, my boyfriend. Which was a weird term to use when you were twenty-nine and your love interest was a few years older than that—and definitely and deliciously a man, not a boy—but I'd take it.

We hadn't yet taken advantage of the room, in a hotel at the bottom of the cliff near the train station. Last night was spent on a plane. And we'd been super busy with our respective bars back in Bohemia, so it hadn't been easy to find time together. But we were actually *together* after a long, tortuous dance. At some point, I'd have a chance to get him alone during this magical trip. Right after I caught my breath and got through our first event this evening.

Thank Dionysus the staircases that twisted uphill between buildings had the occasional landing where I could stop and look at my phone and pretend I wasn't about to die.

And it was a good thing I dug my phone out of my fat canvas messenger bag and looked.

I had a new message from Neil: "Starting to set up. Hope you had a good nap."

Subtext: *Are you on your way yet, or do I have to send out a search party?*

"Be there in ten," I texted back. My navigation app said five, but I had to build in gasping breaks, given the cliff and the warmish late June afternoon.

It was sweet of Neil to let the mixologists on our team have a little rest before the gig, but I was pretty sure the other three were playing tourist. We all had other jobs. Luke usually worked in Neil's bar back home in Bohemia, and Barclay and Melody would soon open a brand-new bar in Bohemia Beach.

I probably should've stayed awake to beat the jet lag. But I'd barely slept for two days getting my bar, Nola, and its co-owner ready for my absence in Florida. To add a cherry to the cocktail of exhaustion, I had trouble sleeping on planes.

So Neil had a choice: cranky zombie or me, Pepper Revelle, my shoulder-length caramel hair pinned back on one side, looking cute in a fluffy fifties-style black dress with white polka dots and a pink crinoline with matching lipstick. I'd added comfy Mary Janes with lacy socks, saucy geek eyeglasses, and my good-luck gator-tooth bracelet. I'd thought about a plaid dress, but I didn't want to offend someone by wearing the wrong tartan.

I resumed my trudge up, passing a whisky bar (scotch whisky, no "e") and a Middle Eastern restaurant that hugged the slope, then refrained from kissing the ground of the Royal Mile once I arrived at the top.

The joyful bray of bagpipes and the chatter of tourists wafted through the air. I consulted my app and crossed the wide, cobble-paved road, where busy shops and cafes anchored towering buildings clad in beautiful gray stones.

I stepped aside to let a group of women dressed in Harry Potter-style robes pass. The one in front wore a sash that said

"Wizard Bride." Her nearest friend's sash said "Witch of Honor."

"Will you look at that hen do?" said a pink-cheeked, gray-haired woman armed with shopping bags who'd pulled up next to me to watch them go. "What happened to wearing a lovely dress?" Then she gave me a once-over and a frown. Perhaps mine didn't qualify. "Not from Edinburgh, are you?"

"No, ma'am. Florida." I looked down at my polka dots. Subtlety wasn't my thing.

"Ah, American. What a peculiar accent you have. Well, at least you're not dressed like a wizard." She marched off and melted into the crowds.

I loved *her* accent. And she'd underscored the first lesson an American needs to know about Edinburgh: It's pronounced *Ed-in-boro*.

I picked up the pace until I reached picturesque Victoria Street, another one of those places in Edinburgh said to inspire the Harry Potter books. I didn't see it, myself. Five-story stone buildings topped with chimneys and peaks and turrets, holding an array of colorful boutiques and eateries at ground level, lined the cobbled lane as it curved down the hill.

I consulted the map app on my phone, looking for the venue. And there it was on the right, its front gently concave, following the arc of the road upon which it sat. A hanging wooden sign declared it The Great Unknown. The bar's exterior was painted cobalt blue, the door red. Mirrored windows on either side of the door offered privacy for those inside while creating a reverse image of the busy, colorful street—and a group of perhaps a dozen women buzzing outside.

Could these be the Archies?

I looked at them curiously as I walked up and tugged at the heavy brass door handle with no luck. Locked.

I knocked, then extracted my phone again to text Neil as a cheerful, round-cheeked woman called out to me. She had long, dark brown hair that she'd probably spent a lot of time curling into perfection. She was possibly even shorter than me, which was saying something. She wore round, thick eyeglasses —so they helped her see, unlike mine, which mostly blocked squirting citrus fruits. She obviously wasn't worried about wearing the wrong tartan, given her neon-plaid skirt and pink Scotland T-shirt.

"They won't let you in yet," she said. I was surprised to hear an American accent, maybe Midwestern. "And we're not sure they'll let us in without an invitation, but we're going to try. I'm Wren Kent."

She stuck out her hand, so I stepped closer and shook it. "Pepper Revelle."

"Oh, are you an American, too?"

"Yep. Florida."

"Sweet! This is my sister, Lark." She indicated a woman who looked a couple of years older than Wren, late thirties, I guessed, wearing a boobalicious red knit top and dark jeans, her almost black hair highlighted with purple. Wren whispered, "We might rush the door. You can wait with us if you want."

"Rush the door?" I wasn't sure I'd heard her right.

Just then, the door opened a crack.

Wren and Lark immediately forgot about me as the cluster of women perked up, squealed and dashed forward, pushing me toward the doorway.

"Hey!" They slammed against me, a few screeching "Arch!" until the door at my back stopped me, hard. I put up my arms, trying to fend them off. It took a second for me to realize what was happening—the Arch Halliday effect. I tried not to panic as I yelled, "Back up!" I would've hated having my insides squished out of me like the cream in a puff on my first day in Scotland.

The women seemed to hear me and took the slightest step back. After a moment, I was able to ease away from the door. It inched open wider ... and Arch didn't appear. The fans deflated with a collective sigh and fell back into their scrum when they didn't see what they wanted.

I saw what I wanted, however, and let out a breath of relief. "Neil!"

He peeked through the slender opening and eyed the fan club gingerly. Then he smiled at me through his trim, dark beard and mustache, his gray eyes twinkling. "You OK? Want to come in?"

"Yes, please." I put my phone away in my bag, felt eyes on me and turned to face the flabbergasted group. Maybe I shouldn't have been so smug, but I couldn't help myself after my near-death experience. "It's cool. I'm with the band."

Wren's mouth dropped open, and I followed Neil inside.

Chapter Two

Neil firmly locked the door behind us, and I had a moment to take in the space.

The Great Unknown was a bar and a restaurant. The kitchen had to be busy, because I smelled good things cooking with a subtle undertone of ale.

Gleaming white floor tiles and soft pink walls suggested this place had undergone a contemporary makeover. Toward the front, sparkling chandeliers and a mirror ball hovered over the dining area, filled with blond wood tables. Farther into the space on the left, a bar of light wood with a stainless top glowed under metal pendant lights. Quality liquors filled the black back-bar shelves.

Black upholstered booths and overstuffed chairs along the wall opposite the bar, accented by fuzzy pink pillows, offered a relaxed place for drinking. Above them, mirrors and what appeared to be engraved book illustrations in ornate gold frames were interspersed with floating shelves holding gilded old books. Some spines said "Scott," others "Waverley Novels."

"Sir Walter Scott?" I wondered aloud. I'd already seen the impressive monument to the novelist near the train station.

"Also known as The Great Unknown," replied Neil, looking good in one of his natty vest-and-trousers combos with a sharp white shirt. "For a long time his books didn't credit him by name."

"How literary. And yet modern. This isn't at all the dark and gloomy whisky bar I'd expected."

"Kind of fits the image Aramach Distillery is trying to project. But don't be fooled. They have a fantastic scotch selection here." He tapped on his phone as he talked, then put it away with an apologetic smile as mine pinged in my bag. "I messaged the group and told the others how to get to the back door. I wouldn't want them crushed by the Archies."

"No kidding. They seemed so nice until they tried to trample me and eat you alive."

I looked back toward the windows. Now I could see through them. The fans were still out there, and as if she sensed me looking, Wren, the woman in plaid, tried to peer in through the mirrored side of the glass. They'd probably have better luck looking into the lit interior when it got dark, but it would be a while since the sun set so late here this time of year.

The room was empty of people except for a few women setting up displays of bottles and swag on a long table at the back. A slender woman with mahogany skin, an elfin nose, a sleek side-parted sixties-style mod haircut and a short green dress gave directions to the other two. They worked in the shadow of a vertical banner that showed a smirking Arch Halliday holding a glass of whisky.

She spotted me with Neil and walked over to us. "You're with the Bohemia Bartenders?"

"I'm Neil Rockaway, and this is Pepper Revelle."

"Izara Abbott," she said crisply, with a bright smile. Her accent was more London than Scottish. "I'm the marketing lead for Aramach. Let me know if you need anything."

"Thanks. I think we have it handled," Neil said. "We have three more coming."

She turned to me. "And I especially look forward to talking to you later."

"Me?" Then I remembered our other task. What exactly did Mark tell these people? I tried to adopt an intelligent expression. "Whatever I can do to help."

Izara nodded and smiled and went off to work again under the gaze of the Arch Halliday banner.

But there was no Arch yet. I might not want to mug him like the fans outside, but I couldn't help tingling a bit at the idea of meeting him. I wondered if he looked like he did on his TV show—muscular with a ready grin and twinkling green eyes and tousled dirty-blond hair.

Arch's series, *Sleekit Sim*, was kind of *Outlander* Lite. He and his cute redheaded co-star Rory Redland played rogues wandering across historic Scotland. They tweaked the noses of the English and got entangled in unlikely adventures. The show featured an occasional anachronism or nod to magic— though no one traveled in time via stone circles. One critic drolly called it a mix of *Rob Roy* and *The Dukes of Hazzard* with a touch of *The Adventures of Brisco County, Jr.,* and everybody loved it, me included.

Would Arch wear a kilt? Oh my gosh.

Down, Pepper. Down, girl.

Neil caught my eye and maybe my pheromones and leaned in for a light kiss. *Ahh.* Definitely better than some movie-star fantasy. Though I still had movie-star fantasies sometimes.

"We have minimal setup to do," Neil said. "This place has a couple of great bartenders who got our supplies for us, and I arrived early to make the Earl Grey honey syrup."

"Is that for the Sherlock & Watson?"

"Yes. A borrowed recipe."* Neil seemed chagrined that it wasn't one of his originals. "I'm saving mine for the big party in Kirkwall."

"Oh, you'll make it your own, and you know it will be delicious. What else are we having?"

"A Bobby Burns."

"Nice," I said. "It's good to have a classic cocktail on the menu, though some scotch drinkers will never have it any way but straight."

"We'll serve the whisky neat, too, or over hand-cut cubes, but interestingly, that's not our client's focus," Neil said. "Though I worry he wants to make scotch into the next vodka."

I chuckled and then brightened as the other three Bohemia Bartenders entered via the kitchen door. "Hey, guys!"

"Hi!" Melody waved, her blue eyes bright. She halted to gawk at the vertical banner of Arch Halliday. I mean, who could blame her? She looked fabulous, as usual, with her blond hair piled up on her head and a short black dress hugging her pinup-worthy figure. Flowers and music notes swirled up her arms.

Luke, who I was sure still crushed on her in spite of his recent forays into dating, pretended not to notice her ogling the banner as he swaggered in wearing a black aloha shirt with white flowers. Its short sleeves showed off his tropical tattoos. He wore his gold-streaked brown hair almost to his shoulders, had pretty brown eyes, and was unusually pale for a Florida boy, making his "Twilight" nickname understandable.

His equally handsome buddy Barclay, with tightly cropped wavy black hair and a bit of manly scruff, wore almost the same

---

* *Created by Kenaniah Bystrom at Seattle's Essex.*

shirt with an inverse pattern, revealing the dragon and other characters inked on his arms. The white background of the fabric popped against his light brown skin as the amber highlights in his green eyes sparkled. I suspected they'd enjoyed a cocktail or two before joining us at The Great Unknown.

"What's up?" Barclay called out.

"Lemon twists or carving ice cubes?" Neil asked.

We both knew Barclay would choose the ice. "Got a knife?"

"And a glove and a mallet," Neil said. "The ice block is in the freezer in the kitchen. One of the staff can hook you up."

Barclay nodded. "If I can tear them away from their fancy snacks."

"They're eating fancy snacks?" Luke asked.

Barclay playfully slapped the back of his head. "They're *making* fancy snacks. Didn't you see them?"

"Oh. Right." He probably didn't notice because he had eyes only for Melody. "I'll work on the twists."

"I'll help," Melody said.

"We'll use those for the Sherlock & Watson. Save the ugly ones for expressing over the Bobby Burns, the Craddock way," Neil said. "We'll get the hint of lemon but garnish them with two Luxardo cherries on a pick for a different look. Pepper, want to handle the *mise en place*?"

"Sure, I'll get us set up. Ooo, do we have little swords for the cherries?" I joked.

"Actually, yes, and they're branded for Aramach Distillery," Neil said.

"Awesome!" I loved cocktail swords. Probably because my very first Shirley Temple as a kid came with a bright red cherry stabbed with one.

I headed behind the bar, stuffed my bag into an empty

cubby, and worked with Luke and Melody to get ingredients and tools lined up. We set up different styles of coupe glasses to serve the two cocktails, as well as rocks glasses for the two types of scotch featured tonight. Neil squeezed lemons.

The cocktail swords were custom metallic purple plastic picks, a nice big size for a pick and vaguely dangerous, with an *A* incorporated into the sword's handle to represent Aramach. We could easily rest a pick on top of a glass—also etched with the ornate *A*—as it skewered the two cherries.

As we worked, more people arrived through the back, including a ruddy-cheeked man shaped a bit like a tree stump, with a facial expression somewhere between worried and grumpy. What was left of his hair was light brown touched with silver. His suit was a bit tight around the middle. He carried two waist-high chrome posts with a length of red velvet rope, the thick type used to keep undesirables out of hot nightclubs, and he headed out the front door with it. In a moment, I heard him barking at the Archies to back away. At least I thought that was what he was saying. His accent was as thick as a bog, especially through the closed door.

"Who's that?" I asked Neil.

"I met him briefly. Magnus Scarth. Security, I think."

Also among the handful of new back-door arrivals was a clean-shaven fortysomething fellow of modest height, with what I suspected was a spray tan, wearing a brown sport coat. He walked right up to Neil. "Neil Rockaway, isn't it? I recognize you from the picture on your book," he said with a smile that, with his curly brown hair, gave him a roguish look.

"Mr. MacIvor?" Neil, mid-squeeze, started to wash his hands of lemon juice so he could shake, but our client—I recognized the name—waved him off.

"Call me Seamus, please." Seamus MacIvor put his

hands on his hips and looked us all over with a pleased grin, his eyes lingering on Melody. "Oh, yes, you'll be just perfect." Which sounded kind of like *pairrr-fect.* I loved it.

Though how could he tell we'd be perfect just by looking at us? And then I remembered our final gig would be filmed for a TV commercial. Melody had been working on finding us the right outfits for weeks.

"We're just about ready to go." Neil looked at his retro watch. "When are you opening the doors?"

"Five minutes. Magnus will let in the invitees, and then our stars will arrive about fifteen minutes after that. We want a full house so Arch can make an entrance."

Stars? Naw, he must've meant *star.* If both stars of *Sleekit Sim* showed up, my head might explode.

"Which of you is Pepper?" Seamus continued, still eyeing Melody.

"That would be me. Pepper Revelle. Nice to meet you." I waved a cocktail sword at him.

His head swiveled, and his smile flickered for a moment. I was never as glamorous as Melody. "Ah. We'll talk in more detail later about our little problem, but keep an eye out. All right?"

"Yes, sir." I'd already met the Archies. Even if they weren't the source of the stalker letters, they were dangerous if you got between them and their idol. Or a closed door.

Barclay appeared with a bag of freshly cut ice cubes and stowed them in the freezer under the bar. He was accompanied by the restaurant's head bartender, a cheerful woman in a leather apron who gave us a few last-minute tips on how things worked and promised to help with any off-menu requests. Modern lounge music started pumping through the sound system. And then the doors opened and the place filled with happy guests.

As a man and woman emerged from the kitchen with trays full of tasty-looking morsels and made the rounds, we got busy shaking the Sherlock and stirring the Bobby Burns, garnishing one drink with a lemon twist and the other with the skewered cherries. We also poured scotch neat or over Barclay's beautiful, big clear ice cubes, depending on what the partygoers wanted.

"I'll take the twelve-year with ice, Hot Pepper," came a familiar voice in a yummy English accent. Yes, I was an accent whore.

I looked up into the golden eyes of hot redhead Mark Fairman. "Oh, wow, I wasn't sure if you'd be here. Thank you! Thank you so much!"

"Whatever for?" Our distiller friend from London took the glass from me, ran it under his nose and closed his eyes, inhaling its smoky-sweet aroma.

"Getting us a job in Scotland, of course! Anyone else we know going to be here?" I looked around, hoping to see botanist Diana Silva, who traveled the world looking for botanicals for Mark's gin. I had a feeling something was brewing between those two.

"Not unless you count Mr. Mixy. He's outside waiting to capture the celebrity arrival with his crew. Apparently he's filming another season of his television show."

"Oh, no," I groaned. There seemed to be no avoiding my ex-boyfriend, a Los Angeles-based celebrity mixologist with a big beard and a bigger ego. I poured a whisky for another guest and handed it over, though I suddenly wanted a drink myself. "Diana won't be here?"

"Not tonight. She's at the botanical gardens. But she'll be

joining us for Orkney." A smug little smile took over his lips. Hmm. Maybe something *was* going on there.

I grinned. "Excellent."

Another familiar face popped up behind Mark.

"I'm here, of course." Mixologist Alastair Markham co-owned London cocktail bar The Dandy Tipple with Mark. He pushed a swoop of blond hair back from his forehead and scowled at our team. "I'll take a Bobby Burns."

"You should be helping these fine people," Mark said idly, "not ordering cocktails."

"We're doing just fine," Neil said.

"As the hired help? At that, you excel," Alastair said with mock politeness.

"Hospitality is what we do," Neil told his frenemy. Alastair, who went to Oxford, liked to make a point of Neil dropping out of that prestigious university to follow his heart—mixology. "It's a calling," Neil said, "making excellent cocktails, ideally for people who can appreciate them."

Barclay snickered at Neil's subtle dig and handed Alastair his drink. Unsure if he'd been insulted, the slender barman huffed and stalked off into the crowd.

"Why do you bring him?" I asked Mark.

"He amuses me. He makes excellent cocktails. And he's had a terrible year, what with the Tipple repairs and his parents undergoing an ugly divorce-by-tabloid. I'm hoping a bit of travel will cheer him up."

"Oh. Poor Alastair." I wasn't used to thinking of Alastair as anything but a grump. Maybe I could help?

"And Victoria is coming as well," Mark added.

"Your Cavalier?" I exclaimed. Mark had an adorable Cavalier King Charles spaniel he'd loaned to me when we visited

London so I wouldn't miss my dear Cavapoo Astra too much. "I love her. Who's watching her now?"

"I paid someone at the hotel a ridiculous amount of money to walk her and stuff her with treats. Fear not. I pamper all the women in my life." He waggled his eyebrows at me and sauntered off as I laughed. One thing I could always count on was outlandish flirting from Mark Fairman.

The room was filling up, and the drinkers kept us busy for another few minutes. After giving another Sherlock & Watson a good shake, I heard something odd above the music and chatter.

I froze. "Do I hear ... screaming?"

Chapter Three

"Yes, you hear screaming," Luke agreed, pausing with his own cocktail shaker in midair to gaze toward the closed door and the high-pitched shrieks occurring on the other side of it. A titter went through the crowd, and the rest of the bartenders also stopped and looked.

Maybe our crew had seen a little too much excitement over the past year or so, but my imagination went wild imagining the bloodbath happening outside.

Neil, ever steady, just chuckled. "I think that means our star has arrived."

"Oh my gosh." I quickly strained and garnished the drink and handed the coupe glass to my guest, a pale woman of about forty who was so distracted she almost spilled it. She gave me an embarrassed, conspiratorial grin. She felt it, too. The Arch Halliday effect. We were going to meet him! Arch! Sleekit Sim himself!

After a breathless few moments, the door opened, revealing a screaming clot of Archies straining against the velvet rope, Magnus's broad back as he extended his arms to hold them at bay, a glint of a white limo, and, after a moment, Arch Halliday himself.

First he waved and blew a kiss to the Archies, who

screamed even louder. Then he stepped into the room, with another man closing the door right behind him.

Melody gasped as Arch took a bow and the crowd burst into applause.

"Rory Redland too?" my friend said. "Be still my ovaries."

I felt kind of dizzy for a second. "Both of them? I think I need a drink." I'd met famous people before but never someone who'd been my computer wallpaper. Today, though, they weren't wearing kilts.

Arch sported a sexy blue suit and tie perfectly tailored to every brawny inch, complementing his ruffled blond hair and scruffy beard. Redheaded Rory, more wiry but still muscled, as I knew from all the times they showed off their pecs on the show, was clad in jeans, a black jacket and an open-collar white shirt. He had a hint of a beard that he usually wore longer on TV. They both looked like they'd just tumbled out of a glossy magazine. And maybe another bar, given how jolly they were.

All of a sudden we bartenders were a lot less busy as the two actors worked the room, shaking hands, signing the occasional autograph, posing for pictures and making their way to where Izara waved at them in the back. Only they took a detour and headed for the bar as the crowd, its energy pumped up a level, got back into drinking and talking.

I pinched myself and tried to breathe as Rory went to Melody ... and Arch came right up to me and smiled. It was like looking into the sun.

"Wha— what can I get you?" I eked out.

He cocked his head with a mischievous look, and then that intoxicating accent touched every word that dropped from his lips. "Well, I suppose I'd better get a whisky, considering."

A giggle bubbled out of me. "Scotch, I presume?"

He gave me a genuine chuckle as I used tongs to drop a

pretty cube in an Aramach rocks glass and doused it with a generous pour of the twelve-year-old scotch. I handed it over carefully, scared I would somehow spill it on his spiffy suit.

"Thank you ...?"

Oh. Wow. Arch wanted my name! "Pepper. Pepper Revelle of the Bohemia Bartenders."

"I've heard of you. All of you." He scanned our team, including Melody, who, oblivious, stared into Rory's eyes as she handed him a Sherlock & Watson. Arch turned back to me. "I'm glad they invited *someone* famous to this party."

At that, we laughed, as did everyone within earshot. And then he grinned and I was able to breathe again as he headed toward Izara and Seamus MacIvor, who looked as if he'd just won the lottery. And why wouldn't he? His pet celebrity glowed like the big star he was, and he would probably help Aramach sell a river of scotch.

Photographers' flashes went off as Magnus let in a cluster of media folks, including Mr. Mixy and his three-person crew, and closed the door behind them. They pressed forward, trying to get shots as Magnus attempted to keep them from running over the honored guests.

Mr. Mixy, known to debt collectors everywhere as Stephan Sully, crossed his arms and let his crew do their job—two guys with cameras and a woman with a boom microphone. He seemed to have a different crew every time I saw him. I wasn't surprised. I couldn't imagine actually working for him. His expression—at least what I could see of it behind the voluminous beard—fell somewhere between smug and annoyed, probably because, as famous as he thought he was, he was sure more people should've been paying attention to him.

Ugh. I didn't need to think about him right now. We had Arch Halliday and Rory Redland in the room!

Izara and Magnus had cleared a small space in front of Arch and Seamus while Rory leaned against a wall, drinking and looking on.

"Ladies and gentlemen," Seamus began after introducing himself, "I appreciate your support of Aramach Distillery as we reach this landmark moment. You've tried our gin." A small cheer greeted this declaration. "And now you're enjoying our whisky. I'd like Arch to tell you a bit more."

The cheer was bigger this time as Arch grinned, shook Seamus's hand and took a step forward. "I'm Arch Halliday."

This declaration was greeted with laughter. There was just something so funny about him introducing himself to a room full of fans, but more than that, his whole demeanor. It was the charm, the charisma that made him so fantastic on screen.

"Ye may know me as a certain Sleekit Sim," he said to more applause. "But I'm here today as a whisky aficionado and, indeed, distiller, as I've a hand in these wonderful whiskies from Aramach. First, we have the twelve-year." He regarded his glass, took a sip and smiled knowingly to the chuckles of his audience. "Ah. It's lovely. And we also have the verra interesting Tropical Timeless Reserve, a single malt that's not only been aged in rum barrels but aged, in part, in the Caribbean, where the hot, steamy atmosphere"—said with a flirty lift of an eyebrow—"accelerates the process and delivers a most delicious, sexy scotch. That's what happens when you take an eight-month holiday in Jamaica."

The guests chuckled, and some headed right to the bar and pointed to the bottles of Tropical Timeless. We did a flurry of pours as he continued.

"Now the world is about to enjoy these magnificent whiskies, and you are the first. So I hope you'll tell a friend or two about them." To the cheerful murmurs of assent, he lifted his glass. "A toast is appropriate, and given we're here in The Great Unknown, where Rory and I've been known to quaff a cocktail or two ..." Arch's friend lifted his glass and grinned. "I'll steal from Sir Walter Scott. After all, he used the word 'sleekit' to describe a sly little mouse in one of his poems."

Everyone in the room lifted their glasses, and Neil quickly poured us shots of the Tropical Timeless so we could join in.

Arch began, "'Here's a bottle and an honest man!' Well, uh, I can't guarantee all that." As he lowered his glass and looked around, everyone laughed. He raised it again. "'What would ye wish for more, man? Wha kens, before his life may end, what his share may be o' care, man?'" He paused dramatically before continuing. "'Then catch the moments as they fly, and use them as ye ought, man. Believe me, happiness is shy, and comes not aye when sought, man!'" Then he said something that sounded like "slan-je-va"* that I'd have to learn to spell later.

Those in the know responded in Scottish Gaelic and drank, and the bar filled with happy noise once again.

"Cheers," Neil murmured to us, and we drank.

"Mmm," Barclay said.

I had to agree. I wasn't into the super smoky scotches, but this one was very accessible, sweet with a touch of fire on the lips, just a hint of peat and an echo of the rum once aged in its barrels. I was kind of relieved. It's always good to know your clients know what they're doing.

"Magnus, now!" Seamus called out to the security man, who'd returned to the door. He opened it, and after a few seconds and a strange bleating sound, a line of about ten bagpipers and a couple of drummers proceeded into the

---

* *Slàinte mhath*

already crowded bar, blasting a merry tune. They snaked through as if they were in a conga line to the clapping of the guests. My heart beat a little faster. Say what you will about bagpipes, but hearing them live and in person was absolutely electrifying.

The man at the end of the line seemed to be having trouble with his instrument. He wasn't blowing on it; he struggled with the plaid bag part, and he actually stuck his hand into it. Before I could think, *That's weird,* he pulled something out.

It took a second for it to register. "Gun!" I cried.

Chapter Four

I wasn't sure if anyone heard me over the bagpipes, and I wondered for an instant if I'd panicked for no reason, because the gun resembled a pistol but also really didn't. It was black and green and funny-looking. Yet the bagpiper lifted his arm and started shooting, *rat-atat-tat-tat-tat*. It wasn't nearly as loud as I thought a gun should be as he waved the pistol around and fired.

"Get down!" Izara screamed at the stars as chaos erupted everywhere simultaneously. The bagpipes yowled to a halt, people hollered and dropped to the floor, a panicked guest knocked down Magnus as the guard tried to get closer to the shooter, mirrors broke, and something hit me right in the chest.

I squeaked, and Neil grabbed my arm and yanked me down behind the bar. I covered my head as a glass shattered above me, trying to come to grips with what was happening. As quickly as the shooting began, it was over. The door slammed. The screams fizzled.

And I heard the weirdest thing. Laughter.

The chuckles started small and then grew, even as a sob or two filtered through the sound of people recovering from a terrible shock.

"It's all right," Magnus called out. "He's gone."

I slowly stood with the rest of my friends and looked around. Then I looked down at myself.

"Pepper!" Neil looked frantic. "You're hit!"

I touched the splotch of pink on my right boob. Or, to be more specific, on my beautiful polka-dot dress where it hugged my right boob. "That bastard!"

"Oh my God, are you OK?" Melody asked, her eyes wide.

"It's paint," I said incredulously. "But it hurts. Was that a paintball gun?"

Neil gathered me to him in a fierce hug, so I hugged him back. He was warm and smelled so nice. Like citrus and spice. Comforting.

"You're going to mess up your vest," I whispered into his ear.

He released me and kissed me and rubbed my arms. "I don't care about my vest." Though he glanced down at the pink smear on it and frowned. "I'm just so relieved you're OK."

"You too." I scanned the rest of the room. "I wasn't the target. Look at this. It's a mess." I thought of our client. "What about Arch?"

We all looked toward the back of the room, where Arch was making a finger gun and pointing it at Rory and laughing. Rory waved his hands, denying whatever Arch was throwing at him. Both of them had multiple pink splotches on their handsome clothes, as did Izara and Seamus and several of the guests. Some of the mirrors were cracked and spattered with paint. Vivid splotches of darker pink marred the pale pink walls. One woman held her head where she'd been hit; a round bruise was already rising, but she wasn't bleeding. Bagpipes gasped and groaned as the musicians rose and turned to each other in apparent disbelief.

"I've called 999," Magnus said as he hustled up to Seamus. "I'm so sorry, sir. I didn't see it coming. Someone knocked me down, and just as I got up again, the gunman bowled me over on the way out. And I'm not properly armed."

"No way for you to stop him," Seamus replied, though he looked furious that someone had spoiled his launch party. "Who was it?"

"That I don't know." A few people headed toward the door, but Magnus held up his hands and shouted, "No one can leave yet. I'm sorry, but I'm certain the police will want to ask some questions."

"Really, Magnus?" Seamus asked more quietly as some guests grumbled. "Do we have to make all this fuss?"

"Someone just shot up your reception, sir," Magnus said. "We must take every precaution. Who knows? He might be waiting outside with something worse."

That thought seemed to give Seamus pause. He quirked his mouth and nodded.

"It wasn't me!" Rory was saying as Arch gave him a friendly punch in the shoulder. "I swear it."

"Aye, we'll see about that," Arch said. He looked around at his stunned guests, who were checking one another out nervously. "Is everyone all right? We like to keep things exciting around here."

His light tone seemed to relax the restless crowd. Maybe it was all a joke, *Sleekit Sim* style. But if it was a joke, who would do such a thing? Rory? Arch? I'd read in some interview that they loved to play practical jokes on each other, but this was a level above, given how many people were caught in the cross-fire. And the bar was trashed.

We didn't have much time to ruminate. Trapped as they were, the guests, some shaken, some sporting pink splotches and looking a lot less fresh than when they came in, hit the bar hard. We served twice as many drinks in the fifteen minutes after the attack as we did in the fifteen minutes before Arch and Rory came in. And then there were sirens. Medical folks arrived to check out the injuries—all light, it seemed—and a couple of uniformed police examined the scene and took pictures.

They were joined by two detectives who interviewed and released the eyewitnesses at a speed that suggested they didn't take the incident too seriously. The dark-haired man in the gray suit talked to the celebrities and Seamus's people. The redheaded female detective, in a dark blue blazer and matching trousers, set up at the other end of the bar to vet the rest of the crowd, so I overheard a lot of the questions.

It seemed no one had seen much. The gunman wore a kilt and looked like all the other musicians. The bagpipers said they'd been hired by an agency and they didn't all know one another, just met up a street over; the bad guy never spoke. And they weren't sure if he even played. As one piper put it, "It's hard to tell when you're in the company of a pipe band going at full blast. But given I heard he pulled the gun out of the bag, it probably wasn't even a workin' set of pipes."

Neither Mark nor Alastair saw anything useful. Mr. Mixy's crew pledged to hand over their footage, but they said they didn't have much.

"I'm sure of one thing, though," Mr. Mixy told the female detective doing most of the interviews. "His beard wasn't real."

"How do you know?" she asked.

"I know." He stroked his huge black beard as if it were a beloved pet cat. I winced. "It didn't even sit on his face straight. And it wasn't a nice one, either."

"I see. Thank you, then, Mr. Sully, is it?"

"You can call me Mr. Mixy." He winked at her, and she turned a stony gaze upon him. He grimaced and turned back to join his crew—but not before shooting me a smarmy smile.

By then, most of the guests, including Mark and Alastair, had left. Seamus told us to stop serving drinks, so the female detective took the opportunity to question our bar team. And we didn't have much more to say than everyone else.

"That was a paintball gun, right?" I asked her. "It looked funny."

She eyed me with her pale blue gaze. "Given no one's dead and the place looks as if the Cat in the Hat got loose in here, yes, it was a paintball gun. How would you describe it?"

"Black and bright green. A pistol but sort of funny-looking, not like a real gun."

"That seems to be the consensus." She took notes anyway as we told her what we'd seen. "You ever see him before?"

We all told her we hadn't.

"Have you talked to the Archies?" I asked, then elaborated to her questioning look. "The Arch Halliday fans who were gathered outside."

She frowned. "They weren't there when we arrived."

Maybe I'd jumped the gun, so to speak, by mentioning Arch's fans. I didn't know the whole story yet about the creepy letters, only that there'd been some. Seamus would no doubt share relevant details with the cops.

The lady detective didn't seem that interested. She moved on to look at the security camera footage from the door.

Magnus ushered the last guests out after Arch and Rory signed a few autographs, so now it was just Seamus's people and us bartenders in the room with the detectives.

"I'm sure it was just a bit of mischief, all in good fun," Seamus told the male detective, "but I can't tell you who was behind it, since no one is confessing." He gave a sidelong glance to Arch and Rory, who were still teasing each other.

"Noted," the detective said. "But a few people were injured, if not seriously, and we look upon such 'jokes' very dimly. You may hear from us again as we investigate further. The CCTV footage isn't very helpful, given the man probably wore a false beard. How long are you in Edinburgh?"

"We're flying out tonight," Seamus said.

"Excellent," the detective said with a smile that implied his lack of patience with shenanigans of the rich and famous. He tucked away his notebook in an inside jacket pocket. "Detective Sergeant, now that our shift is more than over, do you fancy a pint?"

"I do indeed, Detective Inspector," said the woman who'd interviewed us, and out they went. Because who wanted to have a pint at a crime scene?

We finished our cleanup and Izara's crew finished theirs as Seamus huddled with Arch and Rory. Magnus escorted the actors out the back. Then Aramach's head honcho came to see us.

"I hope that didn't scare you off," Seamus said. His brown jacket sported a spatter of pink paint on the lapel.

"Of course not," Neil replied.

"Good. Then we'll have a chat tomorrow when you arrive in Kirkwall. You and Pepper come to see me, all right? I don't know how this happened today, but I don't want it to be worse next time." So maybe Seamus didn't think the attack was a joke after all. His tone gave me a chill.

"We'll be there," I said.

"Arrange it with Izara. You have her contact info," he said to Neil. "Personally, I think I need a drink."

When he walked off, Barclay said, "A drink sounds like a pretty good idea."

Neil smiled and looked around at us. "I just happened to get a late reservation at Panda & Sons. You in?"

"Heck, yeah!" Luke said as we all nodded and grinned. So what if my friends all looked great and I looked as if I'd been attacked with bubble gum? Neil had reservations at one of the top craft cocktail bars in the world.

"Hey, handsome," I said to Neil. "Can I buy you a drink?"

Chapter Five

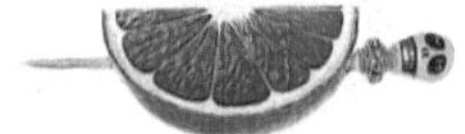

The Bohemia Bartenders met outside our hotel early in the cool, bright morning. We all wore casual light layers—I'd donned a gray denim jacket over a white knit top with black jeans.

I wasn't exactly wide awake, and the pastry I'd had for breakfast just made me more sleepy. So jet lag compounded with a wee bit of a hangover meant it took several seconds for me to comprehend who was about to drive our shuttle bus to the Edinburgh airport.

"Albert?" I blinked as the stocky fellow with short brown hair, a gray-streaked beard and a tweed driving cap loaded my blue roller into the back of the dark blue van.

Albert's broad grin made all the lines in his face smile as he turned to me. "And how have you been, Miss Revelle? Haven't seen you since—September, was it?"

"Yes, that's right. I'm good. Why are you here? Have you moved to Edinburgh?" Albert was Mark's driver and all-around assistant at his estate on the outskirts of London.

Albert chuckled. "So you don't know then? You'll be flying to Kirkwall in Mr. Fairman's jet. I'll drive the shuttle north and take a ferry so you have transportation on the islands."

"That's amazing." I looked at Neil, handsome in a blue

cable-knit sweater, as he put his own suitcase and big bar bag in the back. "You knew?"

"Didn't I mention it? Hard to turn down the offer. Very convenient, given how few commercial flights there are to Kirkwall." Neil had come a long way from being jealous of Mark's attentions. Not that he was ever overt about it, but I knew.

"This is uncharacteristically ... fun of you," I said.

Neil frowned. "I'm fun."

"Oh, I know, you're *definitely* fun," I backpedaled, giving him a quick kiss for emphasis as the other bartenders gathered around, wearing mischievous grins. "This is just, um, unexpected."

"He's taking the jet anyway," Neil said. "And Diana's always on him about not being green enough. He figures he'll earn points by taking more people on the plane."

"Ah," Barclay said. "Kind of divvy up the greenhouse gases?"

Neil chuckled. "Something like that."

"Will we be in first class?" Luke asked.

"It's all first-class on a private jet," Barclay said.

Luke looked skeptical. "Are you sure?"

"Oh, it's very nice indeed," Albert assured him.

"What, you have another offer?" Barclay teased Luke.

Less than an hour later, we settled into our cushy tan leather seats as Mark Fairman's Gulfstream 650ER rolled down the runway. The jet lifted into a cloud-dotted blue sky, headed north to the Orkney Islands.

Mark sat next to Diana and across a dark wooden table from Neil and me. Mark looked delicious, as usual, in brown pants and a chest-hugging butterscotch sweater, weirdly color-coordinated with his cute little spaniel, Victoria, who curled up in his lap. I'd already had a chance to pet her. She wagged her tail double-time when she saw me, but I thought she was even more thrilled that she could still catch a whiff of Astra on my bag. After a rocky start last Christmas, the two dogs became fast friends.

Now Mark scratched behind her floppy ears, and she lifted her chin and opened her big chocolate eyes briefly and sighed before dropping her head and going back to sleep.

The pilot's voice came over the speakers, telling us we were free to move about the cabin, but I was too comfy to budge. I eyed Mark. "How rich are you again?"

He raised an eyebrow. "That's a very American question."

"Sorry. I didn't mean to be rude. Just teasing you about flying around in a private jet."

He chuckled, letting me off the hook. "I don't count the stuff. Often. The thing about having money is that it just keeps making more money."

"If you aren't an idiot. Which you are not," Diana conceded, pushing her short, dark brown hair behind her ears. Diana Silva, English botanist on retainer for Mark's Fairyland Distillery, wore khakis, a white blouse and simple silver jewelry, a variation on her usual adventure outfit. "But as much as you spend on your collections and toys like this, I wonder sometimes."

"I hire well," Mark said. "I'm a lucky man. And I'll let you in on a little secret. I'm not the only owner of this plane. My brothers are all in on it."

Oh, he'd mentioned his brothers before. "The ones in energy and tech and supermarkets?" I asked.

"The very same. What a good memory you have." Mark shot me a warm smile. "Of course, I'm a bit selfish with it. I mean, it's just so *fun*."

The plane really was fun, as was Mark. And so was Neil, in a totally different way, despite my teasing. Especially when I got him alone and I wasn't jet-lagged. Unfortunately, I'd crashed as soon as we got in the door last night after our delicious outing at Panda & Sons.

"Hey, can we get a drink?" Luke called from farther back in the plane, where he and Melody sat opposite each other over another small table. Across the aisle, Barclay read his tablet on a beige sofa, while Alastair Markham slouched against the pillows at the other end, playing on his phone.

Neil looked skeptical. "A little early for a cocktail, isn't it?"

"Not when you're on a plane like this!" Luke answered. "I want the full billionaire experience."

"It's not like we're driving," Barclay added.

"Alastair, make us all something, won't you?" Mark asked.

Alastair huffed and put down the phone. "You can't be serious. They're all bartenders, supposedly."

"Yes, but you know where everything is. Do a round of G&Ts, there's a good chap."

I glanced at Neil, who was trying very hard not to smile as Alastair flounced over to the credenza directly opposite our table and got to work, pulling out Frilly Fairy Gin and Lightning Bug Premium Tonic Water—both Mark's brands—as well as limes, a board, a knife, Collins glasses and a silver ice bucket from the small fridge.

"There's a forward galley and crew compartment as well, but I didn't think we needed full service today," Mark explained.

"Not when you have a brilliant mixologist like Alastair on board." I was sort of teasing him, but I meant it. He was good when he put his mind to it.

Alastair shot me a look, not sure whether to be thrilled or

insulted, then threw together the gin and tonics with alarming speed.

Neil made a strangled noise that would have been a laugh if he hadn't been so polite. But in a moment, he stood, helped garnish the glasses with lime wheels, and served the cocktails to everyone. Alastair took his tall glass and flopped back into the corner of the couch with his phone.

"I should have mentioned there's also coffee in the galley," Mark said.

I'd noticed the heavenly scent of coffee earlier and wondered when I might have a cup. "Maybe I'll follow up with coffee. I'm still on Florida time. I think I can get away with one eye-opener." I took a sip and sighed with pleasure at the bright, fresh flavor of the drink. "And this might be the last gin we have for a while."

"It's true Kirkwall's few watering holes aren't big on craft cocktails," Mark said, "but besides a dizzying selection of scotch, most of them have loads of good gin on hand as well. A distillery like Aramach starts with gin because it's available more quickly and keeps them afloat while the scotch ages."

"Even though they're quick-aging some of the scotch," Neil noted.

"Yes, well, if it's too quick, it's not technically scotch," Mark pointed out.

"Isn't some scotch only three years old?" I asked.

"Yes, and it must be aged in Scotland." Neil knew all the rules.

"Why the big marketing push now?" Diana asked.

Neil swirled his drink. "Seamus feels his whiskies are ready for the big time. Aramach has had small releases of younger whiskies, but he's decided to go full bore into promoting scotch as a craft cocktail ingredient as he releases the twelve-year and the Caribbean-aged whisky. That one meets the aging requirement in rum barrels in Scotland before Seamus finishes it in Jamaica. The theory is that the tropical heat accelerates the aging process, adding more depth in less time."

"It's a theory," Mark said neutrally. His distillery was known not just for gin but for a very nice spiced rum, as well as a successful vodka, and he was always trying something new.

I regarded my drink with its versatile and fragrant gin. "I rarely make scotch cocktails at my bar. I always turn to other liquors first."

"I think Seamus wants to change that," Neil replied. "It seems like a bold move to emphasize cocktails, but once upon a time, scotch punches weren't unusual. That was a long time ago, though, when punches helped mask the poorer quality whiskies."

"And I hear Seamus is experimenting with chipping and exotic yeasts and other interesting if not highly regarded ways of aging his whisky," Mark added.

"Chipping—is that when they put burnt wood into the booze?" Diana asked.

"Toasted chips of select wood," Mark said. "And in some batches, he's also heating the barrels and doing other naughty things."

A corner of my mouth lifted. "How naughty?"

I felt Neil's alarmed gaze on me as Mark grinned. "I don't know all of Aramach's secrets," the Brit said, "but not all distillers are as open to radical imaginings of one of Scotland's national treasures as I am. I look forward to seeing what he's working on."

"Well, I'm looking forward to scouting out the local plants," Diana said, as usual not rising to the bait of Mark's "naughty" comment. Unlike me. But her brown eyes held a spark of amusement. He was definitely growing on her.

"I guess our first order of business will be talking with Seamus about the weird fan letters Arch has been getting," I said.

"And the weird paintball attack yesterday," Neil added. "I have to admit, it scared me."

"Aramach seems to be making light of it, if you read the socials today." Barclay held up his tablet. Even though he was a few feet away, I could clearly see a photo of a laughing Arch and Rory spotted with pink paint splotches.

"Who published the photo?" I asked.

"Some blogger who was at the party. And everyone's picked it up." Barclay scanned his screen again.

"Then there's this." Alastair tapped a button and held up his phone, which came to life with blaring bagpipes.

Neil and I both jumped up to look at the clip, as did Barclay.

"It's shaky video, and it's all over the place," I said. "One of the Archies must've shot it from outside."

"I can't tell which one is the bad guy," Neil added. "Is there any video of the Paintball Piper coming out of the bar?"

"See for yourself," Alastair said. The clip showed the line of bagpipers streaming through the door, though the videographer—a generous description of whoever shot this—was zooming and panning and bouncing and occasionally looking at feet. I briefly spotted the backs of Lark and Wren cheering at the front of the cluster of fans, then the video ended with the door closing behind the corps.

"Everyone's saying it was a prank between Arch and Rory," Barclay said.

Melody nodded. "I think that's what Izara told people. I overheard her answering a few media questions."

"But was it a prank?" Diana asked. "Sounds ghastly to me."

"A good way to spin it, I suppose," Neil said as we sat again at our table.

"Izara didn't seem like she was in on the joke when it happened." I flashed back to her yelling at the stars to get down. I took a deep sip of my drink to quell the wave of nerves that swept through me. "Maybe it wasn't a prank at all. Maybe it was a warning."

Chapter Six

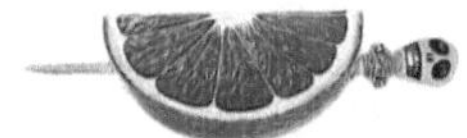

Orkney from the air was a dream of green patchwork islands, rugged beaches and cliffs, scattered homesteads and the occasional wind turbine. It seemed delicate, somehow, with so much ocean around it, but the people this far north—at the same latitude as Anchorage or southern Greenland—endured brutal gales and bitter winters. Delicate they were not.

The jet landed smoothly, and we exited down the stairs with our luggage into a lovely morning. Per Neil's arrangement with Izara, Magnus awaited us with an Aramach Distillery shuttle in front of Kirkwall's tiny airport, since it would take all day for Albert to get Mark's van up to the islands.

"Hey, can I get a ride?" came an all-too-familiar voice as we wrangled our suitcases into the back of the van.

I spun to see Mr. Mixy and his three-person crew striding over to us with enough baggage to start a new colony on Mars.

"I hope not," I muttered as Neil asked him, "Are you going where we are?"

"We're staying at the same inn," Mr. Mixy said. "Seamus hooked us up."

Great. Thanks, Seamus.

On the curb, Diana and Alastair stood with Mark, who

held Victoria by the leash as she strained to sniff one of the big rocks on display.

"We'll call a cab," Mark said after assessing the clown car situation. Just how many bartenders could we fit into one passenger van?

"Thanks for the ride, Mark," I called out.

"Anytime, Hot Pepper." He raised an eyebrow at me, then, to my amusement, winked at Neil. My nouveau boyfriend shook his head, but he wore a smile as Mark's party walked away.

Magnus scanned Stephan and the TV crew and the pile of bags. "Whatever we can't fit in the back, you'll have to hold. But I can drop you off at the inn. Then I have to deliver the bartenders to their final destination."

That sounded ominous. And worse, we'd have to have Mr. Mixy on board.

"Fantastic!" my ex said. He introduced his all-American crew, and everyone squeezed in. I was a second too late to call shotgun, as Barclay grabbed the co-pilot's seat. So I headed to the back after Neil, and unfortunately, Stephan followed us to the last row to sit next to me.

"My book is with my editor," he volunteered as Magnus cranked up the shuttle and rolled out of the airport.

"If she edits you out of it, I'm sure it'll be great," I said.

Mr. Mixy laughed. "You're so funny. She loves it. It's so hot, my agent is on the verge of selling the movie rights before it's even published!"

My stomach flipped. "And I'm not in it, right?"

"Not by name, certainly," he said vaguely.

Oh, crap. "We had a deal."

"No one will know it's you. I even changed the name of the bar."

"The bar changed names anyway." Mr. Mixy and I had worked together in Bohemia before Stephan (not Mr. Mixy back then) revealed his true nature as a bad boyfriend and chronic liar and I broke up with him. That was years ago, when I was a lot more naive, still learning my craft. He moved to L.A., where he proceeded to get social-media famous, land a cocktail-themed TV show and start the autobiography I'd been dreading.

Out of the wreckage of our stupid short-term relationship arose Nola, my New Orleans-themed bar and restaurant, which was doing quite well. I'd just paid off my Aunt Celestine's loan, which had made it possible for me to buy the old bar and renovate it with my business partner, Jorge Listo. And I didn't even have to be famous to make it successful, thank Dionysus.

As we exited the airport property, Mr. Mixy did selfies and talked to his phone, so I mentally shut him out and enjoyed a few minutes of rolling through emerald-green pastures dotted with sheep and bordered by short stone walls.

We passed a few houses in varying shades of pebbled tan before Magnus took a turn or two and entered a narrow lane. The van slipped between outbuildings, and we found ourselves in front of a rambling Victorian mansion with lots of chimneys, a square tower and a gothic feel.

"Why do I feel like I'm about to star in a show on PBS?" Melody said in awe from the seat in front of me.

"Och, aye, Rose Hill House has been featured in more than one drama and mystery," Magnus called from the front as he stopped near the door. "It's a lovely inn now, but it used to be a private residence."

We did the whole boarding process in reverse, exiting the shuttle, extracting our luggage and bringing it into the airy two-story front hall. It had a vintage vibe with a chandelier and intricate floral wallpaper. An elaborate wooden mantel surrounded a fireplace with a couple of chairs in front of it. A wide staircase climbed to parts unknown, and a door marked "W.C." led to a convenient bathroom. A sign pointed to the "Lift" through a doorway in the back of the space. Another pointed down a hallway to the restaurant.

A friendly brown-haired woman in her fifties named Ola greeted us from a reception counter. First she showed us a relaxing room with a handsome brick fireplace, dark wood floors, tall bookcases stuffed with books and games, a pool table, a game table, and comfy brown leather furniture. And more haunted-house wallpaper.

"You're welcome to enjoy the game room whenever ye like. Now let's check you in, and we'll make sure your bags get to the right rooms." Back at the desk, she handed out old-fashioned keys on rose-shaped metal fobs—Melody had her own room; Barclay and Luke would share a double; and Neil and I had one together (yay!).

"We keep the place locked at night, but you can always get in if needs be," Ola said. "One of those keys opens the front door. You can go out the back door, but you can't go in that way. We open the front door to the public in the morning, as we serve breakfast and lunch in the restaurant. It's quite popular. Your breakfast is included, of course. And there's a kettle and biscuits in your room if you find yourself needin' a grain of tea."

"Everything's included," Magnus said. "They're on Mr. MacIvor's account."

"Och, aye," Ola said. "Seamus is very good to us. And to have those cheeky young stars staying with us—it's quite exciting, isn't it?" She giggled like a girl. The Arch Halliday effect again. He set a room aglow, and Rory Redland, no slouch himself, doubled the electricity. In fact, I'd read that Rory had been cast in a British heist movie and had a book coming out about his adventures on the *Sleekit Sim* show. Those two were star power squared.

"All right. Everybody ready?" Neil asked us bartenders while Mr. Mixy's gang went to their rooms to regroup and Ola went off to round up someone to haul the bags. "Pepper and I need to see Seamus MacIvor. I'll have Magnus drop you three off at the venue in town." He nodded at the guys and Melody. "Figure out the lay of the land and where we'll have our supplies delivered for Saturday's event."

"No problem," Barclay said.

"Luke will check the status of our orders," Neil said. "We have a couple of days to sort out any supply issues." It was only Wednesday, but we also had Seamus's problems to work on, too.

"Got it," Luke affirmed.

"Melody will consider our lighting, of course," Neil joked. "And check with Izara Abbott to see what we need to know for the shoot."

"You bet! If we're going to be filmed, we need to look good. Of course, the clothes will help." She wore a sly expression.

"As long as we don't look like the Von Trapp Family Singers again," I said.

"Or vampires," Luke added.

Melody gave him a pointed look. "I'm pretty sure you volunteered to look like a vampire at the film festival, but I'm too nice to mention it. Or your nickname."

"Yeah, Twilight." Barclay wasn't too nice to use the nickname. The rest of us chuckled at Luke's scowl.

"When you're done, text me and we can see where we

stand," Neil said. And then we reboarded the shuttle, mercifully without the Mixy posse.

As Magnus turned hither and yon, we passed a distillery, but I caught only part of the sign. "Is that—?"

"No, it's not Aramach," Neil said. "I believe that's Cliffstone Distillery."

"Very well regarded," Magnus said, though his tone was dry.

"We stock a couple of their bottles at Nola," I told him.

Magnus harrumphed. "I'll take you past the pier so you can have a gander."

A few turns later, after passing low, sturdy houses, a busy fish and chips shop—we would have to check that out later—then a few big stores and industrial-type buildings, Magnus took a right at a roundabout.

"The Peedie Sea." He pointed at a lake-like feature to the right. "And the not-so-peedie sea." On the left, the view opened to a bay, an inviting expanse of blue water.

"It's so pretty," I said. "Is that a cruise ship out there?"

"Aye." Magnus didn't sound pleased. "Sometimes there are two or three. We get up to seven thousand visitors in a day."

"Holy hell," Neil said. "What's the population of Kirkwall?"

"About ten thousand," Magnus said.

"The town doesn't look big enough to hold that many people," Melody noted.

"Not for long, anyway," Barclay agreed.

"Maybe it's good for the shops," Luke replied.

Magnus said something I couldn't understand, but then again, that wasn't unusual. I did get the tone, though: grumpy.

Here were more older-looking buildings of brick and stone, across from the harbor. Tourists crowded the street, and cabs and a few buses lined up to whisk them off to the local attractions.

There were a few bars and hotels among the buildings that faced the water. A wide, substantial concrete pier—nothing like the wooden Florida versions I was used to—and several squat buildings there catered to vessels from ferries to pleasure boats. Then Magnus turned right onto a narrow street that curved right again, crowded with cute little shops and thronged with tourists.

The road opened up into an astounding sight on the left, a colossal building of reddish stone.

I asked the most obvious question ever. In my defense, I was stunned. "That's the cathedral?"

Neil's eyes shone with interest as he looked out the window with me. He loved anything historical, and this place had a monumental energy about it, the echo of centuries.

"Aye, that's St. Magnus." Our Magnus pulled up to the curb across the street from the massive church. Its bell tower loomed over the rest of the structure, which was adorned with stained glass windows and arched entrances recessed in tiers of patterned red and yellow stone. Names covered an imposing, angel-topped stone cemetery gate, memorializing those lost in the "Great War"—ah, to think people thought World War I might be the last great war. The entire complex was spectacular, imposing but also warm, thanks to the color scheme.

Barclay voiced what I was thinking. "What kind of stone is that?"

"Sandstone," Magnus said. "Red and yellow from different parts of Orkney. They started building it almost nine hundred years ago. Of course, there've been changes and updates since then. It was almost falling down at one time, but it was rein-forced with steel girders in the 1960s."

"It's friggin' *huge*," I said. "I mean, given this is such a small town. Not to insult you or anything."

"That's how the earl thanked God for letting him win in battle." Magnus shut off the engine. "And of course it let him honor St. Magnus and court the cult."

"The cult?" I asked as we exited the van. Even if Neil and I had another appointment, I wanted to get a good look at the cathedral.

"Och, it's a long story. The short version is, back when Orkney was ruled by various earls, Magnus's cousin betrayed him at what was to be a peaceful meeting. This was in the early eleven-hundreds. He tried to bargain for his life, but his rivals decided he had to die, and Magnus's own cook was drafted to kill him with an axe."

"Cool," Luke said, and we all looked at him askance. "What?"

Magnus snorted. "His remains were buried up at Birsay at first. There were miracles and what-not, and the cult of Magnus grew to the point where the Bishop of Orkney made him a saint. Eventually, Magnus's nephew sailed over from Norway, overthrew the treacherous cousin's son, and began the cathedral. Rognvald. He was named a saint himself. His and Magnus's remains are both interred here."

"Are you named for him?" Barclay asked.

"No. Named for my uncle." But Magnus wore a hint of a smile.

"I want to see inside. But not now," Neil said. Duty always came first with Neil.

"We'll have time later." I hoped my confidence was justified.

"At any rate," Magnus said, "this is your venue." He pointed to a three-story building of brown and yellow stone across the street from the cathedral, complete with mini towers and adornments that evoked the era noted in the carved sign over the doorway: *TOWN HALL, 1884*. Columns flanked the door, each topped by serious-looking fellows in frock coats carrying weapons, also carved of stone.

"The party is in the town hall?" Barclay asked.

Magnus nodded. "It's an event venue. Very nice. Ask for Fiona. She'll give you the lay of the land."

"All right, let's do it," Melody said. "The sooner we finish, the sooner I can go shopping in these adorable boutiques."

I was pretty sure Magnus rolled his eyes as Neil and I bade our friends farewell and got back in the van. This time Neil sat in the front, maybe to keep Magnus company. Not that he seemed to need it. I was fine with relaxing in the second row and watching us roll back into the countryside—east of the harbor, I thought. We seemed to be circling it, at times on a one-lane road with the occasional "passing place," or so said the signs, to give cars an outlet to avoid head-on collisions.

Finally, we passed through an open gate in a gap in a stone wall. The recently paved lane, bordered by more low stone walls, ascended a rolling green slope. A quarter mile inside the gate, metal letters mounted on a slab of rock announced Aramach Distillery.

It seemed like everything was made of beautiful stones here, maybe because there weren't many trees. I hoped we'd get to see the famous stone circles of Orkney. Part of me wanted to test if they'd whisk me off to another century full of hot Scottish guys in kilts, but it was probably better to get there through fiction. I was a big fan of modern plumbing.

Several buildings at the top of the hill comprised the distillery. The biggest was half modern, half old farmhouse, with the tan pebbled finish that seemed so common here. One had a small pagoda-shaped tower, or rather chimney—perhaps the distillery's kiln for smoking its malted barley.

The whole complex had an unobstructed view of the sea, and its parking lot held half a dozen cars with room for plenty more.

Neil had told me Aramach wasn't doing tours yet. Those would follow the new scotch releases. No doubt the cruise ships, like the one I could see in the sparkling sapphire harbor, would be happy to provide the tourists.

We entered the main building's spacious modern half through heavy glass doors, and my supernose did its best to parse all the smells: smoke and peat. Scotch and sea. A faint hint of wood polish, which made sense, given the gleaming wood floors and the large, circular bar that dominated the lobby.

Exhibits described the distillery and the process. And the whole place was a gift shop, with trinkets and folded shirts and bottles displayed everywhere under strategic lighting.

The curve of the tall cashier's desk in the back reflected the curve of the bar, but no one was there. The map behind the desk showed Aramach's location on the Orkney mainland, and a sign there listed tour prices. Oh yes, Aramach was ready.

Magnus had disappeared, but in a moment, clacking footsteps from the far reaches of the lobby heralded the arrival of Izara, looking sharp in a tight black skirt, green blouse and heels. She didn't seem nearly as composed as she had in Edinburgh—at least, as she had before the paintball incident.

"I'm so glad you're here," she said. "Seamus is in a tizzy. We've had more strange letters."

Chapter Seven

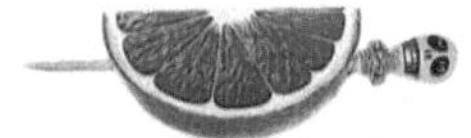

I wanted to move into Seamus MacIvor's office. I probably could have, given how big it was. The view through a long wall of curved glass—a panorama of green fields and the blue sea, and beyond that, the Kirkwall harbor and undulating low hills—would be worth it. The wide white couch looked good for napping, facing a coffee table and comfy chairs by a crackling fireplace. There was a large wooden desk, a rectangular teak table with six chairs for meetings, a bar, a dark wood floor, and shelves displaying bottles and books and bric-a-brac, all lit beautifully.

Even better, a bright-eyed black-and-white border collie trotted over to greet us, licking our hands and soaking up all the love I gave her.

"That's Nessie. Watch out, or she'll herd you." Seamus, more casual today in a sweater and khakis, shook our hands. "How was your flight?"

"Excellent," Neil said. "Mark Fairman gave us a lift."

Seamus chuckled. "Show-off. But a good sort. Arch chartered a plane for us last night, which I appreciated. At least he wasn't mobbed at the airport." His smile turned to a frown.

"Have you learned any more about what happened yesterday?" I asked. "Did Arch or Rory 'fess up?"

"They both say they didn't hire the Paintball Piper, as some of the stories are calling it now," Seamus said. "They each act like they think the other did it, but it was probably one of them."

"Maybe they feel bad because a few people got hurt," Neil said.

Seamus didn't look happy. "Not badly, thank God."

"But the incident seems to have triggered some of Arch's fans," Izara said.

"Fanatics," Seamus amended. "I suppose we'd better talk about this."

He gestured to the meeting table, where someone had already set out a pitcher of water and glasses, and all four of us sat. Nessie curled up on a fuzzy white rug by the fireplace.

Izara pulled a tablet computer and a clear plastic bag stuffed with envelopes out of her chic black leather satchel. Her bag was almost as fat as my canvas messenger bag, which I stowed under the table.

"How long has Arch been getting unusual fan letters?" I asked, pouring water for everyone as my bartender instincts kicked in.

Seamus took a sip of his water. "Before he even invested—in case you didn't know, he has a thirty percent ownership in Aramach—he got a lot of fan mail through the TV show. There was the occasional creep but nothing too egregious. Then he began his promotions for us, and fans began associating him with the brand. Most of them are very nice, and they buy whisky, which I appreciate, even though they aren't your typical scotch drinkers. We expected a higher profile among drinkers with Arch doing promo, but we didn't realize how many of his TV fans would follow him to the scotch. We saw more of them hanging around his events and even coming to the distillery."

"Hence the gate?" I asked.

"We've been glad to have it given all the attention," he said. "But it's usually unlocked, and it'll be open once tours begin. I don't see a real problem with the Archies coming here. Arch is rarely on site."

"Except," Izara said, "sometimes the Archies hang around the entrance on the off chance they'll spot him. The really obsessed ones, I mean."

I glanced at the bag of envelopes. "And the promotions he's doing have inspired more fan letters?"

"A lot more." She shook the bag so the whole pile of letters cascaded onto the table. "This is just a fraction. I'm afraid we invited trouble when we started a social media campaign in which Arch read fan letters on video, so long as the letters were about where they'd want to share a whisky with him. Some of the letters were quite inappropriate."

Seamus snorted. "Steamy love scenes, more like. Some of the weird notes came in the mail, others through a letter drop at our shop in Kirkwall. What we picked up this morning came through that box."

"And you haven't considered just taking away the box?" I asked.

"There's still the post, if they want to send letters," Seamus said. "We thought we might better assess the threat, if there is one, if we kept the box open."

Maybe, if they kept an eye on it. "Do you have any cameras on this box?"

"We have CCTV but nothing on the box." Seamus ran a hand through his curly hair in frustration. "It's not well lit at night anyway. And given thousands of people come down that street whenever the cruise ships are in town, it would be difficult to pick out one person even if we had a camera on it."

Neil gestured to the letters. "What did you get today?"

Izara opened a light blue envelope embossed with butterflies and extracted a sheet of matching stationery. "This was addressed to the distillery." She unfolded it and read:

How could you put him in danger like this? Or was it his so-called friend? Keep him safe or those of us who really love him will do something about it. He's ours. You can't have him. You can't ruin him. I won't let you.

"Signature?" I asked.

"No." Izara laid the letter down so we could all look at it.

"But it's kind of a sideways threat." I pondered the language. "They want to keep 'him' safe—Arch, presumably. And there's some Rory hate there, maybe? But the 'do something about it' and the 'He's ours' is definitely off. And the 'we' turns into 'I.'"

"Like they're trying to speak with the authority of some imagined collective," Neil said, "then get possessive at the end."

"What I get from it is they don't want Arch working with Aramach," Seamus said. "How far will they go to stop him?"

"Or they just don't want him working with Rory." So far, I wasn't impressed by this implied threat.

"We get fan letters for Rory, too, even though he's not associated with the distillery," Seamus said. "Sometimes I think he gets more love than Arch. But I see your point."

"Any other letters worth mentioning?" I asked.

Izara opened a white business-size envelope and pulled out and unfolded a piece of letter-size white paper. On one side was printed the photo of Arch and Rory laughing and covered with ink splotches. Hand-printed words were on the other. She read aloud:

Now you think you have double the fun.
What if something turned two into one?
What if the one then became none?
Don't spoil this for everyone.

It was signed with an awkwardly written "PI."

"It's not the first one we've had signed this way," Izara said.

"What does the signature mean? Private investigator?" I asked.

"Someone's initials? Know anyone of that name?" Neil asked Seamus and Izara. They shook their heads.

"Poison Ivy?" I suggested, and Seamus almost cracked a smile. I read the note again. "Turn two into one?" I grimaced. "Like get rid of one—what? One of the stars? And then turn the one into none? That's super creepy."

"It seems more like a direct threat." Izara's voice cracked as she shuffled through the pile. "A death threat."

"I hope not," Seamus said. "But there's that underlying hostility about 'two of them.' Is this hate for Rory? Or both?"

"Why can't people just write death threats in a straight-forward way?" I complained, thinking of the stupid poems that lured me to a confrontation with my nemesis in New Orleans.

Neil's mouth quirked as he shot me an amused glance. "Wouldn't that be nice."

"Not nice at all." Izara seemed annoyed on top of being upset.

"You're right." I pointed to the pile. "Any other letters you want to point out?"

"Here's another one from PI that was left in the Arch mailbox at the shop about a month ago." Izara slid a small sheet of yellow lined notebook paper from a white envelope like the other one and unfolded it. As in the other note, each word was printed by hand. She read it aloud.

> With every joke and every dig,
> your fate becomes more grave.
> We're not laughing with you, pig.
> You'll pay when next you rave.

"PI is very angry," I said as Izara placed the letter on the table. "They must really hate Arch."

"Is he too jolly for them?" Seamus asked. "I don't get it. Everyone loves Arch. And he doesn't rave. He jokes, yes. But he's not a nutter. *This* person is a nutter. People don't have a sense of humor anymore."

I didn't know what motivated the writer, but "your fate becomes more grave" didn't give me warm fuzzies. "Have you run these by the police?"

Izara shot Seamus a glower as he shook his head. "I didn't want the negative publicity. I talked to a friend in the Orkney police, off the record. He said they can't do much without an explicit threat anyway."

I got the feeling Izara didn't agree with his decision to keep these letters secret.

Neil leaned in for a closer look. "It almost seems like they disguised their handwriting. It's printed deliberately, as a child might write it. Not that I think it's a child."

"A child like that could star in a horror movie," I agreed.

Izara pulled what looked like a greeting card covered in flowers from another envelope and opened it. "This was also addressed to Arch." She read:

My darling,
I love you both too much to let them take you away from me. You don't need the whisky. You need me. I'll keep you safe. I'll take you home. You won't ever have to worry about him ever again.

She set it on the table for us to peruse. The writer, who'd neatly printed the note, had signed it with a hand-drawn heart with wings.

"We call this writer the Flying Heart," Izara said. "Arch has had other letters from this person, possessive letters."

I read it over. "Is this another reference to Arch and Rory? Or a different 'him'?"

"Given the context, maybe Rory?" Neil pondered it for a second. "Some of these notes seem to express more animosity toward Rory than Arch. Though that bit about taking him home—Arch home—gives me pause."

"It would freak me the hell out," I said. "Stalker city."

"This is why we're going to have Magnus around at any

distillery-related events," Seamus said, "not that he helped much yesterday."

"It was a difficult situation." I felt bad for Magnus. He was trying. "Maybe it's too big of a job for one person."

"We'll have a couple of extra people on hand for the party, but that's a closed event and a closed shoot," Seamus said. "That's not what I'm worried about. Arch is exposed all the time. And I'm not even sure what the threat is."

"Maybe we need to talk to Arch," I suggested. "Maybe he has more insight into who these correspondents are, since he interacts with the fans all the time." It was funny—now I thought of him as someone I had to protect rather than a sex symbol. Well, in *addition* to being a sex symbol.

"He was here earlier talking to Blair," Izara said. "Maybe he's still here. I'll take you to her."

"That's good. Let me know if you figure anything out," Seamus said. "This isn't the kind of publicity I'm looking for."

Acid tinged Izara's reply. "Murder would be very bad publicity."

Chapter Eight

"We'll do our best," I told Seamus as we gathered our things and stood to go. I tried to sound confident, but these few batty missives weren't much to go on.

Nessie's ears perked up, and I gave her head a scratch before Neil and I followed Izara out of the office.

"Any chance we can review more of the strange letters?" I asked her as we passed through the lobby.

"I've scanned everything. I'll send you a link to the folder," Izara said. She led us outdoors and along a path that wended through the campus.

"Who's Blair?" I asked.

"The master distiller." Neil had done his homework.

Izara took us into a large building of brick and stone that looked and smelled a lot more industrial inside than the touristy lobby. Big, round copper tanks caught my eye. We found Blair a floor up, where the tops of those tanks—the stills—stuck out of the metal decking, well lit by the peaked skylight above that ran the length of the room.

We found her turning knobs on a machine that looked kind of like a steampunk fish tank, only instead of fish, there were clear globes with clear liquid flowing through them and clear cylinders.

"One moment." Blair, a couple of inches taller than me and pale with short, dark hair, lifted a finger to make us wait as she bent slightly to focus on the tank. She wore a white T-shirt and black overalls embroidered with the Aramach *A*.

Blair turned one of the knobs. After a moment, she walked over to one of the wide paper spreadsheets laid out on a table and entered some numbers. Then she looked up.

"What are you working on?" Neil asked.

She smiled. "This is a funny place to start the tour."

"They aren't tourists," Izara said. "Sorry to interrupt, but I thought they should meet you. Blair Rendall—Neil Rockaway and Pepper Revelle of the Bohemia Bartenders."

Blair's smile grew wider as she shook our hands. "I've heard of you. Here to make something of my whisky, are you?"

Neil laughed. "It's quite something already."

"Thank you." She stuck her hands in her pockets. "I was just cutting the spirit as it flows into the wash safe. Time to collect the heart. We cut out the heads and the tails, which are less desirable." She was getting into tour-guide mode, but I always appreciated a refresher on how the liquid gold was made. "That'll take two or three hours."

She gestured to the four huge copper stills, squat with tall necks, set partly into the metal-grate floor. They were throwing heat, and the equipment made a lot of noise that landed somewhere between the grind of machinery and a waterfall.

"The wash stills and the spirit stills. We distill twice." Blair stood there admiring the beautiful copper vessels, genie lamps for giants, then surveyed all of us. "I could tell you more, but that's not why you're here, is it?"

Neil and Izara looked at me.

I turned to Blair. "Seamus asked us to learn more about the

weird letters Arch has been getting. We'd like to try to determine what the threat is, if any, and hopefully where it's coming from. We thought you might know something."

"Ah. You're the one Mark Fairman mentioned." How many people did Mark talk to here? "I know a lot of things," Blair continued wryly, "but probably not what you need. Would you like a cup of tea?"

"I'm fine," Neil said.

"I'm good." But I was thinking, yes, Neil, you *are* fine.

"I'll take a cuppa in lieu of something stronger," Izara said.

"We happen to have something stronger if you need it." One side of Blair's mouth lifted. "Let's go to my office. It's a bit quieter."

We followed Blair to a small room with a tan carpet and cream walls decorated with framed certificates, bulletin boards covered in papers, and more papers and boxes on the desk. A few different Aramach bottles sat on a bookshelf, along with empty tasting glasses, binders, books and bits of equipment I couldn't identify. A side table held a microwave, a box of packaged snacks and the electric teakettle, which she started up.

It wasn't much quieter in here, even with the door closed. A big glass window showed off the stills in action. Blair would have a great view of her potions from her desk.

She dropped English Breakfast tea bags into two mugs. "Arch is a pain in the arse." Her blue eyes might've held a hint of humor, but I wasn't sure.

Izara and Neil sat in the two chairs opposite Blair's desk.

I left Blair's office chair open for her and stood by the window. "Tell me more."

"I was born here. My da worked at Cliffstone Distillery." She checked our faces and saw we knew what she was talking about—the distillery across the island. "I visited him often at work. He died when I was at university. Heart attack on the job, actually." I marveled at her even tone as she revealed this tragedy. "I loved it there. And I loved him. I wanted to be like him, do him one better. Become a distiller. Cliffstone wouldn't give me the time of day, but I apprenticed elsewhere, worked hard and studied my craft, and when this job came open, it seemed like the perfect opportunity. And Seamus was open to having me aboard. I know what I'm doing."

We all nodded. She certainly gave that impression.

"Seamus is not a traditionalist." Blair poured the hot water into the cups, then tapped her smartwatch before lifting her gaze again to us. "He respects the tradition, but he is willing to take chances. He wants to shake things up. And he happens to think he can sell more scotch if he can reach more people, people who don't necessarily think of scotch when they want a drink."

"Hence the cocktail theme of this marketing campaign," Izara added.

Blair nodded. "Seamus met Arch at some high roller party or another. Arch was looking to invest in a distillery, and Seamus needed the capital. The bonus of having a built-in celebrity spokesman was too much to resist. So Arch came aboard."

"Is he from here, too?" I asked.

"No. Edinburgh." Her reply made me wonder if the Paintball Piper was from Edinburgh, too. "He's charming, I suppose, but he's always coming around for samples and sniffing around the process, and frankly, he doesn't know what he's doing. I've seen his interviews. He acts like he made the whisky. Trust me, he did *not* make the whisky."

"And you find his presumptuousness annoying," I said.

"You understand." She granted me a thin smile. "I think

we're being taken less seriously. Or perhaps *I'm* being taken less seriously. It's partly because of the fandom." She grabbed a packet of shortbread cookies from the table and held it out. "Biscuits? They're made with local butter."

She offered them around, and we munched for a minute. *Oh, wow.* A butter and sugar boost was just what I needed. "Thank you. They're delicious."

"They're my weakness." Blair grinned and looked down at her smartwatch, tapped the screen, disposed of the tea bags in a trash can and looked at Izara. "Milk?"

"Just sugar, please."

Teas doctored, Blair took a sip and sighed. "I don't mean to come across as bitter. Arch has done a lot for the success of Aramach, and I feel sure he'll do more. I'm just trying to illustrate how he comes across. How *we* come across. And there are people in the scotch world who don't appreciate what they consider the 'dumbing down' of scotch."

"Like Cliffstone?" Neil suggested.

"Exactly. Like Callum Cotter at Cliffstone. The owner," she said to my questioning look.

"Would Callum Cotter send threatening letters?" I asked.

Blair took another sip of her tea. "He despises Seamus for pissing in his pool. I don't see him writing creepy letters, necessarily, but making mischief? Hiring the Paintball Piper? It wouldn't surprise me at all."

"Would he do more? Worse?" I asked.

"I don't know. He and Seamus go way back. Something ugly happened between them."

"What?"

"You'll have to ask them."

Interesting. Why hadn't Seamus mentioned this possibility? Maybe he didn't think that whatever happened between him and Callum Cotter was a big deal. But we'd have to ask.

"I don't think I have any more questions. Neil?"

He shook his head but turned to Blair. "Any chance of seeing your kiln?"

She chuckled. "Ah, you spied our pagoda, did you? It's just for show. We don't dry the barley here. But we do peat it, and with Orkney peat, too. We deliver it to a commercial maltser with very specific direction as to how much of our peat to use to get the right flavor profile. Most of the scotch distillers get their malt this way now."

"Interesting," Neil said. "But not Cliffstone?"

"Not Cliffstone," she agreed. "They still have the malting floor and burn their peat with coke on the property for most of their malting. But the old ways aren't always better. It's a lot less precise."

"If precision is the goal," Neil said.

"We can debate that sometime." Blair's eyes held a spark of mirth.

"Thanks for your time," I said to her.

"Nae bother. I look forward to tasting your cocktails on Saturday." She set down her cup and stood.

"Thanks, Blair." Izara set her cup on the table. "I'll be in touch about that new shoot for the website."

"No problem. At least I don't have to dress up for that one."

"Lucky you. I'm going to work more dungarees into my wardrobe," Izara joked, and we headed out.

"Is Seamus still around?" I asked Izara after we got back outside.

"He had an appointment this afternoon, so no. Why?"

"I wanted to ask him about his beef with Callum Cotter."

"I doubt there's anything there," Izara said. "But I'll let him know you want to speak with him again."

I looked at Neil, then Izara. "Maybe we should talk to Arch next. Where do you think he is?"

She lifted an eyebrow. "Probably drinking. I think I can find out." She pulled out her phone, tapped and tapped again. "Try The Whale. It's a hotel bar. You can get lunch there, too. Magnus can take you."

My stomach took the hint and rumbled. The shortbread was just a tease. "Lunch sounds good. Thanks for all your help."

"Let me know if you need anything. Anything at all. I'm worried about Arch and Rory. Those letters are more than unsettling." She crossed her arms, hugging herself. "I've a very bad feeling about this."

Chapter Nine

Magnus drove Neil and me toward the waterfront and stopped behind several taxis lined up near the pier. "The Whale's just down that a way."

"Thanks," Neil said.

"Call me when you need another lift. You have my number?"

"I do." Neil patted the trouser pocket that held his phone.

"See you later," I told Magnus, and we got out. The afternoon was almost warm but not quite. As a Floridian, I gloried in the ability to wear layers and not die of heatstroke. It really was a lovely day.

"The bar is almost across the street," Neil said.

"Let's walk for a minute first."

"Walk and think."

"Exactly."

Kirkwall's waterfront was less busy than it had been this morning. Maybe the tourists had moved on to other attractions. As we gazed out over the blue, the main pier extended into the water to our right, and a shorter arm with the ferry terminal jutted out on our left, sheltering a smaller bay marked by a mini lighthouse.

I took a deep breath of the invigorating sea air as we

moseyed along the sidewalk next to the water. "What did you think of Blair?"

"She's cute."

I whipped my head around to stare at Neil, and he laughed and looped his arm in mine.

"Kidding," he said. "I mean, objectively, she's kind of cute, but I don't think she'd like that word. She seems really smart."

"At least we agree about that." I smiled. I wasn't used to him teasing me like that. "She doesn't like Arch much."

"Or at least she resents him representing not just the brand but the whisky itself."

"And I wonder if she resents Callum Cotter, too. Cliffstone didn't give her a job, and you could say that her father's job there killed him."

"She didn't seem overtly emotional about Cliffstone," Neil said, "but there's a lot to unpack there."

"And I think she's really proud of the job she has now. I like her. She's straightforward. She has a dry sense of humor." I paused. "But we should keep her in mind."

"Maybe asking everybody to be Arch's pen pal gave an open invitation to any crackpot with a grudge against him or Aramach or Seamus," Neil suggested.

"Isn't that the hazard of any fame now? Especially the interactive social media type. People think they own you if you're famous, and they can be just as nasty to people who aren't. The ugly comments. All of it."

"I'm questioning why Seamus has us doing this to begin with," Neil said. "If he thinks these letters are an ongoing threat, he should up the security or get the police involved."

"The police in Edinburgh didn't seem impressed by the Paintball Piper, and Seamus seems worried about bad publicity," I replied. "He wants us to ask around, and I'm OK with doing that. Maybe we'll get lucky. But I know what you're saying. I don't feel equipped to deal with a violent stalker."

"And I don't want you to. I don't want any of us to." Neil stopped and turned to me and wrapped me up in a hug. "At least he's hired extra security for the event. That makes me feel better."

"Meanwhile, Arch is out in the wild," I said dryly. "Should we go check him out? I mean talk to him."

Neil laughed and released me. He was well aware of my *totally* innocent lust for Arch Halliday and Rory Redland.

We turned and walked back to The Whale, located in the ground floor of a four-story Victorian hotel built of beautiful stone. The bar was off the lobby, and beyond it was a full restaurant. I took in the tin ceiling, parquet floors, wooden bar and a blue-and-white painted back bar that evoked the Scottish flag. Scotch whisky filled the shelves—most of it, it seemed, from Cliffstone Distillery.

But all of that was just the backdrop for the Arch and Rory show. In jovial conversation, the two actors sipped from rows of tasting glasses lined up in front of each of them while several people lingered nearby and folks at the tables looked on with fascination.

A female bartender attended to the guys, trying to look like she didn't care that two of the hottest stars on TV were drinking her pours. She did better than I would have. The stars had a gravitational pull that sucked me in and made me forget my purpose. Hell, I wasn't even sure what my name was.

"Pepper!" came a cry from someone on the other side of Arch.

There. That was my name.

Oh no.

Mr. Mixy stepped away from the bar. I realized some of the

people gathered around were, in fact, his TV crew, though they weren't filming. Maybe the stars had asked them not to. But Stephan was giddy anyway. He had a contact high from all the star power in the room.

I didn't know how I'd missed him—well, I did know, because I'd been busy staring at Arch and Rory. But Mr. Mixy was very hard to miss. His purple T-shirt read "Kilty As Charged." He wore a blinding orange pleated kilt ringed by one purple stripe and one reflective one. His sporran—the pouch that dangled in front—was covered in long, orange fur and had two little cow horns poking out of it like a Highland coo. He looked like a Caledonian traffic cone.

"We're doing shots!" he called out to me and Neil.

Arch lifted an eyebrow at Mr. Mixy, as I could see in the mirror behind the bar. "Sacrilege! These aren't shots. We're *tasting.*"

"In quantity," Rory amended, and they both laughed.

"C'mon, Mixy, you're falling behind," Arch told him. Then he looked over at me and smiled, his dirty-blond hair ruffled, his green eyes sparkling, his sage sweater so clingy I wanted to pet it. Heavily pet it.

Omigod. Get a grip, Pepper. Neil is right here. Remember? Neil? Hot nerd mixologist you chased for a year before he succumbed to your charms?

"I know you, don't I?" Arch asked.

"Yes. We met at the event in Edinburgh." I pointed a thumb to my guy. "Neil and I are with the Bohemia Bartenders. Seamus thought we should talk to you."

"Och, aye. Well, you'd better have a drink, then." Arch gestured to the two stools to the right of Rory, which no one else had been brave enough to take.

Mr. Mixy seemed crestfallen at losing my attention, but he

sat on the other side of Arch and threw back another glass of scotch. Definitely not the way to drink the finer stuff, and I was sure this was fine.

I eyed a menu sitting on the bar as I climbed up next to Rory and tried to remember to breathe. "We'll split the Cliffstone flight of four," I told the bartender. I glanced at Neil to confirm.

He nodded, quickly assessing the menu. "I'll try the haggis bites and an order of chips."

Oh, yeah. Food. "And I'll take the fried Grimbister cheese. And water, please." There. Cheese would get my brain working again.

"Coming right up," the bartender said with a friendly nod.

I leaned in a little so I could see both Rory and Arch and spoke quietly. "Given what Seamus told us, it's a wonder you're out and about in public right now."

"So you've been reading my correspondence?" Arch said, well, archly.

"Only what Izara shared with us." I took a sip of water while our bartender poured the flights.

"She's worth three times what you and Seamus pay her." Rory ran a hand through his red hair. "She's a treasure."

"I don't set the salaries! I don't own *that* much of the company," Arch replied.

"You'd better take care of her is all I'm saying." Rory sipped another glass of scotch. It seemed each of them had about ten glasses going.

"I think you both need someone to take care of you," I said.

The two men turned to me with matching mischievous expressions.

"I mean security," I rushed to say.

"I'm touched," Rory said.

"You'd like to be touched, you mean," answered Arch, and they both snickered.

I grabbed one of the newly arrived glasses of scotch and took a sip to mask my embarrassment. Not smoky at all. Interesting. I handed it to Neil.

"Aye, you have a point about security." Arch took another sip. "Rory here will be my bodyguard."

"I don't see how, as I'll be off on my book tour soon." Rory swirled his glass.

"You wrote a book?" Neil asked. Neil, of course, had an award-winning cocktail book of his own.

"It's a memoir of our time so far on the set of *Sleekit Sim*," Rory said.

"And that's not all you're up to, is it?" Arch said. "Don't be modest. You have that adventure show, for one thing."

"What adventure show?" I asked.

"Oh, fun with motorcycles, climbing, kayaking, caving. Doing idiotic stunts in natural settings." Rory waved a dismissive hand. "Just my usual hobbies. It's a travel show. I'm the host."

"And you also have a movie to film," Arch interjected. "We've had a devil of a time scheduling the show around it."

"Tell me more." I sipped the next glass of scotch. I really should ask what these were. This tasted of aging in ... port barrels, maybe? I handed it to Neil.

"Mmm," he intoned as he tasted it.

"It's a little movie we're filming in London," Rory said.

"With two Oscar winners and a killer script," Arch said brusquely. "Drink up and toast yourself."

"I'll toast you!" Mr. Mixy sounded desperate to cut in. "To Arch and Rory!"

They just looked at him for a few seconds, and after it got really uncomfortable, they burst into laughter. Neil and I awkwardly each raised a small glass and took a sip as they drank. We spent a few minutes tasting all our samples—all different, all yummy. Cliffstone deserved its reputation.

I turned to Rory and Arch and tried to get the conversation back on track. "Tell me about the letters. Do you recognize any of the signatures or content? Do you have any theories as to who it might be?"

"Arch should answer this one," Rory said. "He's the darling of the correspondence set."

"I wouldn't be too sure." Neil twisted the third glass in the flight slowly between his fingers, admiring the legs of the whisky sliding down the inside. "Some of the letters seem to be"—he paused—"more hostile to you."

"Ouch!" Rory exclaimed. "Hostile! I admit, I've seen a few of these letters, but I can't imagine one of our *followers* wrote them."

"You say *followers* like you're talking about someone specific," I noted, pleased that my fried cheese had arrived. I took a delicious bite and sighed in pleasure.

"Well," Arch said, "we do have a couple of deeply dedicated admirers who happen to show up wherever we're filming. Even that behind-the-scenes show when we tooled around the Highlands for a week. They always seemed to know what hotel we were staying in, that sort of thing. Honestly, I'm surprised they're not here right now."

"Do you have their names?" I pulled my phone from my bag to take notes.

Arch stared at the now mostly empty glasses in front of him. Was he starting to feel the scotch? "Oh, I don't know. Something like Feather or Flamingo."

Rory hooted. "Flamingo? No, it's birds. I mean, not women as birds. I would never call women birds." He winked at the bartender, who smirked back. "It's their names, like."

"Oh my God," I said. "It's not Lark and Wren, is it?"

"That's it!" both shouted, and I almost fell over in the blast of affirmation.

"Who?" Neil asked.

"I met them in Edinburgh. They were standing outside the bar with the other Archies." I slid an embarrassed look to Arch. "I hope you don't mind that term."

"How could I mind that term?" His smile carved a dimple in one cheek. Not quite as good as Mark Fairman's but close. "Lark and Wren, yes. They're persistent, but I don't think they would do much harm."

"They're quite skilled at stalking," Rory added with a kind of perverse admiration. "They don't seem too bad. Just too— there."

"And the Paintball Piper was a man," Neil pointed out.

"Of course it was a man," Arch said. "Why would a man write letters when he could just shoot us?"

The joke fizzled, and those of us at the bar got quiet. What if the guy *did* shoot them? Shoot them for real?

"Do you think a rival distillery might have anything to do with the letters?" I asked Arch. I didn't want to mention Cliff-stone by name and attract attention in this Cliffstone-heavy bar.

He lifted one shoulder. "That's a verra interesting possibil-ity. We are making scotch in refreshing new ways. Not everyone approves." He tipped a glass toward a bottle of the Cliffstone eighteen-year sitting on the bar. "I've heard through the grapevine that a certain distiller just might be jealous of all the attention we're getting, but it's only a rumor." Arch seemed smug, but why wouldn't he be? He was famous, he was going to make even more money with whisky, and he had all the fans he could want. And a few he didn't want, but we were working on that.

"If you think of anything that might help us find your suspicious correspondents, can you let us know?" I asked him and Rory, pulling cards from my bag and handing one to each of them.

"Of course," Arch said, and Rory patted my hand where it rested on the bar. *Rory patted my hand!* I stuffed another triangle of fried cheese into my mouth. The scotch was going to my head. Or maybe it was the company.

Mr. Mixy cleared his throat at the other end of the bar. It was the sound of a man desperate for attention. "I get fan letters sometimes. They seem obsessed with my beard. And they want to swizzle my stick, if you know what I mean."

Arch and Rory broke into laughter again. I stifled a groan and turned to Neil. "How's the haggis?"

"Not bad. Well disguised with breading and frying." He sipped the last glass of scotch. "This one's growing on me. The peat is really talking."

"Let me try it again." I accepted the glass, took a sniff— smoky—then a swallow. Now that my palate was over the smoke, the whisky tasted woodsy, like a campfire with burnt caramel and just a touch of sweetness. "Cliffstone has quite a range."

The bartender caught my comment. "They have several special releases outside of their usual variously aged single malts."

"And you have a lot of them right there." I waved at the wall of whisky.

"We do. Including some bottles so collectible we have to

keep them under lock and key." Then she went to the other end of the bar to tend to the demanding Mr. Mixy.

I looked at Neil. "Maybe we should go to Cliffstone."

"And talk to Callum Cotter? How can we get in? He and Seamus don't get along."

"Maybe Mark can help," I murmured. "He seems to know all these distillers."

"That's a good thought. Why don't you text him?"

A corner of my mouth lifted. "You don't mind?"

"Of course not. I'm not worried about Mark." Neil's playful gray eyes held mine with a smolder that put peat-burning to shame.

I swallowed. "OK." I texted Mark our request.

My phone rang a moment later.

"Are you in town?" Mark asked.

"At The Whale."

"I'll be there in a moment. I think I can help, but I want to come with you. Diana's wandered off to look at plant life, and I'm bored."

He ended the call, and I looked at Neil. "He's coming here first."

Neil's smolder evaporated into resignation. Then his phone buzzed. Actually, mine did too. We both looked. Our friends were done with their tasks and wanted to meet up for fish and chips.

"Aw, fish and chips!" I said. The cheese hadn't filled me up.

"We'll have to get some later," Neil said. "At least if Mark can get us our meeting."

At that moment, Mark walked through the door with Victoria, her tongue and ears flapping. "I got you your meeting. But we have to go now."

"There you go," Neil said, texting our regrets to Melody, Luke and Barclay. Dang it.

"You look disappointed, Hot Pepper," Mark said.

I slipped down from the stool and petted Victoria, who licked my hand and panted happily with her tongue hanging out. "Just missing a chance for fish and chips, that's all."

"That *is* tragic." He offered me a teasing pout, then turned to the bar, accepting a small bowl with water from the bartender that he set on the floor for Victoria before turning to the guys. "Hullo, my friends. Looks like you're having a grand lunch." He waved at Mr. Mixy and shook Arch and Rory's hands as if he did it every day. Well, Mark did run in more exalted circles than I did.

"Delicious and nutritious," Arch agreed, sipping again. The glasses were almost empty now, and Arch's eyes had a softness they didn't have earlier. Maybe the actors needed fish and chips, too. "Join us, Fairman?"

"Alas, I have an appointment and a cab waiting." Mark looked at me. "Shall we go?"

Chapter Ten

No one claimed the front seat of the taxi, maybe because of the stinky wooden box frame covered in webbing filling the front passenger floor.

"Mind the creel," the grizzled driver said.

So I found myself stuffed in the back between two handsome guys on our way to Cliffstone Distillery, holding Victoria as she sniffed madly. Normally this arrangement might have been pleasant, except the car was slightly smaller than a can of beer, the Cheese of the Month Club hadn't done anything to slim my hips, and the taxi smelled like three-day-old fish. And I still wasn't used to being on the "wrong" side of the road. I clutched the dog in panic whenever we zipped past another vehicle.

Finally, the car climbed the curving route to the Cliffstone complex and dropped us off in front of the distillery. We took a moment to air out and visit the sheep across the street. Mark held Victoria's leash as she barked at a sheep daubed with light blue paint, and it bleated back. The pup watered a thistle, and we turned to step into the road.

"Pepper!" Neil grabbed my arm, pulling me back.

Paying too much attention to the dog and not enough to the un-American traffic pattern, I'd narrowly avoided getting run down by a tiny van as it zoomed by. It sported signage for

Disco Devan, DJ Services, complete with a wee swinging mirror ball hanging from the rearview.

Neil turned me toward him. "You OK?"

"All good." I smiled at him. "You're my hero."

He smiled back. "Don't forget to look to the right."

"Shall we?" Mark sounded a trifle impatient as he tugged on Victoria's leash and beckoned us across the street. An open gate between two handsome old stone buildings drew us in.

A brick-paved courtyard sloped uphill through what felt like a faux medieval village. Colorful flowers overflowed the window boxes. Stonework gave the appearance of age, but this touristy part seemed clean and inviting, as you would want your distiller to be.

To the left, however, signs warned of danger. Under a roof, copper-colored vertical pipes and black pillars labeled "low wines condenser" betrayed this place's more industrial purpose: making high-end scotch and lots of it.

"This way." Mark led us up the slope, past a gift shop and a few tourists sitting on benches, and through a nondescript black door as if he owned the place. A small reception area with a few soft chairs, shelves with Cliffstone memorabilia and an empty desk greeted us. "Callum is expecting us. Stairs are this way."

Down the hall, past more offices, we found the stairs and headed up. A few moments later, Mark, carrying the dog, led us to an open door. "Hullo?" he called.

"Get in here, Fairman," came a crusty Scottish accent, and we all entered to see a smiling Callum Cotter stand up at his desk. He came around and rubbed Victoria's long ears, then shook Mark's hand.

Callum wore dark jeans and a button-up light-blue shirt. He was a good-looking man in his early sixties, with short, reddish-brown hair threaded with silver, a medium beard, and ruddy skin that had probably seen a lot of time in the blustery wind. Or the bar. Wire-rimmed reading glasses perched on his nose.

This office was much more traditional than Seamus MacIvor's at Aramach and not nearly as large. But it was cozy and rich with dark wood and golden lighting. Books and whisky stuffed the shelves behind Callum's obsessively clean desk. On the white walls hung framed photos of people working around the distillery or getting medals at competitions, and several medals were framed as well. A couple of paned windows looked out over the street, the pasture beyond and, in the distance, the blue sea. Were all the views here this breathtaking?

Mark gestured to Neil and me. "Callum, I'd like to introduce two very good friends, Neil Rockaway and Pepper Revelle of the Bohemia Bartenders. They're making cocktails for Aramach's event this weekend and wanted to see the O.G. scotch distillery around here."

Callum's hazel eyes flickered over us. "Pleased to meet you," he said neutrally, and he shook our hands as well. He offered me a little smirk. "I heard they hired you because you were pretty."

"Neil's the pretty one," I said. "I'm the brains of this outfit."

Neil and Mark burst out laughing at my joke, and Callum's smirk turned into a smile. "Then your brain must be the size of the North Sea, because I've read your colleague's book." Callum pointed to his shelves, where, to my surprise, I spotted Neil's *Cutting-Edge Classics: Cocktails with a Twist.* "Though you didn't include much in the way of scotch cocktails, as I recall."

"You're right," Neil said, following Callum's lead as we all sat on the comfy leather-and-wood armchairs, smaller than Callum's big CEO throne. Victoria flopped onto the floor. "But we'll be showing off scotch in our drinks this weekend. Come to think of it, your new Grimleens bottling would do very nicely in cocktails."

Callum lifted an eyebrow, clearly surprised at Neil's familiarity with Cliffstone. He stood and made a selection from a shelf stuffed with bottles and set it on the desk. The label showed the Cliffstone logo and a beautiful twilight photo of the Orkney hills and sea with *Grimleens* in an elegant script font.

"It works well in cocktails because it's one of our few scotches that, frankly, tastes more like bourbon," Callum said. "We hope it will attract more of you Americans to our whisky. That said, I still prefer it on its own." He produced four curvy Glencairn tasting glasses, poured us each a dram and nestled back into his chair.

"Now we're talking." Mark cheerfully held up his glass. "Neil, say something."

Neil, who stored an archive of toasts and quotes in his indeed *very* big brain, lifted his glass as well. "How about Mark Twain? 'I always take scotch whisky at night as a preventative of a toothache. I have never had the toothache, and what is more, I never intend to have it.'"

His quote induced a round of chuckles and lessened the subtle tension, and we all took a sip. Oh, my. Compared with the flight we'd tasted at The Whale, this was sweeter, smoother, yet held a touch of complexity and earth that suggested scotch. But it was only a suggestion.

"Very nice," I said. "Was it aged differently or—"

"We don't do Caribbean aging," Callum cut me off. "We occasionally use a port barrel or another alternative. We definitely don't drop chips of wood in a steel barrel. This is a matter of judicious barreling and blending. Scotch is built on tradition. On the land. On the peat. We have a carefully conserved source here that should last us another three hundred fifty years at least. I am willing to try new things, but quality and tradition are what we are all about. We are not trying to be the social media flavor of the month."

Ouch. I had no doubt his vitriol was directed at Aramach.

"Aren't you doing a new promotion?" Mark asked lightly, his tone a balm to Callum's biting words. "I read about it in one of the entertainment mags. With that lovely actress from the *Fairy Kingdom* movies? Given the name of my distillery, I rather envied your coup." Right. Because Mark owned Fairyland Distillery.

"You don't mean Freya Dearness?" I asked. "She's wonderful."

Callum shifted in his seat, caught by the irony. Maybe his marketing team *did* want Cliffstone to be the social media flavor of the month. "She *is* wonderful. And she's very much in line with our traditional values. She's from Orkney. In fact, she's shooting a new video for us. Very high-end and focused on the legends and history here."

He seemed kind of excited about Freya Dearness, but disdain for anything that didn't fit his "traditional" box was clear. Such as a certain cocky actor who starred in a silly historical adventure show.

"She's about as far from Arch Halliday as you can get," I observed.

"True. He isn't Cliffstone material." Callum chuckled. "Ms. Dearness can't stand him."

"Why's that?" I asked.

"Perhaps you can ask her. She's just come up from Edinburgh."

She was in Edinburgh? She wasn't the Paintball Piper, but that was an interesting coincidence. "If we wanted to talk to her, where would we find her?" I asked.

Callum lifted an eyebrow. "Please don't crowd her. She's filming at the cathedral today."

"You're filming a scotch ad in a cathedral?" Neil asked in surprise.

Callum shrugged. "They shot a quiz show there once. Scotch is much more sacred."

As religions went, he could do worse.

"If you try to see her, I might go with you," Mark said. "I'm a little bit in love with Freya Dearness."

I turned to him. "You're not writing her creepy letters, are you?"

"Ha." Mark showed a dimple. I refrained from fanning myself.

"Speaking of letters," I said to Callum, "has she received any disturbing correspondence from fans?"

He took another sip of whisky. "Not to my knowledge. Then again, we don't have a mailbox in the middle of town just begging for stalkers to drop her a line."

"So you've heard about Arch's letters?"

Callum grunted. "I can guess. I know about Aramach's mailbox. It's hard to miss. Besides, Seamus built a whole promotional campaign around it."

"Do you and Seamus know each other well?" I asked.

"Not really."

Neil absently twirled his glass between his fingers and focused on our host. "Did you both grow up here?"

"He's a late transplant to Orkney. Had a grandmother here, inherited her farm and decided to get into scotch."

"Does that mean he visited Kirkwall as a kid?" I asked.

"Are you here to talk about Seamus MacIvor?" Callum asked. "I thought you wanted to see the distillery."

"We'd like that very much," said Mark. "I've taken the tour so many times, I could probably give it myself."

"Why don't you, then?" Callum said. "I have things to do."

"Thanks for your hospitality," said Neil, ever polite, as we stood. "Can I sign that book for you?"

Callum seemed pleased by the suggestion. He pulled it off the shelf and handed it and a pen to Neil. "Have at it."

As Neil signed the title page, I scanned the photos on the wall. My gaze caught on one showing a few smiling men standing around a big copper still. A little girl hugged the legs of one of the men. I pointed. "Aw, look. Who is she?"

Callum's head snapped up from where he'd been watching Neil, and he glanced at the photo. "A daughter of one of our employees."

I had a theory as to who it was, but I wanted to see what he said. "That's nice. Do the workers always get to bring their kids?"

"No. We don't allow children here as a rule, with the exception of tours, of course, though my son visited occasionally when I could drag him away from his video games. Now he works in our accounting department. He'll take over from me one day." Callum made a motion as if to wave away the photo. "The girl loved to hang around after school while her father worked. It did no harm. Sadly, he's passed from this world. A good man. You know the way, Fairman?"

"Yes. Thanks, my friend. Let's get together for a drink and a cigar."

Callum relaxed into a genuine smile. "Definitely. Have a nice tour. Goodbye."

"Thank you for the whisky," I added on our way out.

Callum grunted again. I'd probably annoyed him with all my random questions. Worse, I didn't get them all answered.

How interesting was it that a photo of Blair and her father —that *had* to be Blair—was on Callum's wall? Guess it just showed how small of a place this was. Callum had nice things to say about her dad, but he was definitely cranky about Aramach and Seamus MacIvor.

If Freya Dearness was from Orkney, would she know more about the men's past? And did their history merit enough enmity for Callum to threaten Arch and therefore Seamus's Aramach? I needed to find out.

Chapter Eleven

Mark kept the tour short, but it was enough to see the differences in the Aramach and Cliffstone operations. Aramach sent its peat away to a company that processed its barley; Cliffstone did its malting on an open floor, old-school, though it was the wrong season for it, so the floor was empty. Cliffstone's warehouse was vast, dark and cool—partially built into the hill, which helped with climate control—and filled with barrels and the sweet, earthy aromatics of aging whisky.

"Callum wouldn't say this, but not all of the malt is done here," Mark confided. "And fifty years ago, the whiskies mostly went into blends. But Callum's father initiated the push to age single malts, and here we are, in a now-revered temple of scotch."

"Speaking of temples," I said as we reentered the court-yard, "should we go to the cathedral and see if we can catch Freya Dearness?"

"Oh, I say, that would be lovely." Mark beamed.

Neil was less enthused. "Callum didn't want us bothering her."

"But he also said we should ask her why she doesn't like Arch." I crouched and scooped up Victoria, in need of a dog cuddle, and Mark handed me her leash. The dog immediately put her chin over my arm and fell asleep. "I don't know if Freya Dearness hates Arch enough to harass him. But she grew up here. She might know more about whatever happened between Callum and Seamus."

Neil sighed. "I suppose it wouldn't hurt to get in her vicinity and see if we have an opportunity. Be subtle about it."

"Ms. Dearness!" I screamed across the graveyard outside St. Magnus Cathedral. "Ms. Dearness!"

"Holy hell," Neil said.

"They're on a break," I told him in my defense.

Mark held tightly to Victoria's leash just outside the cemetery gate—not the grand war memorial gate out front, but a closed metal gate set in a stone wall, across the street from what looked like castle ruins. More cool stuff to see if we had time.

We clustered with a handful of other lookie-loos who'd realized a major movie star swept through the timeworn gravestones in a flowing lavender gown and blue velvet cape, a camera crew filming her every move. Only now Freya drank from a big metal bottle (water, presumably, not scotch) while a woman wearing a hairstylist's utility belt combed and rearranged the star's sable locks. The crew fiddled with their gear, and another annoyed-looking woman with a tablet in her hand glared at us.

It was she, not Freya Dearness, who walked over to confront us. Unlike the statuesque Freya, this woman was birdlike and slight, cute in an elfin way, with pixie-cut blond hair, freckles and gray snapping eyes. I put her in her mid-forties.

"Ms. Dearness doesn't have time for autographs right now, I'm afraid," she said in what had to be a local Orcadian accent.

The other fans let out an "awww" as the blond woman shooed them away. I wasn't going to be shooed.

"Please tell Ms. Dearness that Callum Cotter suggested we speak with her," I said. "It will only take a minute." Well, it could take all day, but I'd try to control myself. "What's your name?"

The woman hesitated. "Elsie Firth. I'm the cultural liaison. I'm here to make sure everything goes smoothly."

"And that no one tramples the graves?" Mark asked.

"Yes, that particularly," she said without cracking a smile.

"Do you work for Cliffstone, Ms. Firth?" I asked.

"I'm a historian and consultant. I work for myself, but sometimes the council hires me to do things like this. Usually I'm busy on a dig, but sometimes I help visiting film crews get things right. Who did you say you were?"

I introduced all three of us and said we'd just come from Cliffstone and Callum.

"I'll ask her if she wants to speak with you. We're on a tight schedule, but she might have a moment." Elsie stamped back toward the crew and the star, who leaned against a particularly large gravestone until Elsie shooed her off. Elsie liked to shoo, apparently.

A minute later, Elsie led Neil and me through the gate and down the path toward Freya and the crew. But not Mark. Elsie wouldn't let him inside the cemetery with Victoria.

"I'll make a very handsome donation!" he called after us. "Please?"

Elsie, unmoved, ignored him as I stifled a laugh. I looked over my shoulder and offered a helpless shrug. Mark pointed at me as if to say, *You'll pay for this!* Or maybe he just wanted me to get an autograph.

All of this rubbing elbows with celebrities had me discombobulated. I was about to meet the star of one of my favorite fantasy movie series. First Arch and Rory, now Freya Dearness? It wasn't like I'd never met stars before. I could actually call Oleanna Lee a friend. But I was just enough of a geek to lose my tongue for a second when Elsie presented us as "these people from Cliffstone."

"I'm Neil Rockaway," he explained, "and this is Pepper Revelle. We're with the Bohemia Bartenders, in town for an event for Aramach Distillery. Something has come up that brought us to Cliffstone. Callum Cotter suggested we might ask you a question or two."

"How mysterious," Freya said with a droll smile. Her Scottish accent was soft, and I could understand her a lot more easily than I could, say, Magnus, whose "to" always sounded like "tae." Then again, she had classical theater training and had to be understood across cultures in the movies. She could probably speak in any accent she wanted.

"It's great to meet you." I tamped down my excitement. "We might want a little privacy." I threw a sideways glance at Elsie, who hovered nearby. The hair lady had already moved away and was chatting with a camera guy.

Elsie scowled.

"Why don't we step inside the church?" Freya suggested. "We can find a quiet corner. We'll be all right, Elsie," she assured her minder.

"Very well," Elsie said. "The south transept door is unlocked."

Freya led us through the door.

The church. A funny way to put it. It was easy to forget the scale of the cathedral when you stood in the graveyard, looking at it from just one angle. It was big from the outside, sure. But the inside hinted of infinity. The architects reached toward the heavens with the soaring ceilings, building something that would inspire awe even in wayward souls like me.

I grabbed a brochure from a table and took in the south transept. It was one stubby arm of the cross-shaped floor plan. If you didn't look up, it was no big deal.

But as we took a few steps inside toward the center of the cathedral and its dazzling height, I realized this niche was so much more than a side entrance. Above the door was a deeply inset, arched stained glass window, with another above it. Toward the top, a huge, round window, its panes framed like a flower, exploded in sunlight. It cast a glowing, angled, lacy pattern on a stone interior wall, also rich with carved details and arched openings. Far above, vaulted wooden beams defined the ceiling. It all drew the eye up and up and up toward the light.

"Beautiful, isn't it?" Freya said in response to my gawking. "I used to come here often as a child. There's so much history here. I didn't know it all, but I'd make up stories to go with the tombstones." She beckoned, leading us along the south wall toward the front of the church, and stopped before one of several inscribed slabs erected between sets of decorative stone arches.

Ornate carved words filled the bottom of the stone. Above them, a woman on her knees pressed her hands together in prayer as she looked up toward a crown held by a hand sticking out of a cloud. Two angels' faces looked on, above an arch spangled with stars and the moon. A rose, an hourglass, and a skull and crossbones completed the tableau.

I leaned in to look more closely at the skull. "Memento mori."

"That's right," Freya said with approval.

"'Remember you must die,'" Neil translated.

"My parents run a church in New Orleans," I said. "I remember seeing these skulls in a book they had on religious symbols. As a kid I always thought they were pretty cool."

Freya chuckled. "So did I. There are several of these here." She looked around. The few tourists in the church were elsewhere, their murmurs indistinct as they floated through the echoing space. "Now what can I do for you?"

I looked at Neil, then spoke. Might as well get right to the point. "We're looking into threatening letters sent to Arch Halliday, who's the front man for Aramach, at the distillery's request. Our inquiries led us to Cliffstone, and Callum Cotter said you—know Arch."

Freya's gentle smile had morphed into a straight line as I spoke. "I know him."

I lowered my voice further. "This is just between us. I know you don't know me, but we're just trying to get at why someone might be targeting Arch. I'm not saying it's you!" I said to her frown. "Just trying to get a better sense of who he is. We are known for our discreet investigations."

That sounded completely ridiculous, especially because my "investigations" usually ended in disasters, most of them loud.

"Weren't you the one yelling my name earlier?" Freya asked.

Neil made a funny noise.

"I'm also known for my persistence?" My reply sounded like a question as I tried to defend myself.

To my relief, Freya laughed. "I'll talk to you. But let's make this long story short, shall we?"

I sighed in relief. "How do you know Arch Halliday?"

"We worked together. One of my first leading roles in London. *Romeo and Juliet.*"

"Really? I didn't peg Arch as a Shakespearean actor," Neil said.

"I'm not sure being in a Shakespeare play makes you a Shakespearean actor," Freya quipped. "I was Juliet."

"Was Arch your Romeo?" I asked.

Her expression was as dry as her tone. "He was not. He played Mercutio, so he was murdered early each night. Not early enough, in my opinion."

Yikes!

"So you, uh, hated him?" I asked.

"Not at first. We slept together, and then I moved on." Freya must have noticed my eyes bugging out. "It's not a secret. Lord knows, he's brought it up in interviews. He's tasteless that way. Anyway, he didn't like me telling him it was over. I think he likes to be the one to make that decision and didn't enjoy being at the other end of the stick. He undermined me with the director. And then he spread some rumors that ruined my chances at starring in a very well-known television drama. But my reviews were good, the worm turned, and I landed *Fairy Kingdom.*"

A huge starring role that made her career. "Where did Arch go from there?"

"The fact that you have to ask should tell you a lot. He bounced around, did some adverts, minor roles in dramas and that sort of thing. He's not without talent," she said matter-of-factly. "He simply has very bad manners."

"I see." And he tried to ruin her career. She was more philosophical about it than I would be.

Neil changed the subject. "Have you received any creepy letters lately?"

A cloud briefly crossed her brow. "Nothing recent. I sometimes do, but they go through my management company, and they tend to weed out the ones they know I don't want to see. Someone's always in love with Aradienne," she said wryly.

Aradienne, the fairy queen in her movies.

"What were you doing in Edinburgh?" I asked.

"Business meeting." She gave me a puzzled look that resolved into realization. "Ah, were you there for the Paintball Piper? Not a very funny joke, if you ask me. Whichever one of them did it should be ashamed. Though I didn't think Rory would be that cruel."

"You know Rory, too?" Neil asked.

"Of course. He's from Kirkwall."

"And you're from Orkney, too, aren't you?" I asked as we slowly walked back toward the south door. "Did you know Rory growing up?"

"Indeed I did. We were in school together."

Wow. A lot of star power for such a small place. "How about Callum Cotter or Seamus MacIvor?"

"I didn't know them that well. I'm closer in age to Seamus than I am to Callum. Seamus spent summers here. He and I were in a summer youth program together once, all field trips to the historic sites. Callum was a guest guide one day, because I remember touring the distillery and him telling us he was going to inherit it all. I never dreamed I'd be filming a campaign for him."

"How old were you?" I asked.

"Let's see; I was about twelve, I think, as was Seamus, which would've put Callum in his thirties?" Freya glanced at her wrist, but where a watch would be was a thick silver bracelet depicting a snake, its head biting its tail. She let out a small huff of frustration. "I don't know what time it is, but whatever it is, I'm well behind it. I'm afraid I must get back to work. They want to shoot me *not* going back through time at the Ring of Brodgar."

I chuckled at the sarcastic stone circle reference. "No problem. Thank you for showing us the tombstones and for talking with us. Would you mind signing something for our friend at the gate? He couldn't come in with the dog, and he's a big fan."

Freya's eyes lit up. "Was that Mark Fairman? He's been in the gossip pages once or thrice, hasn't he? Of course."

Mark would be thrilled that she knew who he was. I dug the cathedral brochure out of my bag and handed it to her with a Sharpie. She wrote a few words and added her big, loopy signature, then handed it all back to me.

"If you're ever in Bohemia, Florida, come see us at our bars," I said. "I'll make you a Sazerac."

"And I'll make you whatever you want." Neil smiled at her. Was he a bit starstruck, too?

"I might need a trip to Florida next winter," she acknowledged, asking us the names of our bars as we exited. We thanked her warmly, and she waved as Elsie ushered her away to the crew.

We headed for the closed gate, where Mark anxiously peered through the bars.

"He looks like a lost puppy at an animal shelter," Neil said.

Victoria was a happier puppy, and she barked as we approached.

"Mark, she knows who you are!" I said as we exited the cemetery.

"You're winding me up," Mark replied in disbelief and delight.

"She's seen you in the gossip rags, apparently." I dug around in my bag and produced the brochure and waved it in front of him.

He snatched it and examined the signature. "Cheeky!"

"What did she write?" Neil asked.

"She said to look her up but only if I bring a bottle of Frilly Fairy Gin for the fairy queen." He grinned and raised an eyebrow.

I looked at the ruins across the road. "I wish we could go there."

"Tomorrow," Mark said. "Neil told me you have an open schedule, and Albert and the minibus should be here by then, so I have a full day of tourism planned for all of your crew and Diana, too. Unless you're still playing detective."

"Maybe we can do both?" I asked hopefully. "I'm not sure where to go from here. Maybe look over the rest of the letters Izara was emailing to me."

"We need to check in with the bartenders," Neil said.

"And get a real meal. I'm starving," I added. "And maybe a nap?"

"Why don't we head back to the inn for a bit?" Neil's eyes sparkled. "Check out the room?"

I stepped closer, put my hands on his chest and smiled up at him. "Do you want to take a nap, too?"

"Good lord." Mark rolled his eyes. "I'd say 'Get a room,' but apparently, you already have one."

Chapter Twelve

This time, we texted Magnus and requested a ride, then talked him into stopping by the chippy, as he called it, so we could get our fish and chips to go: haddock with light-as-air breading and hearty fries. Magnus had to translate for me when the young woman behind the counter asked me if I wanted salt and vinegar. It was more like *saltenvinegar* spoken at the speed of light. Good call, though.

We bought some for Magnus, too, and all four of us sat on a low wall by the harbor and looked at the water as we inhaled huge pieces of delicious fish and Victoria snarfed up strategically dropped morsels. Afterward, I still had a big piece left over in the cardboard box. I hoped our room had a fridge.

I was pleasantly full and drowsy by the time the shuttle got back to Rose Hill House. I looked forward to that nap. Maybe a *real* nap, though having Neil in the same bed would be awfully tempting. Stupid jet lag. It was kicking my butt.

The place was quiet. Maybe the other bartenders and guests were having a siesta, too. Neil and I promised to meet Mark for cocktail hour, whenever that was, and we tromped up the stairs to the pretty but rather chilly room.

The ornately carved ceiling was high, befitting an old house, with a small crystal chandelier hanging from a medallion at its center. The floors were dark, glossy wood and the walls a pale yellow, decorated with a couple of paintings, one of cliffs and the sea, another of boats in the harbor. The large window, above an old-fashioned radiator, looked out over the lawn, with scattered houses beyond and blue water in the distance. An open door led to an ensuite bathroom.

"No fridge," I said, surveying the desk, a comfy chair and a couple of nightstands. "But they brought up our bags."

"Why don't I go look for a place to stow that?" Neil suggested, taking my fish box.

"I suppose we could just throw it away." But I looked longingly at the box. It probably wouldn't be as good later when it was cold, I told myself.

"I'll see what I can do."

"OK, thanks!"

Neil smiled and took the box and left the room. He was a problem-solver. And he was sweet to me. I was a very lucky girl.

He came back several minutes later, after I'd plugged in my phone and shed my shoes and glasses and jacket and unbuttoned my jeans, since there was a lot of fish swimming around in my tummy. I lay on the comfy sleigh bed, propped against the fat pillows, looking up at the chandelier. The light was off, so only the natural, soft afternoon glow from the window winked in the crystals.

I turned my head toward Neil as he closed the door behind him. "Any luck?"

"I gave it away. I hope that's OK."

"Really? That sounds like a great solution. Who wanted it?"

Neil paused a beat. "Mr. Mixy."

"Oh. Well, at least it won't go to waste. But you should've warned me. I could've garnished it with Dulcolax first."

Neil snorted. "I know you wouldn't do that."

"I would be *tempted* to do that, given means and opportunity. Then again, I'm not sure we want to hang out with an intestinally challenged Mr. Mixy. And I suspect we'll see a lot more of him on this trip since he's here for Aramach's launch party."

Neil cringed a little as he sat on the bed and pulled off his shoes. "It gets worse. Mark invited him on the outing tomorrow, though his crew will have to drive separately since they won't fit."

"But Stephan will?" I wanted to be as far from Mr. Mixy as possible. I didn't recall how many seats there were. "How many people can fit in this van?"

"Up to fourteen plus Albert, apparently. Mark and I spoke before the trip, and I had Millie book our tickets for the historic sites, but I didn't know who all would be coming before now. It looks like it'll be us five bartenders, Mark, Diana, Alastair. And Mark has invited Arch and Rory, too. They agreed to go if booze was involved."

"What? Arch and Rory? Really?" I sat up straight. I wasn't sure you could put that much hotness into a passenger van without it exploding from pure sexiness.

"Mark knows them. He knows everybody."

"Not Freya Dearness. At least not yet."

Neil chuckled. "And he hired a guide." He had shed his sweater, revealing a simple black T-shirt advertising his bar, The Junction Box, that fit very nicely indeed. "Plus Izara is coming in hopes of getting social media material from Arch for Aramach, and Magnus will ride along for security."

Neil lay back against the pillows and tugged on my arm so I collapsed next to him. I curled on my side so I could run a hand through his thick hair, dark brown with hints of red. It was neatly cut but just long enough for that. I looked into his eyes, those gorgeous gray irises rimmed in dark blue, then traced his cheekbones and nose and his lips, framed by his trim beard and mustache. Was this guy really mine? Finally?

He grasped my wrist and kissed my finger, then leaned closer and touched my lips with his.

"Mmm." I opened to his heady kiss, snuggling into his lean, muscled body, drinking him in as my chill evaporated in a rush of heat. The nap could wait. He slipped a hand under my top, sliding it around my back, strong and warm. "You're touching my tattoo. When are you going to get one?"

He kissed my neck. "Do I really have to?"

"Just one. It's a bonding experience." I giggled. Then I stopped laughing as he pulled me close and made me forget about tattoos and exes and silly celebrities.

SOME TIME LATER, we made our way to the ground floor and the game room. Our bartenders played pool. Mark and Alastair relaxed on the cushy leather furniture, and Diana browsed the bookshelves.

To my surprise, Arch and Rory walked in and plopped down at the game table. It was maybe 6 p.m. local time but felt earlier given the light coming in the windows, that soft, far northern light that added a touch of magic to everything.

"Finally, someone who can drive the bar cart." Mark gestured to a golden cart loaded with bottles and glasses, bar tools and an ice bucket that had materialized since I saw the room this morning. "Your people are busy, Alastair is 'on holiday,' and we all know you two will delight us with your skills."

"Ha!" Alastair said from the chair where he played with his phone. He never looked up.

"Well, flattery will get you everywhere," I said. "Where'd this come from?"

"Ola. With some help from Seamus and myself, who sent over enough booze to stock it for the week," Mark said. "Who wants a gin and tonic?"

"Sacrilege," Arch said. "I want Aramach scotch."

"Is there any Cliffstone on that cart?" Rory joked.

"Hush. Don't make trouble," Mark said.

"Funny hearing that from you," Diana said with a grin.

"Says the woman who got into trouble today," he answered.

"What?" I asked as Neil stepped up, took orders and made quick work of the cocktails using Aramach's twelve-year and Mark's Frilly Fairy Gin, along with his tonic water. I sliced a few limes on the cutting board as Diana closed the book in her hand and spoke.

"It was the oddest thing," she said. "I borrowed a bicycle from the inn and took a long ride today, as I often do, investigating the wildflowers and other plants. I was examining a lovely blanket of thrift—they call it sea pinks around here—on the edge of a meadow overlooking the sea when I heard voices. I looked up and found people shouting at me!"

"Why?" I asked.

"I'm not sure. I wasn't trespassing. There were only half a dozen of them, perhaps, and they carried signs. My guess is they were bored and anxious for an audience. It's hard to have an effective protest without anyone hearing you, and this area was rather remote."

"Like a tree falling in the forest," Neil said.

"Exactly so," Diana continued, accepting a G&T from him

and coming around the couch to sit next to Mark. "Thank you. At any rate, they called me a tourist! Someone actually shouted 'Begone, tourist!' I'm a botanist!"

Mark snickered, and she glared at him.

"Not only that," she said, "but they carried signs that said things like 'Save the Past' and 'Digging Is Deadly.' I believe one even showed a circle with a slash through it, superimposed over a bottle of scotch."

Arch sat up straight, the ice in his glass clinking. "Which scotch?"

"That one." Diana pointed to an Aramach bottle on the bar cart.

"Huh." Arch sank back into his chair. "That's strange. What do they have against scotch?"

"And Aramach in particular?" I asked, handing a G&T to Alastair, who granted me a brief smile. "Did any of the signs say anything about Arch?"

Arch and Rory both looked at me in alarm.

I swallowed under the pressure of their celebrity gaze. "Well, you know, given the letters, it seems like a valid question."

Diana looked thoughtful. "I don't think so." Just as Arch let out a breath, she added, "Oh, but there was a sign that showed ..." She looked at Arch and bit her lip. "Yes, it was you, I'm afraid, in your kilt, like you wear on your show."

Arch managed a brittle smile. "Did I have a circle with a slash through it, too?"

Diana's smile was also strained. "Um, no. It looked more as if you'd been stabbed with a dagger."

"Diana!" Mark exclaimed as Arch's face turned stony.

"I'm sorry, but that's what it looked like." She turned an apologetic glance back at Arch.

"I don't like the sound of that," Neil said. "That seems like a very explicit threat. One the police should know about."

"Wait a second." Arch's expression changed to one of delight. "That must be from the season two finale. Remember, Rory? When the duke stabbed me and everyone thought I was going to die? I thought that was one of my better episodes. Fans loved it. They went wild online wondering what would happen next. Maybe one of these protesters is a fan."

I couldn't believe he was that naive.

"An odd choice of image," Mark said, echoing my concern. He turned to Diana. "I don't think you should go that way alone again. I don't want you entangled with such bloodthirsty sorts."

She shrugged. "They didn't seem particularly dangerous." But she didn't protest as she usually did whenever Mark tried to warn her off adventuring. Maybe she was shaken, too.

"We need to find out who those protesters are," I said. "If they have a thing about Arch, they might be behind the weird letters."

Arch looked like he wanted to say something, but then he didn't. What was he thinking?

"I think I need another one," he told Neil.

OK, then. At the rate he'd sucked down the first scotch, he was probably more rattled than he let on.

"Diana, maybe later you can show me where you were on a map?" I wanted to show it to Seamus and see what he had to say.

"Of course," she said.

Melody, Luke and Barclay wandered over to grab a drink.

"Good game?" I asked.

"Melody humiliated us again," Luke said, but he didn't seem unhappy about it.

"Too much time spent in bars." Melody grinned.

"Not like everyone else here," I joked.

As the others talked, she sidled up to me. "Did you have a good nap?"

I read the mischief in her eyes. "Didn't get quite as much sleep as I'd planned."

She laughed. "Good. It's about time you had some sleep deprivation."

Neil called over Barclay and Luke, and we had a quick conversation about the hall and the preparations for Saturday. And then we told them what we'd seen today.

"Freya Dearness?" Barclay pursed his lips in a silent whistle. "Man, I'd love to meet her."

"She wants to meet Mark!" I said.

"She what?" Diana looked up from her book.

"Hasn't Mark showed you his autograph?" I wondered if I should've kept quiet. I was rooting for Mark and Diana. Then again, I wasn't going to interfere. If a movie star was going to distract him, that was none of my business.

"She had the cheek to say she wanted to meet me but only if I brought her gin," Mark said. "Ridiculous."

Diana smiled. "A small price to pay to meet someone so famous."

"I want women to love me for my charm, not my gin," he said.

Or your millions, I thought as Diana laughed. But the big goofball did have charm. And stupefying sex appeal. Not to mention a generous heart. Better than millions anytime. I glanced at Neil, who was looking at me, the corner of his mouth quirked up in a half smile.

"She was going to film at the Ring of Brodgar after we met her," I said. "I'd love to go there. Is it on the tour tomorrow?"

"We could go right now if Magnus is available to drive," Neil suggested, "since the sun sets so late here. It might be nice. And then maybe go get some dinner?"

"Capital idea," Mark said.

After a moment of tapping his phone, Neil looked up. "Magnus will be here in fifteen. Enough time to finish our drink."

"Or three," Arch said to everyone's chuckles.

"Great." I looked around. "Who wants to go back in time?"

Everyone wanted to go except Alastair, so Mark made him promise to take Victoria, who was snoozing in Mark's room, for a walk.

"Fine," Alastair said. "So long as you let me know where to meet you for dinner."

At least he wasn't totally unsocial. And at least Mr. Mixy wasn't here. Then again, not knowing where he was could sometimes be as nerve-wracking as knowing.

"Ooo!" Rory hopped up, pulling a buzzing phone from his pocket. "I'll just be a moment." He left the room.

"I'd better hit the W.C. before we go," I told Neil.

He smiled. "Cute. I'm going to start calling the bathrooms in my bar 'water closets.'"

"They'll never understand that in Bohemia," Melody said, and I laughed because it was true.

I slipped out to the lobby and couldn't help overhearing Rory, who was down the hall with his back to me, talking on the phone. "Don't worry. He doesn't have a Scooby, as usual." He paused. "No. Stop freaking out. Yes, I'm being careful." He turned and saw me. I waved awkwardly and made a beeline for the bathroom, disappearing from his view, but I heard him say more softly, "I have to go. I'll see you soon, all right? We'll figure it out. Love you."

Well, that was interesting. I did my business and touched up my lipstick in the mirror and considered what I'd heard. What did he mean by Scooby? Like Scooby-Doo? And who was he talking about? My mind leapt to Arch. Was Rory planning a prank? Was he talking about the Paintball Piper stunt? And who was he talking to? Sounded like a girlfriend.

When I left the W.C., I almost ran into Rory, waiting outside the door.

He seemed amused by my gasp. "Need to spend a penny." But then he just stood there for a second, searching my face. "Pepper?"

"Yes?" He'd given me a start, and now I was starstruck. Rory, aka Kenzie on *Sleekit Sim,* was talking to me.

"You seem like a trustworthy sort. Don't make too much of what you just heard, all right? I don't need the world knowing about my personal life."

"I didn't hear much, which means I don't know much, but of course, I'll be discreet." That was the second time today I'd claimed discretion. In this case, I was pretty sure I could do it.

"Thanks. I appreciate it. And I'm glad you're here to help Arch." His smile seemed genuine. Then he ducked into the W.C.

Wow. I had a moment with Rory, and an illuminating one. He was worried about the crazy letters, of that much I was sure.

At least Magnus was driving us this evening. He could offer some security for Arch. As it was, there were too many people who seemed out to get him, but figuring out who was like trying to grab ahold of fog. Were these fanciful threats? Or something much scarier?

I was starting to understand why he drank so much.

I reentered the lounge to find folks shrugging on jackets and getting ready to go. A few minutes later, Magnus entered the room.

"You're going to love this," he said. "Your favorite stalkers are here."

Chapter Thirteen

"**O**h, no," Rory said.

"Not the birds?" Arch held up his hands. "I mean the women with bird names."

"I believe that's them, yes," Magnus said.

"Is that all?" Arch asked with mock disappointment, prompting laughs.

"That's quite enough, sir." Magnus had squared his shoulders and assumed his role as security guy, determined to protect Aramach's co-owner and spokesman against the stalkers at the door.

"They're mostly harmless," Arch replied.

"Yeah, that's what *The Hitchhiker's Guide to the Galaxy* said about Earth," Barclay said, "and look how that turned out."

"I love that book," Rory replied, and he and Barclay shared a grin.

No one seemed particularly worried that Lark and Wren—at least, I assumed it was the Americans I met in Edinburgh—might be outside, especially if they were alone. But Magnus insisted on holding the door for us and ushering us to the shuttle van as the two women looked on. Yep, it was them.

"Pepper!" Wren called out.

I kind of had to stop. And what was that saying about keeping your enemies closer? Not that Wren seemed like an enemy, but then again, she was part of the crowd that almost crushed me in Edinburgh.

I paused as the others boarded the minibus. "Hi, Wren. How are you doing?" Then I thought about the letters. "How long have you been in Orkney?"

"Oh, we caught a flight yesterday." That must have been right after the event in Edinburgh. So she had time to drop a note in Aramach's box here if she wanted to.

Wren pushed her glasses up her nose. Her round cheeks were rosy in the cool air, and today she wore jeans and a dangerously low-cut black top that showed off her generous curves. Her taller sister, Lark, had on a similar outfit, only her top was the same purple as the streak in her dark hair.

To my astonishment, Arch stepped away from Magnus and toward them both.

What is he doing?

"Sir!" Magnus called out.

Arch waved him off. "Ladies. So nice of you to stop by."

Wren turned toward him, forgetting I was there, and stammered, "Ar-Ar-Arch!"

"That's my name! And don't you forget it!"

"As if!" Lark almost shouted, a grin stretching across her face.

Arch shook Wren's hand, gazing into her eyes, then took Lark's and leaned in and whispered into the big sister's ear for several seconds as her eyes danced in fevered excitement. Then he lifted her hand, kissed it, and waved to both of them. "Farewell, my sonsie lasses!"

They clutched each other and squealed, and I could see why. He'd turned on the charm afterburners and even used a phrase his character wielded on *Sleekit Sim* whenever he broke a woman's heart, which was just about every episode.

I followed Arch onto the bus.

Magnus exhaled noisily as he shut the door behind us and sat in the driver's seat. "Was that really necessary?" he asked Arch, who sat up front with Rory.

"Got to keep the fans happy." Arch wore a mischievous look.

Rory, not so much. "Better you than me. They're a little too close for comfort. How did they know we were staying here?"

"Stalkers have their ways, my man," his co-star replied. "I asked Lark not to tell anyone else where we are. Told her it's our secret. Might as well make the best of it. These ladies haven't threatened me yet."

"That you know of," I muttered from where I sat behind them with Neil, and the actors both turned and gave me a look.

"Seems you also know the lovely birds, do you?" Arch said to me as Magnus drove us out of the property. "Are you a stalker too?"

"Ha! I met them outside the bar in Edinburgh. They and their fellow Archies almost crushed me trying to get to you."

"But they backed off when they saw me open the door," Neil said. "Thank God I'm not a movie star."

Arch and Rory laughed. "Oh," Arch said, "it has its perks."

My imagination ran wild, perhaps not to my credit, but how many groupies had ended up in their beds? It might be pretty hard to resist the right invitation. I mean, not for me. I had Neil. And I had put my more frisky days behind me.

I looked toward the back of the passenger van, where Luke and Melody were talking. "Hey guys," I called to them. "Anyone following us?"

They paused and looked out. "There's a car behind us," Luke said.

Barclay looked, too. "It's a Bimmer," he said with approval. His personal car was an old BMW convertible that he doted on almost as much as he did his sweetheart, Gina.

"More to the point, who's in it?" I asked.

"Arch's girlfriends," Melody said dryly, and almost everyone laughed.

Magnus let out a grunt.

"We won't let them get you," Mark said. "Diana will protect you."

"Works for me," Arch teased.

"*What?*" Diana turned her gaze from Arch to Mark and chuckled. "You're the devil, Mark Fairman."

"I believe the term you're looking for is 'handsome devil,'" Mark said.

He wasn't wrong, and I was pretty sure his sense of humor was growing on Diana. I reached for Neil's hand, and he wove his fingers through mine and looked at me and smiled. I supposed there was something about being happy with someone that made me want my friends to be happy, too. Mark and Diana were very different people, but they had a chance. At least as long as more movie stars didn't get in the way.

The sky now was a mix of silver and gold, silver layers of thin clouds alternating with soft stripes of golden sunlight. We spun through the rolling hills past tan houses and green fields, stone walls and sheep, some fluffy, some skinny and freshly shorn. The occasional towering wind turbine poked up in the landscape, and of course, there was water—we'd round a curve and a glimmering bay would stretch before us. And not a strip mall in sight.

"We'll see more of this area tomorrow," Magnus told us after about fifteen minutes of beautiful scenery. He gestured toward a few tall stones standing in an arc. "There are the Stones of Stenness. My gran told me they were the oldest stones in the British Isles, and she would know."

"Was she as old as they were?" Arch teased him.

"She wasn't Neolithic, no, but close." Whoa, Magnus made a joke! "A farmer in the 1800s destroyed two of the stones to discourage trespassers and toppled another, until local outrage stopped him from destroying more, but the damage was done."

"That's horrible," I said.

"With any luck, he was cursed for his trouble." A minute later, Magnus pointed to a slab of rock standing to the left in the middle of a green slope. "There's the Comet Stone. And beyond it is the Ring of Brodgar."

Higher up the hill was an extraordinary sight: a surprisingly wide circle of standing stones. You could probably fit an American football field in the center of them, without the end zones.

"Wow, that's a lot bigger than in *Outlander*," I said.

"These aren't the stones in bloody *Outlander*." Magnus sounded kind of ticked off.

"Sorry." I couldn't help but make the comparison. "I know that. It's just that they're the only ones most Americans see on TV, other than Stonehenge. This is amazing."

Magnus softened his tone. "They are indeed. Some think there were at least sixty stones in the beginning. Just over half that stand now, but the circle is remarkably intact. Of course, several had fallen and were re-erected in the early twentieth century." He pulled into a parking lot to the right of the road. "And lest you're thinking of trying the *Outlander* route, you won't be able to touch the stones, as they're asking casual visitors to stay outside the ditch at the moment to help preserve the inner path."

"I'm good," I said. "I don't think there'd be much use for a mixologist in eighteenth-century Scotland."

"You never know. You might end up going back to the Vikings," Neil joked. "How's your mead game?"

"I draw the line at fermenting. I just mix stuff."

Mark called to Magnus. "How old is the ring?"

Magnus *hmphed*. "Och, about forty-five hundred years."

Our group got quiet as Magnus turned off the engine and we disembarked. He urged us along, probably to stay ahead of the Archies. The two women had pulled in behind us but parked a discreet distance away, and now it looked like they were arguing. About what? Who got to jump Arch first?

We headed down the path that would take us across the road and to the stones. My mind was still trying to wrap around the fact they were more than four thousand years old.

"This has been here since long before the Vikings ruled Orkney," Neil murmured.

"Incredible." I took in the hill, the stones, the few folks walking on the grass-and-earth path around the circle. Flaxen sunbeams broke through the streaks of silver-blue clouds, adding to the mystical mood.

To our right, a handful of cows, most of them brown and white, stared at us from the middle of a pasture. A couple of them were different—super fuzzy with light brown hair, bangs worthy of Alastair, and big horns.

"Oh my gosh. Are those hairy coos?" I exclaimed, running over to the fence. "I want to pet them."

"I wouldn't recommend that," Magnus cautioned. "Though the kye might lick you if you can get them to come to you."

The coos, or kye, as Magnus said, didn't respond to my own cooing while my friends walked on, so I gave up and rejoined the group.

The meadow around us rippled with color. Where I saw patches of flowers in purple, yellow and white, Diana saw details. "Oh, look at the ling."

"Ling?" I asked.

"The mounds of purple heather you see there." She pointed hither and yon. "Red clover. Oxeye daisies. Eyebright. And is that nipplewort?" She exclaimed over a delicate yellow flower.

"Mmm, nipplewort," Mark mused. "That sounds promising. Shall I pinch a bouquet for you?"

"Certainly not!" Diana wore a horrified expression until she realized he was teasing her—she would never dig up wildflowers at a site like this! Then a corner of her mouth lifted at his double entendre while Luke and Barclay snickered.

Even I recognized a thistle here and there, with purple blooms and spiky stems. Nice to see the national flower showing off for us tourists.

"And the butterflies!" Diana was in raptures. "Oh, a Small Tortoiseshell. Isn't it lovely?" The butterfly in question paused on a flower, allowing me to see orange wings with black and brown markings, black and yellow stripes along the top edges, and bluish-gray accents on the scalloped sides. It was lovely indeed.

The ditch around the ring made the stones feel elevated as we walked along the path encircling it. It was hard to take in the whole ring at once, and we couldn't easily see the few people walking on the other side. Around us was a landscape of gently rolling hills and silver expanses of water.

Our group split up without speaking, taking different

branches of the path around the henge. Mark and Diana and the other bartenders went one way.

I followed Neil, who led us after Magnus, probably so he could glean more history from him, while Magnus trailed Arch and Rory in case any stalkers came along. I looked behind us. Wren and Lark followed us, but at least they kept several feet back. They were starting to freak me out a little, too.

"What's the ditch for?" I asked Magnus.

"I'm not sure. You should ask Elsie Firth—she's a local historian who worked on a dig of the trench several years ago."

"Elsie!" Freya Dearness's elfin babysitter. Or should I say the cathedral's babysitter. "We met her today at the cathedral."

"She knows more about it." Magnus breathed harder as he tried to keep up with Arch and Rory. "I do know the trench was built sometime after the stones were set, dug from the bedrock. It might've held water, perhaps symbolically setting apart the ring, like the water around our islands."

"It's amazing how much of the ring is still standing," Neil said.

"That's the truth," Magnus replied. "Who knows where some of the stones went over the years? And tanks did maneuvers through the stones and ditch for Army publicity shots in World War II. We're lucky they didn't destroy the place."

"We need to do an episode about a stone circle," Arch said. "Tweak the nose of that *other* show."

"I love that idea," Rory replied as we approached two women walking toward us down the path. "Let's talk to—"

He stopped talking. And walking. So did Arch.

So did Magnus.

So did the two women.

I recognized them. And they weren't Wren and Lark.

Chapter Fourteen

"Well, if it isn't the queen of fairyland herself." Arch's tone was teasing, but underneath it was an edge I hadn't heard before.

Freya Dearness faced him, no longer in her flowing gown; now she wore black leggings, a loose dark blue velvet jacket over a white top, and a light scarf. With her was Blair Rendall, Aramach's master distiller, in jeans and a sweater.

"And it's the Rob Roy of the airwaves," Freya replied, her tone cool but cordial. "I heard you were visiting."

"Keeping track of me, are you?"

She smirked and gestured to Neil and me. "No, these lovely people told me."

"Hi, Freya. Hi, Blair," I said as if there was nothing weird about this moment.

"Hello Pepper, Neil. Rory." Freya acknowledged Rory with a friendly smile, and he gave her a little wave.

Magnus nodded at the women.

"Shouldn't you be dancing through the lavender?" Arch asked Freya while Rory stood there, looking amused. Arch must've overheard Neil and I telling the bartenders about her shoot.

"That was earlier," Freya said, a twinkle in her eye. "Now

I'm just going for a daunder around my favorite place with a friend. I missed the solstice, so I wanted to pay my respects. At least I don't need an entourage." We were the entourage, I supposed. "Having trouble with your fans?"

I winced—she got that tidbit from us—and glanced behind me. Wren and Lark were far enough back I didn't think they could hear the conversation, but given their aura of excitement and the fact they were clearly pretending to stop and chat while they stared, I had a feeling they knew who was talking to Arch.

"First, this isn't my entourage." Arch seemed genuinely annoyed. "We're just out for a walk, like you. And second, my fans and I are just fine. I actually own the whisky I'm promoting. Can you say the same?"

"Why would I need to? I do quite well without owning the whisky."

"As if I don't?"

"We'd better be going," Blair cut in. "Nice to see you fellows."

"Nice to see you, Blair," Arch said pointedly. "Maybe we can chat again this week about Aramach's plans."

Blair's jaw tensed for a moment. "Of course. Have a good evening."

As she and Freya passed Arch and Rory, Arch muttered, "Foul witch."

Freya spun to face him, standing straighter, and suddenly all the world was a stage. "Thou sodden-witted lord! Thou hast no more brain than I have in mine elbows." She quirked her mouth and raised an eyebrow, and a moment later, she and Blair were well down the path. They exchanged nods with Wren and Lark and were gone.

"She always did know more Shakespeare than you," Rory teased his friend.

"Och, shut yer puss." Arch trudged forward, Magnus and Neil and I in tow.

"What did she mean about the solstice?" I asked Neil quietly.

Not so quietly that Magnus didn't hear me. He fell back a step to talk with us. "Don't you know? Ms. Dearness is one of our better-known pagans. You just missed the summer solstice observance here. It's very peaceful, very popular."

"So was Arch right about her being a witch in real life?" I asked.

Magnus snorted. "Not to my knowledge. She's certainly no 'foul' witch. She's a lovely lady. Mr. Halliday had another meaning altogether, I'm afraid. Speaking of whom, I'd better catch up." He walked faster so he could get closer to Arch and Rory, and Neil and I let him puff away from us.

"So Freya and Blair are friends." I stated the obvious.

Neil slipped his arm in mine. I appreciated his warmth; the early evening had become chilly, though the sun still hadn't set. "They both grew up here. Makes sense they would know each other."

"But how interesting is it that Blair, distiller for Aramach, is friends with the woman representing the Cliffstone brand?"

Neil tipped his head back and forth as if he were considering the possibilities. "We're all grown-ups. We can work for different people and still be friends. You and I own different bars in the same small place, and we're friends."

"More than friends." I leaned into him, playfully pushing against him. *Hmm.* More than friends. Were Freya and Blair more than friends? Now I really was jumping to conclusions.

"You don't think Blair would sabotage her own employer, do you? Maybe send Arch some hate mail? Especially when Arch gets on her nerves and apparently hates her famous friend Freya."

"Blair seemed to be annoyed with Cliffstone when we talked with her," Neil said. "Not Aramach. She likes what Seamus is doing with the distillery, and he gave her a shot."

"True." We'd made it halfway around the circle. The other bartenders and Mark and Diana walked toward us.

"See you on the flip side," Mark said with a smile. "You have a little surprise awaiting you."

What did he mean by that?

Melody paused and whispered in my ear as they walked past. "What's up with Arch? He looks like he swallowed a lemon."

"Some petty feud with Freya Dearness," I said softly. "We ran into her."

"Damn it! I should've come with you. Oh, well. I got to learn a *lot* about wildflowers." She grinned and trotted off to catch up with the rest of the group.

I regarded the rough outlines of the stones against the dramatic sky. They'd seen a lot of history. And mystery. The circle was eternal, and here we were, tracing the path of millennia.

It also made me think of something else: What goes around comes around. Was something—or someone—from the past sneaking up to bite Arch, maybe thanks to something he did long ago?

"Pepper!"

Ugh. Speaking of what goes around comes around. Here was the surprise Mark alluded to—Mr. Mixy and his crew packing up their gear next to the circle as we approached. They'd picked a pretty spot where the stones appeared to grow out of beds of wildflowers, and beyond them, the water and distant hills, blue in the late-day light, looked like a painted background in a storybook.

"Stephan," I acknowledged Mr. Mixy as the crew hoisted their bags and walked ahead of us toward where we'd come in.

"Arch! Rory! How's it going?" Mr. Mixy was even more excited to see the stars. Which was fine with me.

"Mixy, my man," Arch said. "Did you get some good shots?"

"Oh, yeah. The ring's got this super groovy vibe, you know?"

Mr. Mixy, cultural ambassador.

"But I wish we could've gotten into the middle," he continued. "I would've gone in, but my producer said we needed special permission." He gestured to one of the guys in his crew. The woman with the audio gear looked back with a pained expression. *I feel ya, sister*.

"Need something a little more exciting?" Arch asked.

"Oh, no," Rory murmured.

"Oh, yeah!" Mr. Mixy's eyes lit up. "What do you have in mind? Dave!" he shouted, and one of the guys in his crew halted. "Get out the cameras!"

Dave, a skinny, pale, brown-haired dude, looked tired. Was this the new producer? But he put down his bag, and he and the other guy pulled out their cameras and the woman put her microphone boom together fast. Pros.

"Come on, then," Arch said, and we continued our walk around the last stretch of the circle, with Mr. Mixy following like a puppy. Or like a puppy wearing another puppy on his chin, given the extremely large beard.

We got back on the path that led to the parking lot. I became aware of Wren and Lark, much closer now. Maybe they sensed that note of electricity in the air. Rory wore a look somewhere between resignation and amusement as we got near the pasture fence and a gate I hadn't noticed before.

The cows mooed as Arch stepped up to the gate. "Let's have some fun. You want to pet a hairy coo, don't you, Pepper?"

Uh-oh. A second later, Arch had the gate open and ran into the field, waving his arms. Most of the cows took off running into the distance, but a couple of the conventional cows and a hairy coo ran toward the open gate.

"Pepper, watch out!" Neil barked.

I yelped, turned and scattered with the others. Our other friends who'd just made it to the junction of the paths stopped, not sure which way to go as three cows ran around in a circle and the hairiest one headed right for Mr. Mixy.

"Film it!" he screamed, and his crew stood their ground and captured the scene as the hairy coo waggled its head and long, pointy horns and galloped toward my screaming ex, who dove to the side just in time. He got his colorful hipster shirt and puffy black vest muddy, but given how fast he leapt to his feet, he appeared to be OK.

I was kind of rooting for the hairy coo. While the other cows stopped in a patch of lush grass and started munching, the fluffy cow ran in a wide circle, reveling in freedom, and headed back our way. Mr. Mixy screamed, turned and ran toward the parking lot, his crew filming his flight.

Arch doubled over laughing. Rory wore an indulgent smile as he snapped a picture, then tapped his phone.

The coo had exhausted its energy, it seemed. It slowed and trotted back toward our party, positioned all around the gate.

Should I?

"Coo!" I called. "Pretty cow."

"Are you nuts?" Neil said. "Just stand still."

"I am standing still." I held out a hand to the coo. Any Highland coo who hated Mr. Mixy was a friend of mine. I held my breath as the cow stopped just in front of me, pushed its head forward and bumped my hand with its wide, leathery nose. Maybe it was looking for a treat. Then it ran its fat, wet tongue over my fingers. "Slimy. But cute," I said softly. "Pretty coo."

It sniffed once, decided it didn't like the taste of me, and ambled back into the pasture.

Magnus stepped up. "We should try to get these other cows in so we don't have an incident."

"I think we already have an incident." Rory nodded at Wren and a couple of other folks who filmed the cow fiasco with their phones.

"All the more reason," Magnus said, circling behind the two cows, who seemed happy to dine out.

Mark, sensing action, came up the path with the rest of the party. "Come on, boys. We can do this."

People herding cows without the help of horses or dogs were funny things to watch. But after about ten minutes of comical running around, the men in our party (I'd like to think we women were wise enough not to participate, but it's possible we just didn't want to ruin our shoes) had convinced the two wayward beasts to return to their home. Except Arch. He stepped outside the pasture, pulled out a flask and swigged it as he watched. Mr. Mixy hid across the street while his crew filmed the roundup. When it was over, Rory, who'd helped, headed for the parking lot.

Mission accomplished, Mark, Luke, Barclay and Neil walked over to Diana, Melody and me while Magnus secured the gate. I was a little worried about Magnus. His face was all red, and he was huffing hard.

"Now I'm sweaty." Luke wiped his forehead. "It's like being back in Florida."

"You could take off some of those layers," Melody said in a risqué tone.

We bartenders froze and looked at her. Melody—flirting with Luke? Luke had crushed on her forever and had only recently been trying his luck on the dating apps, in a sign he'd given up on her. And while she aimed her coquetry the way you'd aim a shotgun, at anyone in range, she never flirted with Luke.

"Please don't strip," Barclay said, breaking the tension with a joke.

"Just one layer." Luke pulled his sweatshirt over his head and aimed his intense brown gaze at Melody. Luke was a good-looking guy, worthy of his teen vampire nickname, and though he was more slender than Barclay, he had enough lean muscle to make the T-shirt he wore look like it was painted on. Almost like the tattoos of monkeys, parrots and tropical foliage decorating his arms.

Melody swallowed, her gaze lingering on his chest before she lifted her eyes to his. "Careful. You don't want to catch a chill." And then she sauntered off down the path toward the lot.

We all stood there for a moment of stunned silence.

Magnus had finished having a private chat with Arch, who didn't look cowed at all, so to speak, and he gestured to all of us. "Let's get going."

Thank goodness for Magnus. We headed toward the shuttle, the Archies trailing at a distance.

"I hope this means dinner," Barclay said as we walked.

"We can make that happen." Neil looked at me. "I was worried about you for a minute."

"I didn't mean to worry you, but I thought I was OK."

"Well, I'm glad you got to meet a coo."

"Being licked by a hairy coo was pretty neat," I agreed. Though I really needed to wash my hands. "But seeing Mr. Mixy knocked into the mud and running for his life? *That* was priceless."

Chapter Fifteen

My belly still felt full when I woke up the next morning, thanks to a restaurant dinner that included lots of local specialties, including a glorious selection of Orkney cheeses. But we had a big day ahead of us, and breakfast was in order.

Neil was already gone—I'd learned he was one of those short sleepers who could go a whole day on four or five hours of rest. Talk about a superpower. But he'd sent me a text: "Meet you for breakfast downstairs?"

Yes, please. I felt hungrier already.

I grabbed a quick shower in water that never got quite hot enough, then dressed: jeans, a knit top, a light black fleece, short black boots and my good-luck bracelet, along with silver jewelry and black hot-geek glasses. I pinned up my hair on one side and applied dark red lipstick. And given the forecast, I stuffed my packable yellow rain jacket into my bag, ready for anything.

Including, possibly, pancakes. Did they have pancakes here?

I heard Izara's voice before I even entered the hallway that led to the inn's restaurant. "What on earth were you thinking? Do you realize how bad this looks?"

"Och, all part and parcel of the Arch Halliday brand," said Arch Halliday.

"Well, I'm more concerned about the Aramach brand at the moment," Izara replied as I rounded the corner. "No farmer takes kindly to their cows being set free. And they might've damaged a World Heritage Site!"

She huddled with Arch and Rory in the hall outside the entrance to the restaurant, whose doors were closed. Probably just as well, since I doubted Izara wanted people to hear her telling off the face of Aramach Distillery.

"You'll annoy the locals, and that's the last thing we want, given the protests and the letters." Izara startled as I came into view. "Oh, good morning, Pepper."

"Hi. Hey guys," I added to take in the handsome pair of stars. They seemed less like superstars to me now and more like naughty boys who did not have their mischief managed.

Arch smirked.

Rory smiled. "Hullo, Pepper."

I paused next to them. "What was that about protesters? Diana ran into protesters yesterday that held a sign showing Arch with a dagger sticking out of him."

"She *what?*" Izara exclaimed.

"To be fair, it showed Sim, not me," said Arch. "One of my best episodes."

"But what are they protesting?" I asked.

"Oh, there's always concern about the land, you know," Izara said. "I expect it's the peat protesters."

"There are peat protesters?" And why was I just hearing about this now?

"Peat bogs lock up greenhouse gases," Rory explained. "Some activists have concerns about digging it up."

"But of course everything we do is measured and responsible." Now Izara sounded like the marketing person she was.

I still wasn't sure I had the facts straight. "So they were protesting at Aramach's peat bog?"

"That's my guess," she told me, "though I'll have to ask Diana where she saw them."

And I needed to look at those letters to see if anything mentioned peat or the environment. Great.

They were all looking at me expectantly. As in, expecting me to leave. Message received. I didn't need to be in on every conversation, as much as I wanted to be.

"See you at breakfast?" I moved toward the door.

"Doubt it," Arch said. "The birds are in there. I'm ordering room service."

The birds. Oh, boy. "See you later, then." I assumed they were still going on the tour, despite their stalkers. But maybe Wren and Lark's appearance was an opportunity for me.

I entered the restaurant, spacious with big, modern windows on two sides that looked out onto the misty garden. Maybe this was a late addition to the Victorian manor house. A sign said to sit anywhere, and since I knew most of the people in the room, I had my pick. Neil and Barclay were at a table big enough for six, chatting over coffee. Mark, Diana, Alastair and Albert—yay, he'd arrived!—were at a table by a window. Mr. Mixy's crew was eating together. And Mr. Mixy sat with—Lark and Wren?

Neil caught my eye, and I waved and raised one finger to tell him I needed a moment. He gave me a questioning look and then a smile. An *All right, fine — I guess you can't get into that much trouble at breakfast* smile.

The last thing I wanted to do was talk with Mr. Mixy. But I wanted to see what I could get out of Lark and Wren.

Lark wore jeans and a gray sweater and a purple scarf that matched the streak in her hair.

Her curvier sister, Wren, sported black leggings, a black and red plaid skirt and a black sweatshirt that said "Kilts: Good girls don't ask. Bad girls find out for themselves"—as well as her glasses. They were rounder and thicker than mine but still made me think of, well, me. Her long, dark hair was down.

They were enrapt by Mr. Mixy, who was talking at them over the remains of their breakfast. I kept forgetting Stephan was a celebrity, too, although his show about cocktails was nowhere near as well-known as *Sleekit Sim*. It didn't matter. These ladies obviously loved celebrities, and he was eating up their attention to the point where none of them noticed me approach.

I was distracted for a second by Melody and Luke, heading for the table with Neil and Barclay. Entering together? No. Just a coincidence, I thought. Still, yesterday's moment between them made me wonder if the tide was changing.

I turned to my quarry. "Good morning, campers."

"Pepper!" Stephan and Wren said at the same time.

"Good morning," Lark added.

"I was just telling the girls about our plans for today," Mr. Mixy said. "Tourism and all. We're going to get lots of B-roll, and I'm going to do a piece on how the Vikings drank."

I suppressed my groan. Thanks to his chatter, the women would correctly surmise "we" meant our Orkney tour included Arch and Rory.

"Is Arch coming to breakfast?" Wren asked.

"I'm not sure," I lied.

"Don't worry," said Lark, though she sounded a bit anxious. "I'm sure we'll catch them later."

I didn't know how they maintained their constant state of excitement. It had to be exhausting. But every time the thirtysomething women talked about the objects of their affec-tion, they buzzed like teenagers. Maybe stalking was fun after all.

I sat in the empty chair. "Do you see a lot of Arch and Rory?"

"As much as we can," Wren gushed.

Mr. Mixy didn't seem pleased with the change in topic. Especially because he was obviously the topic until now.

"We've met them at fan events and premieres," Lark said. "And we've seen them on the road, you know, when they're filming in different places."

In other words, when the sisters were in stalking mode. "Do you travel a lot?"

"We have since our mother passed, yes," Wren said. "We spent a long time taking care of her when she was sick back in Ohio. We were glad to do it, don't get me wrong, but she left us enough money to get out and enjoy life. And we decided to travel."

"To Scotland," I said.

"Especially Scotland," Lark said. "*Sleekit Sim* was our escape when our mother was going through cancer treat-ments. We'd all sit and watch and get a chance to laugh, you know? And we wanted to see some of the places in the show."

"And Arch and Rory!" Wren enthused, saying what Lark apparently wouldn't. "We've been so lucky. They know who we are now!"

You bet they do. "Do you ever write them fan letters?"

"I used to," Wren said, "but now that we've met them, I prefer to send little gifts. You know, flowers or a bottle of scotch to their hotel room. And we keep on meeting them, which is even better than a letter."

"Yes, it's better." Lark took a sip of her tea and cast an indulgent look upon her exuberant sister.

"And we can get away from our annoying brother," Wren added.

"Your brother? In Ohio?" I asked.

"Yeah, he's not happy that he didn't get as much as we did from the estate, and he's always nagging us for more." Wren deflated. "But he's kind of a ne'er-do-well, you know? And he never helped out when Mom was sick."

"Let's not talk about Jay now," Lark said. "Not when we're in such a happy place."

"You're right. You're right." Wren sighed. "I just worry about him sometimes. I mean, not that he would hurt us or anything. He's just not on a good road, you know?"

As curious as I was, I didn't think I needed to know those kinds of details. But Wren seemed eager to talk.

"Your dad's not in the picture?" I asked.

"He left when we were little," Lark said.

"Well, my parents basically threw me out when I was a teenager," I said. "And I turned out all right. I found a new home with my aunt, and she's awesome. At least you had precious time with your mother."

"You're right." Wren perked up. "And now we're here, living the dream, and we even got to meet Mr. Mixy today!"

Mr. Mixy swelled up under Wren's adoring gaze. "You can send me a bottle of scotch anytime you want. Or vodka," he said in what he must've thought was a seductive tone. Maybe it was, to someone who didn't know him as well as I did.

"Aw, really? You're sweet." Wren patted his hand. I suppressed a chuckle. In Wren's world, Mr. Mixy was no Sleekit Sim.

Speaking of sweet, she seemed way too sweet to wish Arch

harm. Lark was quieter but of the same mind. Any sort of obsession was worrisome, but I couldn't see them writing stuff like "your fate becomes more grave ... You'll pay when next you rave." Maybe they'd invested too much of their lives in pursuing someone they didn't really know, but I could understand. They'd been through a tough time at home. Maybe they were just letting off a little steam.

"It was nice talking to you." I stood. "I have a breakfast date. Have a great day."

"Oh, we will!" Wren exclaimed. She and Lark exchanged a look.

I was pretty sure I knew what would make their day great. Stalking our shuttle bus.

Chapter Sixteen

Stuffed after a traditional breakfast with the bartenders —with four kinds of meat, little potato pancakes called tattie scones, fried eggs and mushrooms, baked beans and grilled tomatoes—I was fueled for a full day of adventure. And had to struggle not to fall into an immediate coma upon taking the seat next to Neil in the second row of our shuttle.

Mark, in front of us with Diana, handed me Victoria as he stood to address our crew. The pooch licked my face as he spoke.

"Welcome, all, to the Drunkard Express!" We laughed, and Mark grinned. "Albert will drop us downtown first, where we'll pick up our guide, and then we'll start at the Earl's Palace. Alastair has prepared a few dandy tipples that he'll be happy to pour for you when you're ready to indulge, and we have snacks as well. Onward!"

Across the aisle, Alastair looked pleased for once as we applauded. Mark sat, his good spirits brightening the gray day.

"I hope we get a little sun later," I said.

"You're getting the genuine Scottish experience." Mark scooped up Victoria. She licked his face, too, and he gave me a mischievous look. "She's just transferring kisses from you to me."

"I think it's more likely you both have bacon on your face," Neil said.

I guffawed. Probably.

"I'm glad I got my exploring done yesterday," Diana said. "But I hope we'll see more interesting flora today."

"We're going to see *everything* today," Mark said. "Would you like a kiss, too?"

Her eyes widened, and then she realized he was holding up the spaniel to her. "Of course." She took the pup, who licked her hand instead of her face, which blushed a deeper shade of her usual tan as she scratched behind the dog's long ears.

Sneaky flirting, Mark. Very sneaky. I liked it.

The aisle of the shuttle stairstepped up and back to a rear row of three seats holding Izara, Rory and Arch. The two actors looked particularly swoony in nearly identical (and probably expensive) dark brown suede jackets. Maybe Arch picked them up from one of his modeling gigs.

Behind Alastair and in front of Izara was Magnus, on security duty today. In the remaining rows across the aisle were Luke and Melody, near the back, and Barclay and Mr. Mixy, just behind us.

The van had a skylight and luggage shelves above us, perfect for my giant bag, Victoria's trappings, and the coolers with Alastair's concoctions. It was quite comfortable considering how many of us were stuffed in here.

We rolled into downtown Kirkwall and a sea of visitors, Mr. Mixy's crew behind us in a small SUV. And, I was pretty sure, Wren and Lark's rental behind that.

"Cruise ship is in," Magnus noted. "Where are we picking her up?"

"We're meeting her in front of the cathedral," Mark said.

"Who are we meeting?" I asked.

"Our guide," Mark said. "Elsie."

Elsie Firth? The cultural liaison or historian or whatever she was who shooed us yesterday? This should be interesting in more ways than one.

We piled out in front of the cathedral, and Neil produced tickets from an inside pocket in his black rain jacket and handed them out.

"Mr. Fairman!" Elsie called amid the tide of tourists, and we headed her way. She wore dark sturdy trousers and a dark blue rain jacket, the hood covering her short blond hair—practical clothes for a cool, rainy day.

"Call me Mark, please," he told her. "We're in your capable hands."

A short stroll later, we stood opposite the gate where we'd entered the graveyard the day before. "These are the grounds of the Bishop's and Earl's Palaces," our diminutive guide said as we headed down the sidewalk in a pretty green park. A large palace ruin soared on our left, and a smaller one awaited across the road to the right.

She led us to the smaller Bishop's Palace first, explaining it had been built as a residence for the bishop in the 1100s, with a tower added in the 1550s. The interior was wide open, with no roof and ragged stone walls, so I had to imagine floors and rooms to match up with the remains of stairs and fireplaces. In the 1600s, she said, the second Earl of Orkney made it part of a larger complex with the addition of the grand Earl's Palace across the street.

"He wasn't a nice person," Elsie told us as we crossed the road to the bigger palace. "He spent too much and was a despot. His court was full of drunkards who fought all the time. Orkney was famous for its strong ale, and they drank a lot of it."

She sounded like she wanted to shoo away the earl, too.

I sidled up next to her. "Do you lead tours often?"

"Never. I'd be just as happy if we never saw another tourist in Orkney." She lifted a chin at a crowd hovering near the Earl's Palace. "The cruise ships, they're ruining it. The 'attractions' mindset. We should be preserving history, not exploiting it."

"Then why are you guiding us today?"

"Mr. Fair— Mark agreed to donate to a dig we're developing of a Neolithic site we hope might be as promising as the Ness of Brodgar." She took in my puzzled expression and, with an impatient frown, explained, "The Ness was a thrilling find near the Ring of Brodgar with the remains of several structures, including what might be a temple or a grand gathering place. We've found tools, decorations, even the bones of a baby. And the bones of hundreds of cattle that were likely slaughtered for a feast. It's a fascinating place." She assumed a dreamy expression. "I spent a glorious summer on the dig once. The summer of the axes."

"You mean the cloud axe?" Neil had come up behind us. "I read about that. Isn't that more like a stone than an axe?"

"Oh, you know about the cloud axe?" Elsie seemed pleased. "You have to remember that stone tools were the norm then, but the cloud axe was probably more symbolic than practical, given where we found it. It's made of polished stone, a dark blue with swirls of white quartz. Lovely."

This was the most animated I'd seen Elsie, but her excitement dimmed as we got closer to the crowd. The visitors weren't just hanging around. They were staring at the castle, which was blocked off by a couple of official-looking dudes holding up their hands.

"Just a few more minutes," one of them said as he saw us approach. "They're almost done shooting."

"Who's shooting?" asked Mr. Mixy, whose crew had filmed him looking thoughtfully at the walls of the Bishop's Palace.

"Freya Dearness," replied one of the tourists, a fortysomething woman who sounded American. "Hey, aren't you that guy?"

Mr. Mixy puffed up, and his beard became more erect. I swear. "Yes, I'm him. I mean"—a trace of doubt flitted across his face—"I am Mr. Mixy."

"Oh, I love your show!" she said. But her attention was diverted by the camera crew emerging from the Earl's Palace, trailed by Freya in her flowing cape outfit. Some of the tourists rushed forward, and she graciously spoke with them for a moment, shaking a few hands as the official dudes looked nervous. Security? Volunteers?

Oddly, it was at that moment that the tourists who hadn't rushed Freya or noticed Mr. Mixy realized the stars of *Sleekit Sim* were hanging at the back of our group. Magnus went on full alert, holding out his arms to block his charges, as a few of the fans came closer, with Wren and Lark on their heels.

"Arch! Rory!" the admirers called out.

"It's all right, Magnus." Then Arch said more softly, "We're supposed to be promoting our whisky. And making up for being cattle rustlers."

Izara shot him a displeased look, but she nodded at Magnus, who allowed the fans to approach.

The guys extracted themselves after a few minutes and came forward just as Freya left her lovefest, and our group and hers met in the middle.

"Storming the castle?" She wore a wry expression as she scanned Arch and Rory and their "entourage," to use her word.

"No," Rory said. "We forgot to bring our giant." Ooo, *Princess Bride* jokes.

"Well, I'm off to traipse through more ancient history. Toodaloo."

"I think you *are* ancient history," Arch said, alluding to the end of her movie series.

"Don't you mean *legend?*" Freya smiled, then strode away, her cloak billowing behind her.

"Nice exit," Rory said with admiration, and Izara glared at him. I guessed she was Team Arch. "What? She and I both worked here as teenagers. Bet you didn't know that."

"Shall we get on with it?" Elsie called out, completely unmoved by all the star power.

The Earl's Palace fed my imagination, with creepy corridors, intriguing rooms and, again, no roof on top. But one could stand at a centuries-old window and imagine what it must have been like hanging out with the earl and living the Renaissance life.

The mist swirled around us as we loaded up the shuttle and moved on to our next stop, trailed by the Mixy crew and the Archies. This caravan was ridiculous. But we were far from alone out here in the land of Neolithic history; there were tour buses everywhere, fighting for space on the narrow roads.

Our first stop was the Standing Stones of Stenness, which we'd seen from a distance the day before. The stones a farmer half-destroyed back in the day.

And there we found a mythological creature, or at least someone who played one in the movies—Freya Dearness. Again.

Our shuttle mob disembarked as Mixy's crew pulled in, Lark and Wren behind them.

There was barely a parking lot. No ticket-takers. Sheep

loitered around the stones. We had to enter via a simple gate to keep the woolly creatures secured. The mist had dissipated, but the clouds hung low, gloomy and gray.

We met the departing Freya and company just inside the paddock.

"Consorting with sheep?" Arch asked Freya.

She smirked, less patient with him now. "I respect them too much. And I don't need a herd to make me feel important." Her eyes slid over our group to Lark and Wren, who were just coming through the gate.

"You know me. I'm mutton but trouble," Arch quipped as she and her people swept past us and left.

I didn't like being lumped in with the herd, but I understood that Arch was getting on Freya's nerves. And the stalkers were getting on mine. And Magnus's. He seemed increasingly agitated every time they popped up, even if they hovered just outside of strike range.

I had a feeling we weren't doing a very good job of protecting Arch Halliday.

Chapter Seventeen

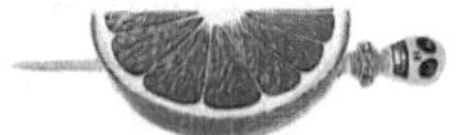

I stood next to Izara as we watched Freya and company get into a big white van and roll out.

"Why is she everywhere we are?" she asked.

I lifted one shoulder. "She's probably thinking the same thing about us."

"Well, all I know is that I don't like how Arch is exposed on this little outing, Magnus or not."

"Any more letters this morning?"

She shook her head. "Nothing unusual. Fan letters and one proposal."

A proposal wasn't unusual? I chuckled. A bride for Arch would have to be a patient woman.

"Did you get the link to the letters I sent you?" she asked.

"Yes, thanks. I don't have any new insights, though." I'd looked through them last night before fatigue caught up with me. There were a few stalkerish notes she hadn't showed us before, including two from the Flying Heart and another from PI, but nothing as creepy as what she'd already shared with us.

I headed to the nearest tall stone slab and listened for the songs of the centuries. Nothing. So I pressed a palm against the rough surface. A few feet away, a sheep *baaahed* at me, and I yanked my hand away. Maybe it wasn't a warning, but why take a chance?

Elsie hustled us onto the minibus fifteen minutes later.

"Lots to see, and I want to make low tide at Birsay," she said. "Just before sunset. Should be lovely if the weather clears."

Next up was Maeshowe, a chambered cairn. To my dismay, the Archies lucked into last-minute tickets, but they behaved themselves. Maybe because Magnus kept glowering at them.

From the outside, the tomb looked like an earthen mound covered in grass. As I bumped my head trying to access it via a low tunnel, I wondered if it was worth it. But inside, it was much more impressive. The guide told us it was older than the pyramids and notable for its alignment with the sun and its runic carvings. Some runes were silly graffiti left in the Viking era, mentioning crusaders who'd broken in, treasure, manly skills, and fair ladies.

"What exactly was that animal shape the guide was talking about?" I asked Elsie as we walked back to the shuttle.

"You mean this animal?" Elsie pulled a pendant out from under her jacket. "Seemed appropriate to wear this today. It might just be a Viking doodle, but it's become one of the symbols of Orkney. Some call it a dragon, some a lion. I choose to call it a dragon. It shares many details with other Norse arts of the period. What some see as a sword penetrating its back, others see as its own tail brought up through its body. Fascinating, isn't it?" Her eyes sparkled as she held up the enameled piece for me to inspect. "This was made right here in Orkney as well."

"Interesting." And strange.

Like the runes. Something bugged me about the runes.

We got back to the visitor center, then strolled to a nearby sweets shop for a cone of some of the richest chocolate ice cream I'd ever had. Mr. Mixy ate a Stenness Monster—a seven-scoop cone—just to have something to film. And Arch bought Wren and Lark cups of ice cream as Magnus freaked out.

I was of the same mind as Magnus. What the hell was Arch thinking?

The snack offered enough of a base to encourage folks to try some of Alastair's cocktails when we returned to our minibus. He'd made a lemon-cucumber gin punch (which I went for) and a scotch concoction with orange and lemon juice, maple syrup, ginger ale and Angostura bitters (which Neil chose, and I tasted).

"Excellent cocktails," I told Alastair.

"Really good," Neil agreed.

Alastair seemed a bit stunned, then said, "Thank you." He visibly relaxed, and a moment later, he was chatting with Barclay about classic cars.

After another half hour on the road, we neared our next stop. From the front, Elsie described Skara Brae.

"It's a Neolithic village around the age of the older pyramids, more than four thousand years old and better preserved than any other such community in Western Europe," she told us. "The village was hidden for centuries, then unearthed by a storm in 1850." She gave us details about its artifacts and structure, which Arch greeted with a noisy yawn.

Elsie scowled at him. "This is one of hundreds of historical sites we know about in Orkney, and there are probably many more. It's thought there's an average of three historical sites per square mile here. Everywhere you see a sheep grazing could be the hidden home of an ancient village or temple. This is a sacred landscape."

The curvy earthen mounds cupping low stone walls could've served as a hobbit condo, only the roofs were long gone. And what a location, on a hill overlooking the North

Atlantic—even if you couldn't see very far over the water, given the weather.

Neil paused with me on the cliff path. "Fog moving in?" Light mist, carried on a brisk breeze, kissed our cheeks.

"It's working on it. Hopefully we'll get our sightseeing done."

"Luke and Barclay don't seem very interested in Neolithic villages."

I snorted. Luke and Barclay were trying to get a fluffle of rabbits to look at them for a picture—there were rabbits everywhere.

"It looks to me like a Neolithic putting green," Arch said to Rory's snickering as our group moseyed back to the parking area. "Sand traps and everything."

"Have some respect," Elsie snapped.

Arch made an "Ooo" face and exchanged amused glances with Rory. I flashed back to high school field trips, when there was always a smart-ass on the bus making fun of everything. I mean, I could be a smart-ass, but it wasn't my full-time job.

It was late afternoon on the cusp of evening by now, and the ice cream and shuttle snacks didn't stop my tummy from growling as we again boarded the van.

"Hey, Mark. We need real food," Luke called out, echoing my stomach's demands, which I appeased with black jelly beans from the tin in my bag.

"Food is next on the schedule," Elsie interjected.

"Next" meant another fifteen minute drive north to a tea room with a gorgeous view and lots of sandwiches and soups on the menu.

"I'm starting to get tourist fatigue," I confessed to Neil as I dug into a delicious ham and cheese sandwich and looked out over Birsay Bay. The bank of fog had crept closer, and the sky swirled with shades of gray over a steel-blue sea. "Do you think we can talk Elsie into a nap?"

"Only if it has historical significance," he joked. He nodded at the view and a green island with rocky cliffs crowned by a squat, white lighthouse. "I think that's where we're headed."

"How? Please tell me there's not a boat involved." Especially with as rough as the water looked.

"I don't think so. The receding tide is supposed to let us pass."

"Is a troll going to demand a password?"

"Or a toll?" Neil's eyes grew speculative as he picked at the remains of his salad. "This place seems so rich in mythology, who knows? There might be a price for crossing a bridge that magically appears and vanishes."

"You're freaking me out."

He smiled. "Just playing with ideas. I'm kind of blown away by this place. So many layers of history. It reminds me just how temporary our time is. We're just a blip. A pebble pushed up on the shore by a wave and washed back out to sea with the tide."

"You're philosophical today." I leaned in and kissed his cheek. "I guess we better enjoy the moment."

"I guess we should." He stole one of my potato chips.

"Hey!"

Neil laughed as Mark stood and called, "Ten-minute warning. We're on a schedule!"

Our next stop was nearby, and it wasn't the island. By this time of day, it seemed, all the tour buses had gone to ground, so we had the Birsay Earl's Palace, another ruin, all to ourselves. Robert Stewart—an illegitimate son of James V, who was king of Scotland—built it in the 1500s.

We learned this and more from Elsie in the van, who

added, "Saint Magnus was buried near here, and reports of heavenly lights, odd smells and miraculous healings led to the development of his cult. The local bishop was reluctant to support the cult until he was struck blind and had his sight restored by the grace of Magnus, or so it was said. He oversaw the removal of Magnus's bones, which were moved to Kirkwall and St. Olaf's church there. And eventually the cathedral, when it was built."

"Do you believe in miracles?" Luke asked.

"St. Magnus miracles?" Elsie smiled like a teacher indulging a dim student. "What's more likely is that the bishop struck a deal with Rognvald, the earl who began building the cathedral, to foster the cult. Rognvald got support, and the church got power. Religion here was very much about politics."

Now in our rain jackets, we wandered around the battered stone walls. Mr. Mixy's crew got some shots. Drizzle came in waves, and the fading light went even more gray as the evening wore on. The chill wasn't pleasant, and soon, some members of our party returned to the shuttle to warm up.

Yet Wren and Lark had doggedly followed us into the ruin. They clapped as Arch and Rory enacted a mock sword fight around the remains of the castle, keeping us entertained as Izara shot video. In the absence of sticks, they'd borrowed a long ice scraper and a squeegee from the van's stash of tools and chased each other, swatting and whacking when they found an opening.

"You're not so good now, are you?" Arch challenged his opponent. They faced off in the open lawn after dashing in and out of the crumbling walls for a while, breathing hard after all the exercise.

"Give me a sword, and I'll show you how good I am." Rory

made a feint with the squeegee. "You haven't beaten me yet on set."

"That's not fair." Arch waved his ice scraper in Rory's direction. "I would've beaten you that day at the priory, but you made me faint."

"It was one little prick. Can I help it if you faint at the sight of blood?" Rory lunged, and he and Arch exchanged a flurry of blows.

"Amateurs," Elsie muttered, then called out, "All right, it's time to see the Brough of Birsay and stop ruining our history."

Rory looked at her. "It's hard to ruin ruins."

"Ha!" Arch poked a distracted Rory in the tummy with the ice scraper. "Got you."

Rory raised an eyebrow at him. "A palpable hit. But I don't think it's a mortal wound." With a flick of the wrist and the squeegee, Rory disarmed Arch, whose mouth dropped open in surprise.

"Don't hurt him, Rory!" Lark called out, almost like she actually believed he might.

"Children!" Izara called. "Come along."

The guys laughed and gathered their weapons, and my spirits lifted at the prospect of enjoying the finale of this long, interesting, exhausting day. I wanted to see the island, of course. But I also wanted to curl up in my warm hotel bed with Neil.

First, adventure. I was in Scotland, after all.

"I'm not liking the looks of this fog," Albert said as he parked in the lot near the rocky causeway that had emerged from the sea with the ebbing tide.

"I don't know if I've ever seen a haar that thick." Rory scanned the view, his eyes dancing. "This could be fun."

"Or," Magnus muttered as he eyed Wren and Lark's car, which was pulling in next to the Mixy crew, "a fine disaster."

Chapter Eighteen

Like a cloud that had fallen to earth, the fog moved in quickly across the water, obscuring the island and most of the craggy crossing we would use to get there. A couple of vehicles sat in the lot. But if their occupants were on the island, it was impossible to see them. The Brough of Birsay was wrapped in vapor as thick as pudding.

"Remember, we're only going to stay for an hour or two," Elsie told us. "It may seem like a small island, but there's a lot to see, and it's easy to get distracted. First, there are wonderful views." She glanced out the window, grimacing at the fog. "Usually. The lighthouse was designed and built by ancestors of writer Robert Louis Stevenson. And the remains of the Norse and Pict settlements may interest you. Some of you." She glared at Arch and Rory.

"And don't forget the tammie norries," Rory said, unperturbed.

"What are those?" I asked.

"Puffins," Magnus answered.

"Yes, you might get lucky and see puffins on the cliffs. Don't get excited and fall off," Elsie warned. "There are caves. One, Walty Reid's Hole"—this, predictably, inspired snickers from Barclay and Luke—"is named for a somewhat legendary figure, perhaps a man who hid from the press-gangs that would force young men into naval service, often leaving young mothers on the islands as virtual widows. Or perhaps he's a trickster, one of the fairies." Her humorless smile suggested she didn't think much of such stories. "The caves are quite dangerous to explore today, so beware. And don't linger. Be back in the car park in, say, an hour and a half, just to be safe. We don't want anyone trapped by the rising tide."

With that, we exited the shuttle and headed for the stone stairs that wound down to the beach. A narrow, zigzagging concrete walkway cut through the center of the rocky expanse between the mainland and the island—we'd seen it from the road. But now the path vanished into the fog, which grew thicker by the second.

Magnus looked around and spotted Wren and Lark heading for the stairs behind us. He hurried after Arch and Rory as they descended.

Unease prickled my skin. I understood Magnus's worry. Even without the Archies, this place seemed dangerous somehow. Maybe it was just the prospect of being trapped by the tide. Rushing water and nowhere to go. It brought to mind that awful night during Hurricane Katrina, all those years ago. I touched the good-luck bracelet I got in New Orleans and tried to banish bad thoughts.

"Ready?" Neil asked me.

I looked up at him and summoned a smile, took a deep breath, and began my descent into the gloom.

The barest outline of the island appeared fleetingly as we reached the beach, then the bank of white enclosed it again. Gray, green, brown and yellow rocks littered the sand. They looked like giant river pebbles, almost flat.

As we moved toward the crossing, the fog allowed us to see only a few yards at a time. Now, a colony of rocks poked up and surrounded the concrete walkway—tilted, thin beds of weathered stone, with shallow tidal pools in between.

The narrow causeway offered the only sensible path through the wet, rocky terrain, and we took it in single file, the passage revealing itself foot by foot. The folks at the front of the line vanished into the fog—Arch and Rory and Magnus. Mark, with an excited Victoria, and Diana followed, then Mr. Mixy and his crew, Alastair, Elsie, and we bartenders, with Neil bringing up the rear.

Wren and Lark followed. Again. They'd hung back till our whole party was under way, but I could hear their chatter as a murmur behind us. The fog didn't come in on little cat feet, as the poem said; instead it laid a great soft cat paw over all of us, distorting sounds and chilling me to the bone.

"You OK?" Neil asked.

I'd slowed down without intending to. "I'm fine. Just kind of caught up in the landscape. It looks like another planet." The angled rocks resembled mini mountain ranges, some covered with seaweed. In places, swaths of bright green growth coated the lowest, wettest slabs. It looked dangerously slick, making me grateful for the walkway. Which soon ran out, leaving us to clamber over a bed of rocks, varying wildly in color and size.

As we moved forward, details of the near shore of the island emerged, its bulk a greenish shadow in the dusky light. It was after 10 p.m. and still daylight. Almost sunset, not that you could tell. But what light there was seemed to fade the farther we went.

"I don't think we're going to see the sunset," Neil echoed my thoughts.

"I just hope we see puffins."

Finally, we reached the edge of the island. A steep path

allowed access to the top of the layer cake of grass and wild-flowers and stone.

I breathed a sigh of relief as we reached the meadow. Nearby, a small building faded into the fog like everything else. Anything beyond it was essentially invisible until we got closer. Features revealed themselves slowly, as if an art restorer lifted layers of gray grime to show the colors underneath.

Our party had scattered into oblivion already, though I could hear voices here and there and occasionally make out a figure moving through the gray. We checked out the building, located near a complex of low stone walls, the remains of Viking houses.

"This sign isn't comforting." I gestured toward the door of the stone hut.

If you are stranded on the island,
dial 999 and ask for the coastguard.

"Let's not do that," Neil said, humor in his tone.

"That would be extremely embarrassing." But I smiled at the idea of being stranded with Neil on an island. I'd prefer it to be warm with palm trees and coconuts and possibly rum, but whatever. At least here, you'd only be stuck till the next turn of the tide. On a night like this, however, the experience would probably be miserable.

"Where next?" He looked uphill. Basically everything was uphill from here. "The lighthouse?"

"OK. If we can find it. I know we saw the island earlier from the cafe, but now that we're on it and visibility sucks, I have no idea how far away the lighthouse is."

"If only it was lit." Neil was right. No light pierced the fog.

We found a path and took what had to be the long way

around, near the cliffs around the south and then the west side. If we got close enough to the edge, we could look down. The sea of fog revealed only glimpses of the water. The view was really unnerving, like floating in space.

A young couple with a boy passed us going in the opposite direction, downhill toward the ruins, and gave us a friendly nod. Then we came upon a crevasse in the cliffs where Barclay and Luke were exploring down below us. Which we only knew because they called to us first.

"Pepper! Neil!" Luke shouted.

"How'd you see us?" I asked. They appeared as fleeting shadows below, moving between leaning walls of rock.

"Can't miss that yellow jacket!" Barclay yelled.

"Be careful on the way back up," Neil called back. For once, I appreciated his cautious nature.

Climbing the hill was good exercise, and it kept me warm. But the views continued to disappoint. Most of the time we swam in a white, ethereal mass of vapor. The fog wasn't uniform, but it was so thick we had almost no confirmation the sea lay beyond the cliffs.

Finally, the white lighthouse emerged from the murk, its lines firming up to reveal a pretty tower sticking out of a roof whose crenellated cutouts belonged on top of a castle. Solar panels arrayed against the fence weren't getting much love this evening.

And it was getting darker. "Time?" I asked Neil.

He checked his vintage watch. "We have about forty-five minutes or so."

"OK, good." I took a deep breath of the damp, cool air as we moved as close to the cliff as we dared. "It feels lonely up here. Like we're the only people in the universe."

I jumped as I heard a rustle and spun around to see shapes emerging from the fog.

"Baaaah." A sheep stood there, staring at me. Then more sheep emerged behind it, all fluffy and round with skinny legs and perky ears. They hadn't been shorn yet.

"Sheep." Neil stated the obvious. "We're not alone in the universe."

"They're cute."

"They look hungry." He gave me a humorous look.

"I don't think they eat mixologists." But as we turned away from the lighthouse toward the grassy track, the sheep followed us. "What the hell?"

Neil chuckled. Another sound echoed through the fog. Voices. "There you go. People. Somewhere. See any puffins?"

We walked several steps closer to the cliff and peered into nearby ledges, but the angles and the fog made it difficult. "Nothing. It's like we're floating in a cloud."

One of the sheep had followed me. "Baaaah."

"Sorry, fuzzball," I said. "I don't have any snacks."

The voices became shouts. A distant bark answered, though from another direction, I thought. Victoria?

"I wonder what that's about," I said as the voices died away.

Neil shook his head. "Probably Arch and Rory goofing around again."

I chuckled.

Then I heard the scream.

I grabbed Neil's arm on instinct. "What was that?"

"*Who* was that?"

I spun about and jogged to the footpath that wound over the grassy crown of the hill, startling the sheep, who turned and trotted down the slope and vanished into the mist. Neil was hard on my heels as we headed opposite the way we'd come. I hoped it was toward the origin of the scream.

"Careful," Neil said as I slipped on wet grass and almost fell. "The cliff is right there."

"I'm aware." The jolt of adrenaline sent my heart into overdrive.

A wail cut through the fog. "Noooo!"

I bit back a curse as I imagined what that scream could mean.

The cliff is right there.

I picked up the pace as much as I dared. It was like running through a dream, a nightmare, with no idea what lay beyond the next few feet.

Someone emerged ahead of us, moving quickly toward us, a flowing figure, cloak billowing, the mist seeming to make way for her. She halted when she saw us, and so did we.

I looked at her in shock. "Freya?"

She sucked in a breath of surprise. "Have you seen my crew? I seem to have misplaced them."

"No. Who was shouting?"

"I haven't the faintest idea. Perhaps it was Arch's fan club." Her usual sarcastic tone was there, along with unmistakable stress. She strode past us and vanished into the folds of the mist.

I looked after her. "What is going on?"

"I don't know. We should keep walking. I still hear someone, and they aren't happy."

He was right. I'd heard another sound. A wail? It chilled me. I nodded and resumed our trek, Neil right behind me.

A figure materialized in the cloud.

Izara. Standing on the edge of a jagged section of cliff, weeping.

Within seconds of one another, other people appeared as well—Diana and Mark, holding back an eager Victoria. Mr. Mixy and his crew. Wren. Elsie. Magnus.

"What is it?" snapped Magnus, red-cheeked, out of breath.

"Izara?" I asked more gently.

She gulped in sobbing breaths and looked up at me. "He's gone. He's gone!"

Chapter Nineteen

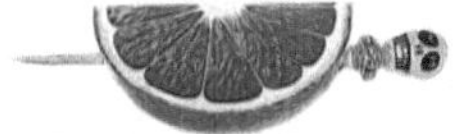

"Who's gone?" I asked Izara.

Her big brown eyes brimmed with tears. "Rory," she whispered. Then, as if she couldn't hold my stunned gaze, she looked away, out at the invisible sea.

My stomach dropped. No. Not Rory. Not adorable, funny, lovable Rory.

A terrible silence descended on the others who'd arrived.

"Hang on. Let's just take a minute," Neil said. "Gone where? What happened?"

Izara pointed over the edge of the cliff.

Wren uttered an anguished cry and buried her face in her hands.

At that moment, Lark appeared out of the fog, her face stricken. "Did you just say what I thought you said?"

A few seconds later, Arch arrived. "What is it?"

"Rory ... he ... I think he fell off the cliff," Izara said hoarsely.

Arch's face went white.

"Oh, sweet Rory. Arch!" Lark exclaimed. "Thank God you're OK!"

Just as I had the thought *What a weird thing to say,* a look of fear, revulsion—I wasn't sure what it was—crossed Arch's face.

He took a step back—which also happened to be a step away from Lark.

"It can't be," he said. "Not—it can't. Have you looked for him?"

"Of course I've bloody looked!" Izara barked. "Can *you* see anything?"

The horrible dream sequence was now all too real, and we were so deep into a cocoon of fog, all I could see right now was the nearby rocks. I edged closer to the cliff.

"Pepper," Neil hissed.

"I know. I'm just seeing if I can see ... anything." Jagged ledges and no guardrails. Movement. Shapes lifting and landing —were those the puffins? And below—I couldn't see straight down without getting closer, but I got the idea as I edged along the brink. Even ten feet down, the fog obscured every- thing. The water was invisible, but I could hear distant waves crashing against the cliffs.

"We were looking at the puffins," Izara said. "Or trying to. I was trying to find a safer spot. He stayed here. I'd lost sight of him. Then I heard him scream. I thought I heard him on the path, but when I got back here, there was no one. I—I thought I saw someone, though. Someone else moving away. But maybe my eyes were playing tricks on me. I'm not sure of anything right now."

Holy crapnoodles. A witness? Or a killer?

One of these people?

Freya?

Arch stepped toward the edge. "Rory!" he bellowed. "Rory!"

We all stood there in the dream, like when you're frozen in place in a nightmare. We waited for an answer that didn't come. Arch looked like he was going to throw up. Then we snapped out of the trance and all moved closer to the cliff, spreading out, trying to spot our fallen friend.

"Rory!" Arch called again. "Where are you?"

"Mr. Redland!" Magnus echoed, his voice rough.

No response. After a few minutes, we spun to a halt, coalesced around Izara.

"Magnus, weren't you with them?" I asked him.

"Arch and Rory lost me when they ran up the hill. *They* ran after them." He pointed accusingly at Wren and Lark. So much for security. "Where were you when it happened?" he demanded of the women.

"Walking on the path a little ways down the hill," Wren said.

"I was behind her," Lark said. Wren shot her a look of puzzlement, and her sister added, "I stopped to look at some rocks."

"I thought I saw her on the path." Elsie nodded at Wren.

"You didn't see what happened?" I asked Magnus.

"No." The catch in Magnus's voice almost broke my heart. "I'm calling 999."

"Yes," Elsie said, looking grim. "You must. They can retrieve—they can find him."

Oh my God. She was about to say "retrieve his body." I shivered, stepping farther away from the cliff's edge as Magnus made the call.

One of Mr. Mixy's crew held up his camera as if to film, and Dave, the producer, waved him down. Dave was a decent dude.

I looked from him to Mr. Mixy. "Did you guys see anything?"

Dave shook his head.

"No," Mr. Mixy said. "I wish we had. Sort of. I mean, I don't wish—"

"The police will likely want to see your footage anyway," Mark cut him off. "You should be prepared to share anything you have."

"We can do that," Dave said grimly.

"Where's Alastair?" Mark sounded concerned.

"He was headed back to the causeway, the last I saw him," Elsie said. "With the other woman—"

"Melody?" I asked. "Our blond friend?"

"Yes," Elsie confirmed.

Mark let out a breath. "That's a relief, anyway. No one wander off now."

I looked at Neil, thinking of Barclay and Luke, playing in that crevasse that now seemed to me like a death trap.

Neil already had his phone in hand, texting. His shoulders relaxed, and he looked up. "Luke and Barclay have just arrived at the causeway and are on their way back."

"Which we'll have to do very soon," Elsie pointed out. "No doubt emergency services will want to talk with us, but they can do it from the other side. They won't want to take all of us off the island once the tide comes in."

"She has a point," Mark said.

"Someone has to tell them where Rory—where it happened." I didn't want to say "fell." Or voice any of my other suspicions. "So they get a head start on where to search."

Diana looked at Izara. "Perhaps he's all right," Diana said softly. "We don't know."

Izara lowered her head and said nothing. What could she say?

Magnus spoke up. "It wouldn't be the first rescue we've had on Birsay. I'll stay with Izara. We'll get a ride. Go on back to the hotel." He squinted at Arch. "Do you think you can stay out of trouble?"

Arch, uncharacteristically speechless, lifted up his hands, surrendering.

"We'll keep an eye on him." Mark looked at Neil, who nodded in agreement.

I turned to Wren. "You and your sister will probably need to give a statement, too." I assumed the police would meet us on the other side of the causeway. And I definitely wanted them to talk to the Archies, just in case.

"Of course." Tears filled Wren's eyes, and her shoulders shook. "My God. Rory."

Lark just nodded and pulled the sobbing Wren into a hug.

I hoped Diana was right. That Rory was still alive. But the silence when Arch called his name? It was so loud, it drowned out the crashing waves.

BY THE TIME our party got back to the causeway, there appeared to be fewer tilted rocks on either side of the walkway. But of course, that wasn't it. The tide was rising. Water sloshed around our path. The walkway was still accessible, but I had this feeling of the ocean closing in. Of everything closing in, even the fog, though now it seemed to bleed orange and red, eerie and ominous. Sunset light, maybe. Not that we'd seen the sun for hours.

As we made our way across, single file, with Arch between Neil and Mark and me right behind Neil, the flash of blue lights cut through the haze. It had to be some sort of emergency vehicle or vehicles waiting at the parking lot. And I heard a droning motor sound that I suspected might be a boat, but I couldn't see anything. The emergency responders were admirably quick.

I was afraid to hope they might actually find Rory alive. The cliffs on that side of the island were high and perilous. This much I knew despite the fog; we'd seen the island before the haar, as Rory called it, moved in. Gravity was a bitch. The rocks were unforgiving. And how could they see anything? These conditions weren't exactly safe for the rescuers, either.

My phone buzzed in my pocket; I'd left my bag in the minibus. I paused on the slippery walkway and checked it.

"What the hell is going on?" Melody texted me. "A cop is here asking questions. They say someone fell off the cliff. Are you all right?"

I paused. Typing the words made it too real. "Neil and I are all right. It's horrible. Looks like Rory fell. Be there in a few minutes."

"OMG no!" she texted back.

One pasty young officer, snazzy in his uniform hat with the checkered band, awaited us in the lot with the police van. To my surprise, he didn't take much time interviewing us; he seemed more concerned with the rescue operation and kept talking on his radio.

"Name?" he asked. "Where are you staying? Phone number?" And he wrapped up with, "Did you see the incident?"

The universal answer was "No."

But was that true for all of us? And what about Freya and her crew? The white van, the same one I'd seen them drive earlier today, was gone.

"Did you see Freya Dearness?" I asked him. "We saw her about the time it happened."

His eyes lit up. "Freya Dearness was here? I missed her.

That's too bad. I love her *Fairy Kingdom* movies. She's from here, you know."

"I know. Are the rescuers on their way?"

"The Stromness Lifeboat is circling to the back of the Brough. They've had to stand down the helicopter, unfortunately, given the fog."

Worse and worse.

Meanwhile, he was treating the fall like an accident, and maybe it was. But given everything I knew, given the weird letters, and given the fact I actually *liked* Rory, I wasn't going to just let this go.

"Drinks all around," Mark ordered once we got back aboard the van, his mood somber. I wasn't used to seeing somber on Mark. He sat and petted Victoria. Diana reached out and squeezed his shoulder, and he laid his hand over hers.

Alastair produced a bottle of Aramach's twelve-year, and we accepted shots of scotch in small paper cups.

I looked back toward the island as we rolled out of the parking lot. The fog was still thick, but hints of light pierced the cloud. The lighthouse was finally lit. Maybe it would help the rescuers. But would they be able to help Rory?

Arch sat in the back row by himself, also looking out the window, silently drinking. What was going through his head?

His best friend, gone. Would he be next?

Chapter Twenty

"I'm glad I'm not the one who has to break the news to Seamus," I told Neil after we'd changed into fresh, dry clothes—jeans and sweaters—in our hotel room. "I feel like this is my fault."

"Oh, Pepper." He wrapped me up in a hug, and I sniffled. "This was no one's fault."

I reluctantly released him. "Are you sure about that? Izara thought she heard or saw someone nearby. What if they pushed Rory? I should've figured out who was targeting the guys by now."

"First, you've had, like, a day to figure it out. Second, our job was to look out for Arch. And third, Rory is a pretty nimble guy. A strong guy. It would take a lot to wrestle him over a cliff. I'm afraid this was an accident."

"Maybe." I imagined the scene. "But what if he was leaning over anyway, looking for puffins? Or crouching on the edge? It wouldn't take much to tip him off balance and send him over. And in the fog, he might not have seen anyone coming."

"Yeah, like we didn't see Freya until she popped out of the fog like that."

I nodded. "That was totally freaky. She seemed upset. Do you think she could've done it?"

"I don't know. She didn't seem to have any animus toward Rory when they met earlier. Arch, yes, but not Rory."

That got me thinking. "The guys were dressed a lot alike today. Their hair is different, but if it was damp, it might've been hard to tell them apart. The light wasn't great, and the fog was insane. Someone could've made a snap decision and thought it was Arch."

"A stalker, you mean?"

"Whoever his enemy is. Yes. One of the Archies? Or someone else?"

A corner of Neil's mouth lifted. "It might've been a sheep."

I smiled. "I think we can provide an alibi for the sheep. There were other people on the island today, too."

"We don't even know where all the people in our party were," Neil mused. "We should do a poll. Want to go downstairs and see who's around?"

A couple of minutes later, we found the rest of our bartenders working on a puzzle in the game room. Mark and Diana had the couch, with Victoria curled at their feet, and Alastair lounged in a chair, eyes closed, his feet up on the coffee table. Albert was there, too, lining up pool balls and shooting them into pockets with uncanny accuracy.

Small plates scattered about showed they'd raided a board laid out with chunks of cheese, pieces of crusty bread, butter, nuts, honey, slices of sausage and grapes. Bottles of water and beer poked out of a metal bucket full of ice, next to an electric kettle and a wooden box stuffed with a selection of tea bags. The bar cart was still loaded, but I didn't see anyone drinking cocktails.

I grabbed a piece of cheese and was not disappointed. The flavor was sharp and rich. "Where did all this come from?"

"Ola left it," Mark said. "Thought we might need a snack. Kettle's on if you need tea."

"Have you seen Arch?" I asked.

"Not since he went up to his room. Given what happened and his nerves about the Archies, can you blame him?" Mark must have noticed Arch's reaction to Wren and Lark, too.

"Of course not," I replied.

To my relief, the Archies hadn't followed us here. I didn't know where Wren and Lark were staying, but I hoped it was far away.

We'd dropped Elsie in downtown Kirkwall. Izara and Magnus hadn't come back. Mr. Mixy wasn't here, either.

"Heeeyyy." Mr. Mixy appeared in the doorway, Dave just behind him. Mr. Mixy headed right for the cheese board. "Don't mind if I do."

Maybe him being here was a good thing. At least from the perspective of asking him questions. Not from the perspective of me always wanting to smack him.

"Stephan. Dave," I greeted them. "Where were you when it happened?"

"Not close." Dave pulled a beer out of the bucket and popped off the cap with an opener. "We were filming around the remains of the old church site farther down the hill. Heard a scream and figured we should check it out."

"What about other people?" I asked. "Did you see anyone in the area?"

"Not really," Mr. Mixy said. "Saw a couple of young guys earlier."

I pictured hit men. "How young? What did they look like?"

"College age, and they dressed like it," Dave said. "They sounded English. One of them said they came over to the island in a dinghy they'd rented off some fisherman and were worried about getting back in the fog."

"Sounds like tourists, boating in that sort of weather," Diana scoffed.

"The fog won't make it easy for the rescuers." Neil's words cast a pall over the already glum room.

I poured myself hot water and dropped a satchel of Earl Grey into the cup. "Melody, did you see anyone on your way out? Anything suspicious?"

She sat at the game table with Barclay and Luke, all of them drinking water. She looked like she'd shed a few tears, too. "Not that I can think of. Alastair?"

Alastair, stretched out in his chair, never opened his eyes. "We saw one couple wearing hideous vomit-green macs with a matching child. Suspiciously American."

"Sounds like the family we saw earlier," I said.

"Did anyone else see other people?" Neil asked.

"Only if plants count as people," Mark said.

Diana elbowed him. "I think we might have seen the same family in green, briefly, some time before it happened."

Albert sank the last in a line of balls and looked up. "I believe I saw them as well, in the car park, several minutes before I saw Freya Dearness and her crew get into their minibus."

Her crew. That was another group of people I hadn't considered. I'd barely given them a glance at the Stones of Stenness and in Kirkwall, but I didn't recognize any of them. But what if ... "Was it the same crew she had earlier?" I asked Albert.

"I assume so, miss, but they all wore hooded jackets in the foul weather," he said. "Miss Dearness appeared just before

Miss Melody and Alastair arrived and just before the police as well."

So Freya found her crew and pretty quickly, if they got off the island that fast. But her hasty exit didn't account for her movements when it happened.

Freya didn't seem to have anything against Rory. But they'd known each other a long time. They shared a lot of history I wasn't privy to.

"Neil and I ran into Freya right after it happened," I told our friends.

"Really?" Barclay sat up. "Did she say anything?"

"She said she was looking for her crew," Neil said. "She seemed to be in a hurry."

"Flustered, I'd say," I added. "But then again, trying to get anywhere in the fog fast was frustrating and stressful. I wonder if she would agree to talk to us?"

Neil almost choked on his sip of water. "What, are you going to ask her if she killed someone?"

"No." Probably not. "I just want to ask her what she might have seen."

"You know whom she might speak to." Diana, clutching a teacup, tipped her head toward Mark.

He raised his eyebrows. "Who, me?"

"That's right!" I pointed to the bar cart. "She invited you to look her up. All you need is a bottle of gin. We just happen to have Frilly Fairy on hand."

Mark sighed. "The things I do for you, Pepper."

I smiled before I remembered why smiling felt odd. "You're doing it for Rory." I disposed of my tea bag and added sugar to the cup. "I take it no one has heard from Magnus?"

"Let me text him." Neil pulled his phone from his pocket and tapped the screen.

A bottle of Skull Splitter ale in hand, Mr. Mixy wandered to the pool table.

"Want to play?" Albert asked.

"Sure, but I warn you, I'm really good."

Albert just smiled a small smile and racked the balls in a triangle.

Mr. Mixy picked a cue from the rack on the wall. "I'm starting to wonder if I'm getting too famous. I don't want someone else to try to kill me."

"I don't think you have to worry," I told him. "You're not as famous as Arch and Rory."

"I could be!"

"I thought you didn't want to be?" Barclay teased him.

"Well, I guess I do, but I don't want crazy stalkers. Just the good kind." He frowned as Albert lined up on the cue ball and broke, exploding the balls in all directions and sinking one.

"What are the good kind of stalkers?" Luke asked.

"The cute kind who want to have sex with me."

Melody looked at me, stuck her tongue out and made an "ew" face.

Albert dropped three more solids into pockets. Mr. Mixy missed his shot.

"That Wren is pretty cute," he continued as Albert sank two more balls. "She kind of reminds me of you, Pepper."

I tried not to barf at Mr. Mixy's attentions. "You've certainly inspired *me* to have homicidal thoughts."

"Thanks." He grinned as if I'd given him a compliment, then flubbed another stroke.

I glanced at Neil, who rolled his eyes and glanced at his phone again.

While my friends sipped and nibbled and held low,

murmured conversations, Albert finished beating Mr. Mixy—
he must log a lot of time in Mark's billiard room.

I found a chair and drank my tea and tried to sift through
what had happened. Another thing puzzled me. Izara's main
charge today was Arch. He was the front man for the whisky
brand she had to promote. Yet she'd been hanging out with
Rory on the island. Had she finished her work for the day? Or
could Izara have done something to Rory? There was that
moment when she looked away from me that felt kind of odd.
But maybe she couldn't deal with facing the tragedy. I totally
got that. And maybe she felt guilty the way I did. She wanted
to protect the guys, too.

The telltale buzz of Neil's phone caught my attention. He
looked at his screen, then at me. "They still haven't found him.
Magnus says the conditions are dangerous and they're going to
suspend the search until morning in hopes that the fog will
clear by then. They'll get a coast guard helicopter out from
Inverness as soon as they can. They're going to get Magnus
and Izara off the island by boat."

"Ugh." The decision wasn't surprising; it had taken us
forever to get back to the hotel in the pea soup, and boats and
helicopters didn't have the luxury of roads. But the delay
wasn't good. If Rory survived his injuries, he needed attention
as soon as possible.

"And they're treating it like an accident, given the lack of
evidence to think otherwise," Neil added. "At least for now."

I kind of wished the police would step in and figure it out.
The truth was, an accident seemed most likely. But those
letters made me think otherwise. Where there's smoke, there's
fire, or so they say. And how did the Paintball Piper fit into all
this?

More to the point, why would anyone push Rory off a cliff?

Chapter Twenty-One

"I'm so sorry, Seamus," I said. "I feel like we should've figured out who was writing the letters by now. Or at least been smart enough to protect Arch and Rory better."

Neil and I sat in the comfy chairs in Seamus's office, facing him on the couch in front of the fireplace. There wasn't much to see out of his big windows this morning—it was gray and misty but not foggy like it was the night before. The rescuers had been searching for a couple of hours with no luck.

"It wasn't on you." Seamus scratched behind the ears of Nessie, who sat leaning against his legs. The collie seemed to know he needed comfort. Seamus looked like he hadn't slept at all. "Magnus was there, wasn't he?"

"But Arch and Rory gave him the slip, and the fog was impossible," Neil said. "I don't think it's anyone's fault, unless someone did push Rory."

"I know what you're saying," Seamus said. "It might've been an accident. But it shouldn't have happened. And I'm concerned about Arch being in danger. Magnus was up practically all night; the searchers brought him and Izara to the lifeboat after they halted operations around midnight. I've told them to get some rest and then to stick tight to our star until this is resolved. Izara will check in later this afternoon."

The weight of what he was saying pressed down on me. Could I help him resolve this—solve this?

"Have you spoken to Arch?" I asked.

"Aye, and I've told him not to play any more games with the Archies. He's to ignore them and politely ask them to leave him be."

"Hey." I'd remembered something. "Our friend Diana saw protesters the other day who carried at least one sign targeting Arch. Izara and Rory mentioned they might be concerned about the peat?"

Seamus's brow creased. "They don't want us digging up the land, but that's the eternal story, isn't it? Someone always wants to dig up land for a shopping center or a car park. But I'm a traditionalist when it comes to Orkney. That may surprise you, given our marketing angle, but it's true. And it's my land. I inherited it from my grandparents. When my grandfather died, I helped my grandmother by cutting the peat so she'd have fuel in the winter, until I helped her modernize the house —some people still burn peat for heat here. And now we cut the peat in a measured way for the scotch. I don't see anything wrong with that."

He sounded defensive, and I got that. But he hadn't ruled out a threat from angry protesters.

Neil spoke. "Do you think Arch will be all right for tomorrow's events?"

Seamus sighed. "I hope so. I think so. The director's in from London. He'll be here shortly to brief me on the plan. You might as well stay for a minute. Do you have everything you need?"

"Luke told me the gooseberries will be delivered first thing in the morning to the venue—they're for the garnish on the star cocktail, the Tartan Goose," Neil said. "They were the hardest to acquire, but everything else is well in hand. I'll make the syrups and start the orgeat later today, and we'll squeeze fruit tomorrow and prep garnishes before the shoot."

There was a knock at the door. "Enter!" Seamus called.

To my surprise, Izara stepped in, wearing a sharp gray pantsuit. But fatigue dripped off her.

"What are you doing here?" Seamus sprang to the bar, got tea steeping in a cup, and added sugar packets and a spoon to the saucer.

"I couldn't miss the meeting with Alan. He's been my primary contact." She accepted the cup from Seamus—points for Seamus—and sat next to him on the sofa. Nessie moved over to her and rested her head on Izara's knee.

"My God, did you get any sleep last night?" Seamus sat, too.

"What happened after we left?" I asked her.

"It was dreadful, frankly. I don't know what I was thinking —that a helicopter would descend out of the mist, pluck Rory off the rocks and then take us all home? The big boat arrived, and they sent over the small boat with a couple of rescuers, who took several minutes to find us. Twilight was settling in, that long twilight we have here in Orkney in the summer. Which meant it was even more difficult to see anything in the fog. They poked around the rocks a bit, but the big boat couldn't come in close because of the conditions, and they finally told us they'd have to give up till morning. Then they had to get us off the Brough by means of the little boat. We got wet anyway, trying to get to it."

"How awful," I said.

"Then we had to wait even longer while they rescued a couple of young fellows who'd lost their dinghy. It got swept away by the tide."

"Insane," Neil said.

"When did you get back to town?" I asked.

"The lifeboat—that's the large boat—took us to Stromness, and someone gave Magnus a ride home. I took a cab. Honestly, I'm not sure when it was. I'm so tired."

"Did you get any better sense of what might have happened?" I asked gently.

She set the cup on the coffee table, placed the tea bag on the saucer and stirred in the sugar, then sat back, not saying a word for several seconds. Struggling. "No," she finally said, petting Nessie's head.

"The rescuers have had no luck this morning, either, I'm afraid. They fear he might have been washed out to sea." Seamus twitched at a soft buzz, then looked at his smart watch. "Alan's here."

"I'll go get him." Izara took a long sip of the tea, set it down and was gone.

In the couple of minutes it took her to escort her charge, we moved to the conference table, and Seamus set Izara's tea at her spot, then offered us some, which we declined. I was full of another big Scottish breakfast from the inn. Nessie curled up on her favorite fuzzy rug by the fire.

Izara entered, towing a tall, skinny man in a long white coat that looked like it was covered in colorful graffiti. He wore it over a black T-shirt, black jeans and black-and-white Converse. He sported a dark buzz cut and eyeliner that showed up starkly against his pallid face.

"Alan! Welcome," Seamus called. Nessie came over and gave the newcomer a sniff. "Alan Woodsy, this is Neil Rockaway and Pepper Revelle from the Bohemia Bartenders."

Alan scanned us up and down. "Acceptable. As long as your colleague dresses you appropriately." Had he been talking to

Melody? "But I *must* know. Who is that divine man outside with that *divine* dog? I *must* have them in our film!"

I couldn't help a chuckle. "That's Mark Fairman. He's coming to the party." Mark had joined us with the intention of going into town and hunting down Freya Dearness while Diana roped Alastair into visiting the Broch of Gurness, another ancient village.

"Well, he must also be in my film," Alan said. "The closed shoot precedes the party, if I have the schedule correct?"

"Yes, indeed." Izara sat and greeted her tea with a small smile.

"And the dog? Please tell me we can have the dog." Alan dropped into the chair next to her and made eyes at the teapot.

A corner of Seamus's mouth lifted, and he arose to fix a cup of tea for him, too. "I don't see why not. Nessie not pretty enough for you?"

Nessie, who'd returned to her rug, lifted her head and tilted it at Seamus.

"Oh, she's a fine dog, of course," Alan said, "but I want *froufrou. Frou* and *frou* and *frou*!"

"Victoria will love that," I said.

"Victoria?" Alan exclaimed. "Is that the dog? Oh, we must get her a blingy collar. Like diamonds. I want *all* the sparkle. You will have the most sparkly scotch that has ever been sipped in Scotland! And I want sparkly cocktails, too!"

I glanced at Neil, who wore a pained expression.

"I trust you completely, Alan." Seamus handed him a teacup. "I'm sure we can do some kind of sparkle. Neil?"

"Sparkle?" Neil grumbled. "Is he kidding?"

We sat side by side behind Albert, who gave us and Mark and Victoria (on my lap—the dog, not Mark) a lift into downtown Kirkwall on the minibus. Or it would be more accurate to say Mark was giving us a lift, since he'd provided the shuttle.

"There's that sparkly stuff that's all the rage in vodka drinks in the glam bars," Mark said. "What's it called?"

"I don't do 'sparkly stuff,'" Neil said. "I make craft cocktails."

"But we have to keep the client happy," I teased him. "Maybe disco ball garnishes?"

Neil grunted. "That wouldn't be terrible, but they don't fit with anything I planned, and getting them here in time would be a challenge."

"Maybe you need actual sparks," Mark suggested. "A little fire-throwing?"

"If this were a tiki event, fire dancers would be perfect," Neil said. "It's not."

"But sparks could work." I stroked Victoria's soft ears. "Or the right light with ... ice. Carved ice. Barclay could carve ice cubes, and we could pour a little scotch over them. Lots of reflective sparkles in the ice."

"But Seamus wants craft cocktails," Neil pointed out.

"Oh, it's just for a shot in the promo video. And I don't think he'll mind if he shows off his scotch as a sipper, as well as a great ingredient for cocktails. A sexy, *sparkly* ingredient."

Neil, next to me, let out a breath and some of his tension. "That's reasonable. It might even be good." He kissed my cheek, which warmed at his touch. "Thanks, Pepper. I'll run it by Seamus and get Luke to hunt down a sparkly swizzle or something. And Barclay can figure out the ice setup. Maybe I can do something with smoke."

I smiled as I saw his brain working. "Sounds like a plan." I liked to see what happened when circumstances pushed Neil out of his comfort zone. He always rose to the occasion.

A chime had Mark pulling his phone out of his snazzy jacket's pocket. He looked especially yummy today; no wonder Alan Woodsy got all excited. "Callum has relinquished the secret location of Freya Dearness," he announced after perusing the screen. "It's the hotel above The Whale, where we all met up with Arch and Rory."

There was a beat of silence at the mention of Rory.

"I have to go to the hall and get some stuff done," Neil said. "Pepper, I think you should go with Mark."

Mark raised his eyebrows. "A chaperone? I promise you, I'll be on my best behavior."

"When are you ever on your best behavior?" I asked Mark.

"Pepper's good at asking questions," Neil said.

"Ah, I see," Mark said, pretending to be hurt. "I'm the big juicy worm on the hook and Pepper's the angler."

I chortled. "I'll try not to ruin your budding friendship with Freya Dearness."

"Ha." He sniffed. "I'm only doing this because you asked me to. Ms. Dearness might be a little too much star power for me. Getting too close to the sun is a good way to get burned."

Which again made me think of Arch and Rory. There was a lot of star power to go around. And Rory got burned.

"Let's do it," I said as Albert stopped the shuttle near the docks. There weren't nearly as many tourists today. No cruise ships, I presumed. "As long as Freya doesn't throw me out."

"Or try to kill you." Mark handed me Victoria's leash and harness.

I slipped it over her head as the pup wagged her tail. "Gee, thanks."

Chapter Twenty-Two

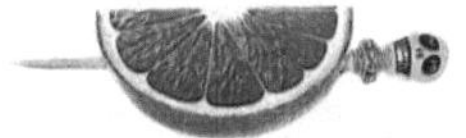

"Mark Fairman, I presume?" Freya Dearness said with a smile as she opened the door of her hotel room. Then her face fell. "And ... Pepper?"

"Good morning," I said with all the chipper I could muster, which was pretty good since I wasn't much of a morning person. And this had not been a chipper morning.

"Come in, then," she said in a wry tone. She took the bottle of Frilly Fairy gin out of Mark's hand and headed toward a credenza, where she plunked it down among a couple of bottles of Cliffstone scotch, a few vases of varying heights stuffed with flowers, and an enormous fruit basket still wrapped in plastic and a showy light blue ribbon.

"Thank you so much for your time this morning. I've wanted to meet you forever." Mark's gushing seemed genuine, and Freya perked up at his admiration as she led us farther into the suite. I let Victoria out of her harness so she could explore.

"I've seen you at a fundraiser here and there, from a distance." She gestured to the soft furniture in a seating area around a fireplace, sat on the couch that faced it, and patted the cushion next to her. "You make the rounds of the social pages, don't you?"

Victoria took her invitation first, jumping up on the sofa, sitting next to her and looking up at her expectantly.

Freya looked at her, then at Mark, then rolled her eyes and started petting the dog. Mark showed a dimple and sat next to Victoria while I took a chair.

"Would either of you like a drink?" she asked.

"I wouldn't mind a scotch," Mark said.

I jumped up. "I'll pour." It wouldn't hurt to soften up Freya with whisky.

"No ice for me, Pepper," Mark said.

"Same." Freya seemed to accept my position as entourage mixologist and turned to Mark with a smile. "Have you been to Orkney before?"

"Yes. I'm friends with Callum and Seamus MacIvor as well."

"It seems we know several of the same people."

"I'm still amazed at the talent produced by this place." Mark's subtle reference to Rory got no reaction from Freya.

"Orkney still feels like home to me. Though I no longer own a place here. I'm thinking of investing in one, but there's a severe housing shortage. Everyone seems to be turning their flats and cottages into holiday rentals for the tourists."

By now I'd found the rocks glasses and filled them with generous pours, which I presented to Mark and Freya. I took a small one for me in hopes of fostering a convivial atmosphere in which I could ask awkward questions. I sat in a chair kitty-corner to them and closer to the fireplace. Its ceramic log flickered with a gas flame. Very atmospheric. Not that warm.

"Some people seem annoyed with all the tourists," I said, picking up on her comment.

Freya looked up, as if surprised I was still there. "Some of the merchants love them, but they tend to be seasonal. Other people miss the quiet. This is a beautiful, magical place, but sometimes I wish there weren't so many people here. It wasn't like this when I was a child. Appearing at the top of a few 'best places to live' lists hasn't helped. Yet I understand the appeal."

"Which your ad campaign for Callum will ..." Mark searched for the word.

"Exploit?" She quirked her mouth. "I like to think our film will celebrate the history here."

"So you were filming on Birsay yesterday?" I asked.

A cloud crossed her brow. "As much as we could. My director got some atmospheric film in the fog, but the shoot was a total mishanter." By her tone, I assumed she meant disaster. "We couldn't get much film of the rocks and cliffs at all. We're planning to go to Yesnaby this afternoon and try our luck." She paused. "When I saw you, I'd been separated from my crew. They wanted me to emerge dramatically from the fog, and then I got turned around and went in the wrong direction."

Maybe a very wrong direction. I got right to the point. "Did you see anything unusual?"

Victoria took that moment to roll over and invite Freya to rub her belly, which she did. "Are you looking into the accident yesterday? I saw something about it on *The Orcadian*'s website. Who fell?"

I looked at her in shock. "Didn't the article say?"

"No," she said pleasantly.

I debated what to tell her. If she knew, she knew, and she was an excellent actor to pretend otherwise so convincingly. If she didn't know, what was the harm?

"It was Rory Redland," Mark said softly, beating me to it. "The rescuers are still trying to find him."

Freya's hand froze over Victoria's belly. The dog pawed at

her, and the star resumed stroking her, slowly. She looked up at Mark. "Rory?" she whispered. "It can't be true."

"Didn't you hear the scream? We saw you right after it happened," I said.

"I suppose I did, but I was so anxious to find my crew that I didn't think much of it." She turned her big violet-blue eyes to mine. They shone with tears. "Tourists, you know. People play and shout."

And release bloodcurdling screams when they're pushed off a cliff.

"You grew up with Rory, right?" I hated to push her, but I wanted to know more.

"Yes."

"The authorities think his fall was an accident, but given some of the letters Arch and Aramach have received, we're considering other possibilities," I said. "You mentioned a youth program you and Seamus attended once. Was Rory part of that?"

"No."

I tried not to show my frustration. "Then can you think of any reason that, say, Callum and Seamus should hate each other?"

She sipped her scotch, looked at Mark as if to ask *Did you have to bring her?* Then she sighed and replied to me. "I have no problem with either man. Seamus and I were friendly, though we didn't know each other well. Callum and I obviously have a business relationship. But something happened during that program that set off an enmity between them that, frankly, I've never understood."

Now we were getting somewhere. "Can you tell us more?" Mark asked.

Absently scratching Victoria's belly, she continued. "As I

mentioned, we were just kids. Seamus was twelve. He tried to start a romance with another girl a couple of years younger than he, and as a sponsor of the program, Callum practically threatened to take him behind the woodshed and beat him unless he gave her up."

"Was it *that* kind of relationship?" I knew kids started young these days, but twelve and ten? Ick.

Freya must've seen the look on my face. "Of course not. It was all very innocent, and she checked the 'no' box when Seamus sent her a note asking to be her boyfriend. Callum has spoken badly of Seamus ever since. I don't know why he reacted so vehemently. The girl was a daughter of one of his employees, but still."

I blinked. "Was it Blair?"

Freya looked at me sharply, then turned back to Victoria. "It was," she said after a moment. "But as I said, nothing came of the romance. And Callum backed off when another orga- nizer had a word with him. Callum keeps his dislike on a low simmer these days, though Seamus's foray into distilling scotch in Callum's backyard still annoys him."

"Callum made that clear when we spoke with him." Mark took a sip. "This is fine scotch. He has nothing to worry about."

"Why would he be so angry?" I asked.

"I don't know." Freya kept her eyes on Victoria. And then I realized she had an idea but didn't want to talk about it. "I think I need some time to myself," she said, standing abruptly. Victoria hopped to her feet on the couch, looking up at her with her sweet brown gaze. "I have to prepare for my shoot this afternoon. I hope you understand."

"It was lovely meeting you." Mark rose and extended a hand, and she shook it. "Thanks for the autograph."

Her composure returned in an instant, and she smiled. A small wisp of a smile. "It was my pleasure. Perhaps we'll meet again at ... at a better time."

"I do hope so." He employed one of his radiant Mark smiles. "Enjoy the gin. Victoria?"

The dog hopped down, put her paws on his leg, then followed his gesture and trotted over to me. I secured her harness, then pulled a business card from my bag and laid it on the coffee table.

"In case you think of anything else," I said to Freya. "It was very nice to meet you again."

"Was it?" Freya's sarcasm was back. "Enjoy your visit to Orkney."

A moment later, we were back in the hallway and descending the stairs, not saying a word till we got back to the street. The sun peeked through the clouds.

"What did you think?" I asked Mark as we walked along the waterfront.

He took Victoria's leash from me and let her sniff as we went. "I was about to ask you the same thing. She seemed genuinely upset about Rory."

"She's also a very good actress." Then I felt bad about saying it. "I know. That's not fair. She seemed to like Rory. And we don't even know if Rory was just collateral damage for someone's grudge against Seamus or Arch."

"Someone like Callum?" Mark said. "I never realized his disdain went that far back. But I don't think Callum was at the Brough of Birsay yesterday."

"Maybe someone who works for him?"

Mark stopped, giving Victoria a moment to water a lamp-post. "Like Freya? She didn't seem invested in his vendetta, if you can call it that."

"You're right." My phone buzzed in my messenger bag, and I took a minute to extract it. I'd received a text. The sender was listed as Unknown. I was about to write it off as spam when the words made me stop.

"You want to know what happened. I can tell you. The Earl's Bedchamber at noon. Come alone or miss your chance."

"What is it?" Mark asked.

"A text from someone who says they can tell me what happened. But they want me to come alone."

"Bad idea," he said instantly. "Where?"

"The Earl's Bedchamber?"

"That sounds fun." A dimple showed for only a second.

"I think it's a public place. It has to mean the Earl's Palace. We were just there yesterday."

"You mean the one here in town?"

"It's certainly more accessible than the other one." I looked at my phone: 11:44 a.m. "It's almost time. I have to try."

"I don't like it, Pepper."

"It'll be fine." I got excited at the idea someone might actually tell me what was going on. And I was desperate for answers. "Look, if you have time, you can wait on the grounds while I go in. Just try to, you know, be subtle about it. They might know we know each other, and if they spot you, they'll know I didn't come alone."

"Pepper, there are very large *open* windows in those ruins."

"Remember all the tourists yesterday? They're not going to try anything hinky." I hoped.

"I'm going with you," he insisted.

I got distracted by Victoria, who'd paused to sniff what looked like a piece of fried fish.

I was about to warn Mark about her interest when a seagull swooped out of the sky, snatched the bit of fish and hopped a few feet away to snack on it. Indignant, Victoria launched herself at the gull, who took off flying down the length of the ferry dock, fish in its beak. The dog yanked the leash right out of Mark's hand as she dashed after the bird.

"Victoria!" he shouted, running after her.

"Thank you, Victoria," I murmured to myself as I turned around and jogged to the corner, heading down the street that would take me to the cathedral and the Earl's Palace. I told myself she'd be all right. Victoria ran toward a low-traffic area, and Mark was in better shape than I was. He'd catch her in no time.

And maybe I'd get enough information from my mystery texter to catch our sinister scribe.

Chapter Twenty-Three

Jogging wasn't my thing, so I'd slowed down by the time I got to the small ticket office on the grounds of the palace. And there I found a familiar face—Elsie Firth, chatting with the twentyish blond man behind the counter.

"Hi, Elsie." I paid the admission. With fewer tourists around today, I had no trouble getting a ticket. "Giving a tour?"

"Pepper, isn't it?" Her mouth formed a flat line. "I've agreed to show an American couple around the palaces." She checked her phone. "They're late."

I was about to be late, too, but I found what she said curious. "I thought you never gave tours."

"This couple has Orcadian ancestors, and like Mr. Fairman, they're donating to our society's next archaeological investigation. Sometimes it falls to me to keep the donors happy."

"That's nice of you."

"I do what's necessary," she said. "And it's a pleasure to share the stories of our heritage. How are you today? Shouldn't you be bartending or something? I understand you have a big party to prepare for."

How'd she know about that? I supposed we might've

discussed it during our all-day tour yesterday. "It's tomorrow. Are you invited?"

"Oh, goodness, no. I read about it in *The Orcadian*. The show must go on, eh? Even under a cloud." She gave me a knowing look.

I didn't want to discuss Rory's disappearance in front of the ticket guy. "Yes," I acknowledged. "We have a job to do. By the way, can you tell me where the Earl's Bedchamber is in the palace?"

She glanced at the puzzled ticket-taker. "Go ahead," he told her. "You can tell her a lot more than I can."

"I just want the location," I said. No doubt Elsie knew her stuff, but I didn't need a historical lecture right now.

She raised an eyebrow. I could almost hear her thinking, *Philistine.* "It's upstairs off the Great Hall."

"Great. Thanks!"

I left the round hut and jogged over to the entrance. Or really, fast-walked, still out of breath from my jog over here. I should start running or something at home. My walks with Astra did nothing to train me for all this physical exercise.

No one guarded the door. I looked around as I entered the palace. A couple of fortysomething women meandered through the vaulted corridor of the lower floor, chatting in an English accent. I heard the cries of children, and two boys popped out of one room and into another. From the earlier tour, I knew these rooms had been used for storage and other things. One used to be a kitchen, with a giant fireplace you could stand in. Nifty but not what I needed. I pressed on, looking for the stairs.

By the time I'd wended up the twisting steps to what they called the first floor, I'd already lost track of where I was. The first room I stepped into had a sign indicating it was a bedroom, but it wasn't the one I wanted. It had probably been a guest room, and it was empty.

Moving on and up a few more stairs, I found myself in the grand hall, where the earl would entertain guests with roasted meat and beer and, presumably, wenches. It no longer had a roof, but it was easy to imagine a feast in here, with its massive fireplace and large glassless windows.

And it was empty. No tourists, no mysterious informant. Maybe in the bedchamber. I scurried across the hall and through a doorway at the far end.

I moved into the earl's chambers—first, a reception area or dining room—and past a couple of dark doorways I had no time to explore. At least one had spiral stairs that didn't go anywhere. I'd climbed them on my previous visit.

I ended up in another room with a modest fireplace and, again, no roof. And a sign told me this was it: the private bedchamber of the earl. It said this was where Earl Patrick would get frisky with the ladies. His first son was born out of wedlock, though his father, Robert, was the one with the reputation for "carnall copulatione." I tried not to think about Renaissance sex while I wondered where my informant was.

A rounded alcove with open windows bumped out here, offering views of the grounds. I stepped over to it and looked out. The two boys I'd seen earlier ran around the lawn, screeching. If one didn't know better, you'd think they were murdering each other.

And then I got a very creepy feeling and spun around.

I'd heard footsteps. From where?

No one was there. For a second.

And then a hooded figure glided into the room. Had they been hiding in that closet or whatever it was outside the entrance? No, I thought. They'd been up the spiral staircase to nowhere, the one that led from the earl's sitting room. That's why I hadn't seen them. Clever.

My informant wore a dark green cloak, possibly wool. The hood drooped low to conceal most of their face. They could have been a cosplayer or an escapee from a fantasy film. But I could tell there was a mask under the hood as well. The cloak was so voluminous, it effectively hid the figure beneath. This person was certainly taller than I was. Who wasn't?

Whoever this was, they didn't want me to identify them.

"Who are you?" I asked anyway, stepping away from the windows. I didn't want the Cloaked One getting any ideas.

And then voices echoed from the Great Hall—Elsie, talking to her tourists. She must've decided to start up here, much to my annoyance.

The cloaked figure held up a hand—clad in a fancy suede green glove that flared at the wrist. The cloak concealed the other hand.

Oh, crap. Did this person have a weapon?

"This was the earl's office. He could work in here or receive guests ..." Elsie's voice floated in to us.

And my informant spun in a swirl of fabric and ran.

I froze for a few precious seconds, then lurched forward, trying to catch them. "Wait!" I shouted. By the time I'd made it to the big banquet hall, the Cloaked One had disappeared.

Elsie and a gray-haired couple wearing bright yellow and blue windbreakers appeared, stepping out of a small room off the main hall. "Pepper. Did you find the bedchamber?"

"Yes, thanks!" I called as I ran for the stairs.

It was no use. As quickly as I could move, which wasn't super fast on these treacherous stone steps, the cloaked person was faster. I spent a minute or two looking into all of the small rooms on the ground floor—perhaps a strategic mistake, given there was no one suspicious in sight when I popped out the door of the palace.

No one was watching the door when I emerged, but the blond guy from the visitors' center walked my way. I ran up to him. "Did you sell a ticket earlier to someone in a cloak? Or see someone in one?"

"A cloak?" He gave me a blank look. "No. I would've remembered."

"Do you have many visitors in cloaks?"

He grinned at the question. "Sometimes. People want to take pictures of themselves in the ruins."

"Would anyone else have seen them?"

"We're a bit thin-staffed today. Derek has been living in the toilet at the community center all morning." He grimaced. "He just took over for me in the visitor center. Did you have a problem with someone in a cloak?"

Only that they wouldn't talk to me and ran like a scaredy-cat when they saw me. "No."

"I'll keep an eye out." He smiled indulgently and walked toward the door of the palace.

"Pepper!" I turned to see Mark striding toward me with a happy Victoria scampering in front of him on her leash.

"Oh, good, you caught her!" I exclaimed, bending over to pet her when she arrived.

"Oh, good, you haven't fallen out of a window," he said dryly. "That was very naughty of you, running off like that. Did you meet your informant?"

"I suppose you could say that. They showed up looking like they'd escaped from a Renaissance fair, wearing a big green cloak with a hood, and ran when someone else got close—Elsie, actually, and a couple of tourists."

"Then I suppose Elsie isn't your informant."

"Safe assumption. And they weren't much of an informant. I want to talk this over with Neil."

"Of course you do." Mark smiled, and we turned back toward the cathedral. "But I'm more than just a pretty face, you know."

Chapter Twenty-Four

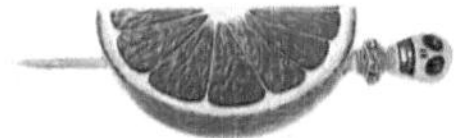

It turned out that talking with Neil wasn't an option just then, as he was neck-deep in event prep when we got to the hall. Mark made his excuses and departed with Victoria, but first he gave us Albert's number and told us to call him whenever we needed a ride.

While Neil made syrups and, with Luke, organized supplies arriving at the hall's kitchen, I got into helping Barclay and Melody set up our space at the back of the town hall banquet room. A crew of burly guys had assembled a sleek bar there consisting of three wide arched segments with translucent walls that resembled frosted glass. They were basically empty boxes, and the whole thing would glow with LED lighting. We put glasses and other things where we needed them, making sure we had a fridge and places for everything. We had no running water here, but given we wouldn't wash glasses—just stow the used ones in crates to be returned to the rental company—we could make it work.

The bar sat in front of a stage that resembled an altar, given the gorgeous triptych of arched stained glass windows that rose behind it, each featuring historical figures. Big arched windows ran the length of one wall, facing decorative pilasters on the opposite wall. The ceiling was arched, too, and decorated in coffered geometric patterns.

Chandeliers dangling clusters of huge bubble lights hovered far above us, but Alan Woodsy ran around directing the building crew on a new lighting project—assembling large, black metal arches over the middle of the space. One was already up, and multiple mirror balls of different sizes hung from half of it. A worker was adding more. And the pieces of a second arch lay about the floor among a fleet of uncovered banquet tables.

"These tables must go!" Alan yelled at the already busy men. "No one wants big square tables in the middle of a dance party. What happened to the cocktail tables I requested?"

"Mr. MacIvor said he wanted tables for the party," one of them said. Clean-shaven and put-together, he had the look of a supervisor, with a logo on his shirt. "He didn't specify what kind."

"Please check with him, determine where the rentals went, and assemble them and make sure the table lights work. Can you do that?"

"Aye, but I don't know what you mean by lights," the man said.

"The tables look like tall cocktail glasses, and the bowls light up. Did no one show you my shot list?" Alan threw up his hands in exasperation while the men shared a look and, I was pretty sure, a chuckle.

"We'll be glad to take a look and replace the tables," the supervisor said, no doubt mentally calculating how many work hours he could add to Seamus's bill.

"So how was Freya Dearness this morning?" Barclay asked me as we pulled rented cocktail glasses out of crates and lined them up by type behind the bar.

"Weird." I paused, reconsidering. "That's not fair. She

seemed upset about Rory. But I get the feeling she's not telling us everything. She also said Callum has had it out for Seamus ever since she and Seamus were kids and Seamus tried to get Blair to be his girlfriend. Blair's dad worked for Callum at the time."

"Do you think he was being overprotective?" Melody picked up a glass that didn't meet her standards and polished it with a dishtowel. She'd been spot-checking them as they came out of the crates.

"Freya seems to think so," I replied. "Callum still speaks of Seamus as if he's an insect to be squished, but I don't know if he really hates him enough to target Arch."

"Or Rory," Barclay added.

Just then, Neil and Luke emerged from the kitchen.

"How's it going?" Neil asked.

"Getting there." Melody pulled a coupe glass from the lineup and polished it.

"Hey." I gave him a smile. "I was just about to tell these guys about my morning."

"You mean talking to Freya?" Luke asked, folding his arms on the bar top and leaning in to watch us.

"More than that." I recapped the conversation with Freya. "And then I got a text on my phone telling me to meet a mystery informant to find out what happened."

They all stopped working and stared at me.

"You didn't," Neil said. I wasn't sure what the "didn't" referred to.

"Yes, I got a text, and yes, I went to meet the mystery informant. But it didn't exactly work out." I told them about the Earl's Palace encounter as Neil's face grew more and more agitated.

"Pepper." His frustrated tone said it all.

"DON'T DROP THE DISCO BALL!" Alan screamed, and we turned to see one of the workers on a ladder bobbling a big ball as he tried to hook it to a chain hanging from the completed arch. "They cost a bloody fortune!"

"It could be worse," I said as the ladder man recovered his balance and secured the ball on the hook. "I could have to hang disco balls for Alan Woodsy."

"You have more than enough balls already," Barclay joked, and Melody tittered.

Neil rubbed his brow. "Why didn't Mark go with you?"

"Victoria escaped. Briefly." And I escaped Mark, but I didn't go there. "More to the point, who asks to meet me in a castle, comes dressed like a cosplayer, then vanishes before they can tell me anything?"

"Someone who didn't want to be identified," Luke said.

"Someone who's scared," Melody added.

"Someone who dresses up as a fairy queen in the movies?" Barclay suggested.

I handed a spotted glass to Melody. "The cloak made me think of Freya, but we'd just seen her. Did she change her mind and want to tell me something in private? Why not just talk on the phone?"

"And how would she get your number?" Luke asked.

"I gave her my card. But my number is available online if you know where to look. Any word on Rory?"

Neil shook his head. "I just pinged Magnus, who said the rescuers haven't found him. A helicopter and boats have been searching since early this morning. They even had a couple of climbers checking the rocks. They were poised to give up the search. And the forecast is calling for more fog."

"How awful." Melody set down a sparkling glass, her face mournful. "Izara came through earlier. She seemed worn out."

"She was up most of the night, I think." I turned to Neil. "Where is Magnus?"

"At the hotel." Neil looked grim. "Arch hasn't left his room. Magnus is hanging out downstairs, making sure no one gets to him."

Guilt came crashing back into my heart. I should've been able to save Rory. And we still had to look out for Arch. "Maybe we should check on him."

And see if he remembered anything else from the Brough of Birsay.

WE GRABBED a late lunch before calling Albert for a ride back to the hotel. He dropped us at Rose Hill House, then headed out to chauffeur Mark to Diana and Alastair for more touring. I'd love to see more of the sights, but I also knew I'd function better if I had a nap. By the time I got over this lousy jet lag, it would be time to go back home.

The other bartenders wanted to do some bar-hopping and dinner later, after a siesta, so we agreed to meet in the early evening. Which gave Neil and I time to check in with Magnus.

We found him in the game room on the couch, a *Scottish Field* magazine in his hand. But his fingers were slack and his head tilted back, resting against the cushions, his eyes closed. His clothes seemed rumpled—I was pretty sure he wore the same outfit he'd worn yesterday, a sport coat but without the rain jacket.

Just when I feared he might be dead, a snort-snore erupted from his nose, and he lifted his head. "What?" he barked, then blinked and sat up. "Oh, it's you. Sorry. I didn't mean to fall asleep."

"I'm not surprised. You need to rest," Neil said. "Any news?"

Magnus pulled a phone from his jacket pocket and glanced at it. "No. Nothing. They've essentially given up the search." He swallowed as if he was trying to digest a mountain of regret. "I can't wrap my mind around what happened."

"Me neither," I commiserated. "Is there any other news? Anyone else come around?"

"If you mean the Archies, they tried."

"Wren and Lark?" I asked.

He nodded. "I heard them in the lobby and told them they weren't welcome here. They said they were just here for lunch, and Ola got annoyed with me and told me I couldn't ban them from the restaurant. So I sat in the lobby and waited until they left. Ola's given me access to the front-door camera on my phone, so I'm getting alerts to people coming and going. I'm keeping an eye out in case they return."

Geez, Magnus wasn't fooling around. "Have you spoken to Arch?"

He frowned. "I knocked on his door when I got here this morning to tell him I'd be downstairs if he needed anything. He just mumbled that he was fine. Wouldn't even open the door. But maybe that's for the best."

"So he hasn't left the inn?" Neil's question made me wonder if he had an idea that my cloaked informant could be Arch.

"Definitely not," Magnus said. "He's allowed to leave, of course, but I'd prefer he not go anywhere until he's needed tomorrow."

"Would it be OK if we checked on him?" I asked.

Magnus narrowed his eyes at me, as if I might be a danger

to his charge. Then he let out a breath and leaned back against the couch. "Aye. Let me know how he is—if he'll speak with you."

He gave us the room number on the top floor, and Neil led the way—to the stairs. This place had a tiny elevator, and it smelled funny, but I wouldn't have minded a ride up two stories. Especially because they were tall floors with lots of stairs between them.

I told myself how much more cheese I could eat tonight after all this climbing. At the top, we found Arch's door, and I hauled in a couple of deep breaths.

Neil smiled. "You ready?"

I quirked my mouth at him, stepped forward and knocked. "Arch?" I called. "It's Neil and Pepper."

There was no answer. I had a bad thought. What if Arch *wasn't* there? What if something had happened to him and Magnus didn't even know? Or he'd left of his own volition? This place had a back door, for exits only—unless someone let you in—and Magnus monitored the front.

I knocked again, harder this time. "Arch, we'd like to speak with you for a minute, please."

Something like a groan filtered through the door, and a few seconds later, Arch opened it.

He looked like hell. I mean, cute, sure, but not his usual roguish charming self. His normally adorably mussed hair just looked like a mess, and he wore one of the hotel's white terry cloth robes open over a gray T-shirt and tight black boxer briefs. Which would have made pre-disaster Pepper very happy but now just made me worried.

Amusement flickered through Arch's eyes as he saw me look, and then he tightened the robe around him and tied the belt. "Come in, then. Is there any word?"

"I'm afraid not." Neil didn't add that the search had been abandoned. "We wanted to see how you were."

"You mean if I'll be all right to do the shoot and the party tomorrow?" I couldn't mistake his sarcasm—or the smell of whisky as he picked up a glass from his bedside table and took a swallow. A nearly empty bottle of Aramach's Tropical Time-less Reserve sat there as well. "You can tell Seamus I'll make it."

"That wasn't what we were going to ask." I tried to be gentle. "We just wanted to be sure you were all right."

"I'll never be all right, all right? Rory's gone. I never thought—I mean, he's a good friend. My co-star. My buddy. He's—was—" Arch choked on his words, took another sip of whisky and plopped down on the bed.

I looked around while he tried to compose himself. Clothes were strewn over the sofa and chair—this room was a lot bigger than ours and had its own gas fireplace, though it wasn't on. More clothes spilled out of an open suitcase on a rack. The desk by the door was a jumble of papers piled on and around an open laptop, with more crumpled papers crowding the floor around the plastic trash bin. The computer screen showed an image of Arch in a scene from *Sleekit Sim*. A memory of a happier time. This was not a happy room.

"Can you recall anything else from yesterday? Something that might tell us more about what happened?" I started picking up the papers scattered on the floor, setting the pris-tine ones on the desk and throwing the crumpled balls into the bin.

"No." Arch took another sip of his whisky. He set down the glass and lay back against the pillows, giving me an exasperated look. "Leave it. Go away, now. Tell Seamus I'm fine."

"No worries," Neil said. "Sorry to disturb you. I'm just sorry about what happened."

"So am I," he mumbled, sounding half asleep already.

"Wait a second." Among the wadded balls and the flat pages on the floor—from a script, I thought—I'd spied a folded piece of paper with handwriting on it. Without even thinking about it, I opened it and glanced at the contents. "Oh my God."

Chapter Twenty-Five

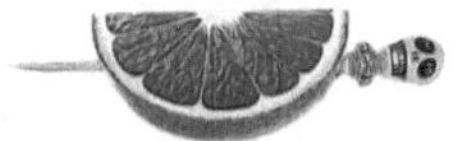

"What is it?" Neil asked as I stared at the piece of paper.

"A handwritten letter. '*My darling, I love you both too much to let them take you away from me. You don't need the whisky. You need me. I'll keep you safe. I'll take you home. You won't ever have to worry about him ever again.*' Arch, when did you receive this?

"Huh?" He lifted his head and dragged his eyes to me.

"This letter. It sounds like one Izara showed us."

The star's gaze was cloudy. "I don't know."

"It sounds *exactly* like one of the letters she showed us." Neil looked over my shoulder.

Adrenaline rushed through me. "Somebody must have slipped this under the door. They not only know where you are, they wanted to be really sure you got the message. They were so determined, they dropped an identical message in Aramach's box. When did it come?"

"I didn't notice it." Arch was in such a state, I wasn't sure if he was capable of noticing someone sticking a letter under the door. Or in his face. But it couldn't have arrived today.

"It had to have come yesterday or the day before." Wednesday or Thursday, I thought. "The other letter arrived in the box Wednesday—or maybe even Tuesday night. And it was before Rory—"

Arch closed his eyes and covered them with one arm as I continued the thought in my head: The letter came before Rory was pushed over the cliff. Maybe written by someone who told Arch he wouldn't have to worry about "him" ever again.

"It's even worse," I continued. "They got to your room. They got into the hotel."

"Not today," Neil said. "Not with Magnus keeping an eye on people coming and going."

"Right. Like I said, it had to be from yesterday or before, since the wording matches the other letter." A dark thought occurred to me. "Whoever wrote it might even be staying here."

"What does it matter now?" Arch growled.

"It matters because you're in danger," I insisted.

"Get out. I need to rest."

Neil gestured to me. "We'll leave."

"Please be careful," I told Arch, taking the letter with me. "Don't open the door unless you know who it is."

"I'm sorry I opened it just now," he grumbled.

Great. Arch Halliday hated me. But we had to look after his interests. I couldn't let anyone hurt him, especially after what happened to Rory.

I tucked the refolded letter into my bag and followed Neil to the door. "Take care, Arch," I whispered and got a grunt in reply as I closed the door behind us.

We took the stairs down a floor to our room. I dropped my big bag and wandered to the window while Neil used the bathroom. The skies were clouding up again, and it looked as if rain, maybe even fog, was developing over the distant water.

"That was really weird," I told Neil when he emerged.

"You'd think he would've seen the note earlier."

"Maybe, maybe not. Did you see that room? He's a slob," I said to Neil's snort of amusement. "But who sends the same stalker letter twice?"

"It would've been convenient if they signed it," he remarked as he kicked off his sturdy black sneakers.

"That's another thing." I found my iPad and rummaged through my files till I found the scanned letters Izara had sent me. It took just a minute to lay hands on the twin letter. "The one Izara showed us did have a signature, that angel heart thing, the one they called the Flying Heart. This one didn't."

"Who knows?" Neil said. "Maybe they forgot."

I grasped for an explanation. "Maybe they signed their real name accidentally and realized it at the last minute and cut off the bottom of the letter before they stuck it under his door."

He chuckled. "Sure, why not? Maybe they were just trying to be mysterious. Maybe they use a different signature every time and ran out of ideas."

I snickered. "Now you're making fun of me. I think I need to give this to Magnus."

"That makes sense. Take a picture of it first."

"Already on it." I placed the unfolded letter on the desk and used my phone to snap a photo. I grabbed my key and stuffed it in my pocket before heading for the door.

"And then we'll take a nap?" Neil's husky tone heated me to my toes.

I gave him what I hoped was a seductive look. "I'll be right back."

I DID NAP. Eventually. And Neil and I met up with Barclay, Luke and Melody, along with Mark, Diana and Alastair, for a little barhopping. Then we headed to an Italian restaurant near the cathedral for a late dinner.

Tendrils of fog crept down the narrow street, wisps for now, but just seeing it gave me chills, even though it wasn't cold. It was a reminder of what had happened yesterday, and I had trouble focusing on my fresh, delicately seared scallops and pasta swimming in a buttery garlic sauce.

I'd just told my friends about Arch's persistent stalker.

"So nice, they wrote it twice," Barclay said grimly.

"The wording—it sounds like a threat to Rory," Diana suggested.

"Which makes it seem like he was pushed," Luke added.

"I think I agree with you." I sipped my Italian fizzy water. "Given the ambiguous wording of the letters, I wonder if Rory was the target the whole time. But why?"

"Oh, I think Arch is the subject of at least some of them," Neil said.

Mark tilted his wineglass to make his point. "When you have that many fans, you're bound to get a variety of nutters."

I pointed my fork at him. "I'd prefer it be one person we can easily find so we can make sure this doesn't happen again."

"Who writes letters anymore?" Alastair picked at his spaghetti carbonara. "Why not email?"

"Because hiding your tracks in email is difficult if professional investigators get on the case," Neil said.

"Which Seamus needs to do. Or maybe we need to go to the police ourselves and tell them our suspicions." But even as I said it, I knew that was a ridiculous idea. What evidence did we have?

"What would you tell them?" Diana asked.

"I don't know, exactly. We don't have enough information." I jumped as my phone buzzed in my bag, which leaned against my foot under the table. I dug it out while the others talked about the yummy food. I had a new text from an unknown source.

I gasped when I read it.

When I looked up, everyone was staring at me.

"Another text?" Neil asked.

I nodded. "It says, 'Let's try this again. Birsay tonight at low tide. The cliffs where it happened. I have answers. Come alone.'"

Storm clouds rolled over Neil's face. "No."

I didn't like "no." Even if it came from Neil. "You know I have to go."

Then everyone spoke at once while I reread the message. Whoever this was had a flair for the dramatic. I just hoped they didn't have a flair for murdering people. I couldn't see why they'd want to hurt me. It wasn't like I was close to figuring out who was making the threats or who pushed Rory. Or was I?

"Albert will give me a ride, won't he?" I asked Mark.

"Give *us* a ride," Mark replied.

"That's ridiculous," I said. "I'm supposed to come alone. Not with a whole clown car."

"I resent that remark," Luke said.

"You're the clowniest of them all," Barclay ribbed him, and Melody chuckled.

"*I* don't want to go." Alastair sipped his wine and gave me a smug look.

"Gee, thanks," I said dryly.

"I am going with you," Neil said. "This is nonnegotiable."

"Or what?" I set my jaw and stared back at him.

Everybody got quiet. When I saw the angst in Neil's eyes, I softened. A little. Then he reached out and took my hand, and I was a goner.

"OK. I'll take you with me, and only you," I told him. "If Mark lends us the van. But we might have to split up on the island if I want to get any information from this person."

Mark looked out the windows onto the narrow street, where the gray crept in, oozing, thickening. The fog was back. "Your person might have trouble seeing you both if it's as bad as last night. Which could work to your advantage."

I seized on this idea. "Yeah, Neil. You could stay nearby and let me meet them by myself."

"They also might be counting on the fog to hide their approach." He squeezed my hand. "Are you seriously going to the edge of the cliff where Rory died? Where he was probably pushed, maybe by this person?"

"I'll stay away from the edge. I'll be careful and on alert. Rory wasn't careful." I knew I was grasping at straws, but I really, really wanted to figure this out, and this was my chance.

"We'll play it by ear, all right? If they want you, they're getting me, too." Neil's hand felt warm wrapped around mine.

I didn't want to lose him here. Or there. Or go high-diving into the rocks. "We'll figure it out. We will. And if Albert drives us, he can see who's coming and going at the lot."

"Of course you can have the minibus," Mark said. "What if we came along and stayed with the vehicle?"

"You might scare them off." Neil surprised me. And made me happy. He was entering operational mode, which meant he was on board. "I think it should just be me and Pepper."

"Should I reply to this person?" I mused.

"I think so," Diana said. "You want to encourage them to show up."

"Keep it simple," Neil suggested.

So I typed back, "I'll be there." I kept looking at the phone, but there was no further response. Conversation turned to other topics, and we finished our meal, though I was less enthusiastic about it as I considered what we might be facing on the island.

Neil pulled out his phone and angled it toward me. I looked at it with him as he called up the tide schedule for the Brough of Birsay.

"It'll be late," he said. "Low tide is 11:15 p.m."

"Late and darker than it was last night."

"But not totally dark," he pointed out. "It doesn't get totally dark here in the summer."

"Close enough in the fog." I considered the time. It would take at least a half hour for Albert to drive us out there, plus add ten or fifteen minutes for caution on foggy roads. And then we had to hike across the causeway and climb up to the cliffs on the far side. We could get to the parking lot by ten thirty if we left soon.

Neil turned to Mark. "Do you think you can summon Albert for us? Is that going to strand you here?"

"I can always hire a cab," Mark said.

"So could we," I suggested.

"Nonsense. Albert is reliable in any situation. And I doubt you'd have luck finding a cab to take you all the way out there on this foggy night." Mark pulled out his phone and tapped on the screen. "On his way," he said after a moment.

"Then I guess we are, too." I looked at Neil, who waved at the server and wrote a mock signature in the air, asking for the check.

I caught Diana looking at me as the others chatted. She murmured, "You will be careful, won't you?"

"I'll do my best." I felt Neil's eyes on me. "I mean, yes, of course I'll be careful. Aren't I always?"

I pretended not to hear Neil's soft groan. Diana, who'd had plenty of excitement traveling the world doing research, looking for unusual botanicals for Mark's gin, just smiled.

I took heart. She was a kick-ass adventurer. Why couldn't I be, too? I mean, if you ignored my issues with running and my need for regular doses of cheese, I could be an explorer or a pirate. A little meeting with a mysterious informant atop a cliff on a tidal island in the fog wasn't going to intimidate me.

Chapter Twenty-Six

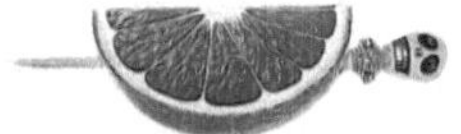

"Are you mad at me?" I asked Neil as Albert drove us carefully over the hills through the thickening fog toward the Brough of Birsay.

"No, of course not. But I wish there was a better way to confront your texter." He sat next to me in the front row behind Albert, but this time, we were the only passengers.

"The only other way would be to surround them and catch them as they come off the island via the causeway, but they probably have some way of ensuring a crowd doesn't come with me. Maybe they have a camera set up somewhere, aimed at the lot. Or a friend. I don't know. I also worry about what a desperate person will do when cornered. They were clever enough to wait until it was late to ping me so we'd have trouble bringing any kind of official posse."

"That's true. But why such an elaborate setup?"

I shook my head. "They're protecting their identity, I guess. I hope I at least find out who this is before we're done."

"I'll be on the lookout, Miss," Albert said from the front. He'd been so quiet, I'd almost forgotten he was there.

"Thanks," I said. "You have our phone numbers now." We'd made sure of that before we set out. "If you see anything weird, ping us."

"Ping me," Neil requested, "to keep Pepper's phone clear for mysterious callers."

"Signal permitting, I will." Albert made a good point. The cell signal there seemed to come and go during our last visit. Maybe our traveling phone plan was to blame.

We'd left our rain jackets in the minibus when Albert drove us into Kirkwall earlier in the evening. I donned mine, zipped my phone into one of the pockets and stowed my bag under the seat as Albert pulled into the empty parking lot for the Brough of Birsay.

I didn't have a weapon. I hadn't brought my cocktail knife to Scotland to avoid problems at the airport. But maybe that was just as well. I didn't trust my stabbing skills unless my informant was a particularly lethargic piece of produce.

Neil and I got out of the van and headed down the stone steps that led to the beach and the causeway. Not that we could see much of the causeway—just the start of it. Which was more than we could see the previous evening. Maybe the fog wouldn't be so bad on the island.

That was a good thought, but it didn't bear out. Once we got on the zigzagging concrete walkway that cut across the bed of tilted rocks and seaweed and tidal pools, the fog seemed to thicken.

"What is the deal with the fog here?" I asked Neil in a hushed voice.

He turned his head briefly to look at me; he was leading the way. "I read up on fog after you went to sleep last night." Of course he did. "There are several types. I think this is what they call an advection fog. Something about warm air moving over a cool surface. Anyway, they had a fog like this several months ago across northern Scotland that went on for a week."

"That's crazy."

"Explains the wind, too. This kind of fog can happen when it's windy."

And it *was* windy. I'd worn my practical boots during our outing this evening, but I'd optimistically chosen a cute, thin V-neck tee to go with my jeans. My bright yellow jacket whipped around me and didn't block much of the chill. I began to understand the British obsession with a cup of hot, sweet, strong tea. How nice it would be right now to curl up with a tea, or maybe a whisky, in a cozy love seat with Neil by a fire and forget about all this skulduggery.

We reached the rock-strewn beach at the end of the walkway and picked our way across. As the steep bank marking the edge of the island appeared out of the fog, I listened hard but heard nothing but waves and the occasional cry of a seabird.

"Did you notice the parking lot was empty?" I asked Neil.

"Maybe we beat your person here?"

"They'd have to show up pretty soon to catch low tide."

"Maybe they got a ride earlier," Neil said. "Albert will tell us if he sees anything on his end."

If he could. I glanced at my phone as we climbed up the ramp to the grassy surface of the island. I had one flickering bar of signal. Not great.

When you could see it, the island resembled a round cake that never rose properly on one side; the grass was its green icing. The highest cliffs were on the side of the island where the cake had risen to its full potential—where the meadow sloped up and away from us.

A wet, salty, earthy smell filled my nose. It took me a second to get oriented. "Ruins there"—I gestured right—"and shack there." I pointed to the left.

"Where the 'call 999' sign was," Neil confirmed. "I think we might have to go past that, then angle right, over the center of the island, if we want the short way to the cliffs."

"The short way is the best way." Not that we could see up the path very far in the fog. It was darker than yesterday, too.

Just as we got past the hut, Neil halted and pulled his phone out of the pocket of his jacket—at least its black color might help him hide in the fog, if necessary.

"Message from Albert. I think it was sent a few minutes ago, judging from the time stamp. Another vehicle arrived, and four people are headed over the causeway."

"Did he get a look at them?"

Neil's eyebrows came together as he glanced again at his phone, then looked at me. "He thinks it's Mr. Mixy."

"Oh, crapnoodles." I didn't think Mr. Mixy was my informant. But he could seriously mess up my rendezvous.

My phone buzzed. *Uh-oh.* I pulled it out and read it to Neil.

"It's from Mark. 'I'm so sorry, Pepper. The Mixmeister cornered us in a pub and found out about your mission and said he had a divine calling to protect you or some rubbish.'" Ugh. Mr. Mixy had been prattling on about helping me ever since his near-death experience last Christmas, but I thought he was finally over it and back to his usual self-absorbed programming. I read on: "Mark says, 'I was very good and quiet, but some of your colleagues were in their cups and more loquacious. Look out. With luck, he'll be far enough behind you that it won't matter.'"

"The only luck we have is bad luck," Neil said.

"You're my good luck." My smile was frayed at the edges, but I meant it.

He tried to smile back. "Let's get up there and see if we can draw out your informant."

But to my dismay, voices reached us from the ramp. Mr. Mixy and friends were right behind us.

"This isn't going to work," I said. "If he follows us, I won't get to meet the informant."

"Or the killer. Maybe this is lucky after all."

"You know we have to do this. I have to do this." I had an idea. "You could distract Mr. Mixy while I go to the top of the hill."

"That's not what we agreed on."

"You're here, aren't you?" I stepped closer to him. "I'll scream like my life depends on it if I'm under any threat at all. I'll tell them there are other people on the island and they won't be able to escape without everyone knowing about it if they try to harm me."

"Like your life depends ... Pepper, you're killing me."

"No one's going to kill me today. Or you. Trust me. Please?" I asked. "I swear I'll scream. Or run. Or otherwise get out of the way."

Mr. Mixy's voice came to us, far too close. "She can't be far. The island isn't that big." There was a response I couldn't make out, then Mr. Mixy again: "Come on, Dave. This'll be great footage, rescuing Pepper from a killer!"

Argh. There he was. The selfish Stephan I remembered.

"Here's what I'll do." Neil sounded resigned. "I'll tell them I've agreed to wait for you here. And I'll direct them to Barclay and Luke's crevasse. Remember?"

"Oh, yes. Tell them I had to go to the bottom of that to wait. That should keep them occupied for a few minutes."

"As soon as they're out of sight, I'll be right behind you. Try to stay away from the cliff, OK?"

I gave him a quick hug. "We've got this." And before he could change his mind, I charged uphill on the path.

In just a minute, he was out of sight, but indistinct voices reached me through the fog. The path branched off to the right, but I wasn't sure that would work. I needed to get higher. Worst case, I could keep climbing up, go off the path wherever I wanted—as long as fences weren't in the way—then follow the cliff around to where Rory vanished.

I kept going and was rewarded with another split in the path. I looked up and caught the glow of the lighthouse through the fog to my left. Well, that was convenient. I angled right, away from it and toward the cliff where Rory had met his end, hoping I wouldn't meet mine.

That thought slowed me down a little. I had to stay sharp and aware of my surroundings. But like yesterday, the fog veiled everything beyond about ten feet. I paused, caught my breath, and listened. All the sounds seemed distorted. Were there voices? Were there footsteps?

There were waves far below, I thought, though their rush and retreat seemed entangled with the wind. Birds cried, still awake in this weird semi-twilight, this high northern summer where it never got dark.

It was dark enough. Gray. Chilly.

I climbed again, toward the sound of the waves, and after a few minutes, I reached what seemed to be the path between the lighthouse and where Rory had fallen. I didn't remember passing this junction yesterday, but we must have. We'd been running toward the screams.

I bore right, walking slowly, looking around, trying to see. Rocks jutted out of the fog to my left. *The cliff is right there.* I heard Neil's warning again in my head.

But where had Rory fallen? Was this it? Or there? I edged closer to the precipice, looking down over the ledges. Small winged shapes like flying water jugs swooped up and out and back—puffins, I thought. I really wanted to see a puffin up close.

And then the sound of feet running toward me startled me. Just as I spun to see who it was, my foot slipped on a mossy patch and my feet went out from under me. For a second, I thought I'd land it as I belly-flopped at the downward-sloping edge of the cliff. But my momentum and the slick rock had other ideas.

No. No! I can't be this stupid. I can't let Neil down. The killer is coming for me!

All these thoughts went through my head in an instant as I desperately tried to grab for any kind of handhold as I slid, feet-first, over the edge.

The last thing I saw as I dropped was a round shape with a narrow face, its baleful glare the sum of all my fears.

"Baaaaah," it said.

Chapter Twenty-Seven

I'm still here.

That was my first thought. Well, after a stream of vigorous curses, which felt great after months of trying to clean up my language.

I was doing that thing they do in the movies, hanging on to a cliff. Cliffhanging. *Gah!*

What they don't tell you in the movies is that the actor either has a big fat cushion under them, waiting to break their fall, or they're filming the stunt horizontally. I'd seen the documentaries.

And in reality, actors are not generally clinging to a wet, slippery rock that abruptly crumbles under their fingers.

Which was what this tiny overhang did within the ten seconds I'd hung all my hopes on it.

"Ow!" I cried as I slid down the rock face, grasping for any kind of hold.

And then my feet hit something solid and almost flat.

I hugged the cliff and sucked in a breath. I held it. Was this real? Was I alive?

"Baaaah," my sheep friend called. *Friend, ha.* Then I thought I heard it trotting away.

Duh. Yes. I was alive, and so was the killer sheep.

Not a killer. Just sheep, I reminded myself. I was sure no

sheep were around Rory when he died—the sheep were following Neil and me and ran away, and Izara didn't mention any in the vicinity. So there was likely still a killer out there, as well as an informant.

And I was down here—where? First, I gingerly looked down to where my feet were stopped—on a ledge. Good. Not a wide ledge, not a perfectly level ledge, but I had eight or ten inches to work with and a small sub-ledge a couple of inches lower.

As I looked down, my glasses, already askew from the fall, slipped off my face and spun into the fog below. A weak clatter followed.

At least I didn't need them to see. But they were cute, dang it.

A small, fluttering shape distracted me. It was one of the butterflies Diana had been so excited about, a Small Tortoise-shell. Its movement in space reminded me just how much space there was between me and the rocks below. Only I didn't have the luxury of flying. I tried to calm myself. A butterfly probably wouldn't kill me unless I let it startle me. I had to focus.

Priorities, Pepper. Step one: Don't fall. The ledge was slippery as snot, and worse, it angled downward slightly toward the invisible sea, where the waves sizzled. Staggered ledges beneath me gradually faded into the fog, though they didn't look friendly. It wasn't like I could stairstep down without bouncing. Even if I made it to the bottom in one piece, what was there? Rocks? The North Sea? I shivered.

So step two was to get back up to the top somehow. The way up was more vertical, with occasional crevices and bulges and, in fluffs near the top, clumps of pale yellow and burgundy flowers. Would any of these crannies work as handholds?

I wasn't a rock climber. I once went to a "fun" sportsplex with climbing walls for my friend Cali's birthday party. Her surfer boyfriend was into adventure sports. I got about halfway up the kids' wall, tumbled down and retreated to the complex's cafe to eat pizza.

I didn't want to climb without help, up or down. This was impossible.

My eyes focused on my bracelet. I'd worn it in other impossible situations. But as superstitious as I'd become about my talisman, I knew it wouldn't magically get me out of here.

I startled and almost fell again when a stout little bird landed on the ledge near my left hand. I wasn't holding on to anything at this point unless you counted digging my nails into tiny creases in the rock face, but I'd mentally glued my hands and the rest of my body to the cliff in hopes of not falling.

I took a long, slow breath, relaxed slightly and examined the bird. Well, this was one way to see a puffin up close. He cocked his head and stared at me curiously, his orange-rimmed eyes set into the sides of his almost round head. A black and orange beak, which looked almost triangular from the side, protruded from a white face. The top of his head and back were black, his round belly white, his webbed feet orange and wide with nasty-looking black talons, great for clinging to rocks.

He was adorable.

"Hey," I said. "Can you go fetch the magic eagles?"

He burst off the cliff with an explosion of little black wings. But since this wasn't *The Lord of the Rings*, my hopes of him accomplishing his mission weren't high. Maybe I should've asked the butterfly.

Time to start screaming. "Neil!" I shouted. "Neil! Help!"

There was a rustle above. I carefully tilted my head back to look up. I couldn't quite see the top of the cake, as it were, but I didn't think I'd slid more than about nine or ten feet. Funny, it had felt like a hundred.

A head poked over the edge of the cliff, hooded. My informant? Did the sheep accomplish what this person intended to do anyway? I held still and tried to identify them.

But in the mist and gloom, all I saw was a face in shadow. Would they help me? Or find a way to hasten my fall?

"Help?" I croaked.

"Oh, Pepper. I didn't mean for this to happen," came a familiar voice in a Scottish accent. The figure tugged back the hood of the robe, and I almost toppled off the cliff in pure shock.

"Rory?" I squeaked.

It took my brain a few seconds to catch up with my eyes. Rory was alive! Thank Dionysus. But how? What happened? It was a St. Magnus miracle!

"I'm glad to see you," I said. "Can you help me get out of here?"

Rory nodded. "I'll try. I have a busted arm. And I don't want your friends to see me."

"Neil's with me. He should be right behind me. He's a good guy, you know. He sent the others off on a wild goose chase."

"Fine," Rory said. "Then he can help me."

Another, deeper, angry voice cut through the fog. "What have you done to Pepper?" *Neil!*

"Nothing! She slipped and fell. She's right there. I'm here to help."

"Oh, my God. Rory?" Neil sounded closer now.

"We can talk about my resurrection later," Rory said. "We have to get Pepper out of here, and I need to get off the island before the others see me. I want to lie low for another day or so."

"Why? Never mind." Neil called out, "Pepper? Are you OK?"

"Down here!" I said. "I'm stuck."

Neil and Rory both poked their heads over the ledge.

"Ever do any rock climbing?" Rory asked.

"I fell off the kids' wall once during a friend's birthday outing." I didn't mention the pizza. "Should I try to climb out?"

"No," they both said.

"I should call for help," Neil said.

"They won't send a helicopter in the fog," Rory replied. "Anything else might take too long."

"Please hurry!" I called. My boots kept slipping in tiny, terrifying increments on the slick ledge.

"We can do it," Rory told Neil. "There were a few things I found in Walty Reid's Hole, perhaps something we can use. Wait a couple of minutes." And he disappeared.

Wait? No problem. I wasn't going anywhere. At least I hoped I wasn't.

"Pepper." Neil's call was more gentle this time. Mist swirled about his face, about all of him that I could make out. He looked like a ghost. "What happened?"

"I slipped and fell."

"You said you'd stay away from the cliffs."

"I was trying to figure out where I was. And there was a sheep."

He was silent for a beat. "A sheep?"

"It startled me. And the rocks were wet. And—"

"It's all right," he said. "Just try to relax for a minute. We're going to get you out of here."

"Rory said he hurt his arm somehow. So he will definitely need your help. And I guess we should honor his wish to keep him away from Mixy and company until we hear his story."

"We will if we can, but the priority is making sure you're safe."

I heard Rory's approach this time, his steps pounding on the earth above as he ran up to our position. One of my feet slipped again, and I gasped and grabbed the puffin's empty ledge and tried to inch closer to the cliff face. "Neil?"

"I'm right here. Hang on."

Rory's face came in view. "All I have is a rope. It was stowed in the cave. I think it's sound, but without a harness and the rest of my gear ..." He thought for a moment. "I could rig up a prusik, but there's the time issue, and I'd probably have to come down and help you, and with my arm hurt—"

"I could help," Neil said.

"You a climber?"

"No." Regret tinged Neil's voice.

"Then you shouldn't. It'll be too technical on a face like this. I have one good arm. You have two. Let's get a rope around her and pull her up."

Great, they were going to rope me like a calf. Or a coo. "Uh, how is that going to work?"

Rory looked down. "Give me a moment."

A minute later, Rory lowered a bright green and blue rope with a loop tied in it, a sturdy-looking knot securing it. "Put this around your waist."

I blinked up at him. That would mean moving.

"Put one hand through at a time," he said. "Slowly."

I froze as two puffins landed on the ledge next to my hand, checking me out. No magic eagles, then. Fine.

Gingerly, I lifted my right hand from the wall of rock and

tried to catch the rope loop, which swung in the wind. I teetered as I grabbed it and plastered myself against the wall again, my heart off to the races.

"You're doing great," Rory said. "Get it over your head, then get your other arm through. It's a bowline knot, so it will tighten as we pull it. I've got it tied around my waist up here since there are no trees or decent rocks for an anchor. Neil and I will get you up, but we're going to need you to do some climbing. I'll direct you."

"I fell off the kids' wall!" I reminded him.

"But I wasn't there," Rory said with the kind of confident charm his character in *Sleekit Sim* wielded to get Arch's Sim out of sticky situations.

I closed my eyes and took another breath. This was what I had to do. Imagine I was in a *Sleekit Sim* episode. I was a daring lass, and an adorable hero—two heroes—would help me get out of this.

I opened my eyes. "OK. I'm ready. Let me get this rope on."

I painstakingly worked the loop over my head, under my arms and down a bit, pulling on it so it was snug around my waist.

Neil crouched, leaning back, holding the rope. Rory, who'd shed his Renaissance cloak to reveal an all-black outfit beneath, lay on his stomach next to him, gripping the rope with his presumably good arm after it passed through Neil's hands. I hoped Rory had a strong enough body to be the anchor. Oh, who was I kidding? I'd seen him without his shirt often enough in *Sleekit Sim*. The dude was ripped. But I was no light lassie.

"Try to get a higher handhold somewhere. I think I see one above your left hand," Rory said.

"OK." I reached a little higher. Not much of a handhold. More of a dainty finger hold. "Now what?"

"See that short ledge up to your right? Put your right foot on that," he told me.

"Crap," I said, anticipating losing my semisafe perch. But I did as he said, and the rope went taut around my waist as they pulled, giving me a touch of confidence. But putting weight on the step meant my left foot would be searching for purchase. One of the puffins cawed next to me, sounding like a drunk playing a kazoo, and I almost lost it. "Shut up!"

Rory laughed. "Made a friend, did you? Commit to the right foot and try stepping up a couple of inches on your left."

I did, and my left foot, or rather toes, found purchase. Rory was the rock whisperer. And the rope was taut. But if they let go, I had no doubt that I'd plummet. I was off my ledge now, the ledge that had saved me.

"We have you." Neil's voice was strained. His tone said, *But please hurry*.

"A few more feet," Rory said. "You can do this."

And so they led me up, one harrowing step at a time. Another puffin landed on their spectators' ledge, and all three of them watched as I made my way up—and, once, slipped and dangled and scrambled for a second that elicited grunts from my would-be rescuers before I found a toehold again.

"Sorry," I called and looked up. Oh my gosh. Neil's dear face was right there, just a foot or so away, and so was Rory's.

"Can you reach me?" Neil asked.

With my right hand clasped onto a mini ledge, I extended my left arm out to him. Keeping one hand twisted around the rope, Neil held out his right hand and clasped my wrist.

"Wait a second, Pepper," Rory said. "Push off with your hand and feet when I say go, and we'll haul you up."

"OK."

"Three, two one—go!"

I did my best to spring off my minuscule holds in the rock as Neil heaved, Rory helping. And then I was halfway over the edge, grabbing with my right hand to pull myself up, and they dragged me to the top. I fell into Neil, knocking him backward onto the ground, and lay there on top of him, hugging him, breathing hard as he squeezed me. I looked up to see Rory slumped over as he sat, gulping huge breaths. We all stayed that way for a minute.

And then I heard voices and rolled off Neil and sat up.

"Wheesht!" Rory held up a hand, telling us to be quiet. He pulled a phone out of a pocket in his black sweatshirt and tapped the screen. "All right, I have someone picking us up at the car park. Tell your ride to leave."

Neil didn't look happy. "I'd rather not."

"Do it, Neil," I said. "Rory saved me, with your help. It'll be all right." I turned to Rory. "Thank you."

"Least I could do. I happen to know what that's like." His smile was grim.

"How are we doing with the tide?" Neil also pulled his phone out of a jacket pocket and tapped it, presumably texting Albert.

"We'll just make it." Rory stood. "Let's go before your friend finds us."

Mr. Mixy, my "friend." I supposed he was trying to help. But Mr. Mixy was about as helpful as a leaky cocktail shaker.

We headed away from the voices, circling around the eastern edge of the island—but not close to the edge. I made sure of that. We eluded Mr. Mixy and crew and saw no one else as we got back to the tidal causeway. Water had started to slosh over the concrete path, so we trod carefully.

Rory, carrying his cloak, pulled his sweatshirt hood forward to conceal his face, but he needn't have worried. Albert had left the parking lot, and only Mr. Mixy's rental SUV remained.

The fog still obscured everything beyond our immediate surroundings, though it was a bit thinner here. But the world felt darker, too. It was after midnight and as close to night as Orkney got in the summer, a deep dusk enhanced by the fog. The lighthouse shone, a point of light barely penetrating the sea-hugging cloud that lay between us and the island.

I stood there for a moment, looking in the direction of that light, wondering if Mixy and company would emerge from the fog. They'd better do it fast if they didn't want to wade across. I felt a teeny tiny spark of guilt. But they shouldn't have been here in the first place!

Then again, maybe I shouldn't have either. I was damp, my yellow jacket was smeared with gunk, my boots were probably ruined, and my filthy jeans had at least one rip from the rocks. My hands felt rough, and my nails—which I kept shortish for work—were a wreck. But at least I was alive.

The low buzz of an engine approached. Beams of head-lights cut through the mist, preceding a compact car in a hurry. It tore into the lot and stopped in front of us.

We looked at Rory.

"Get in," he said as he headed for the co-pilot's seat.

Neil and I exchanged a glance, evaluating our chances, then climbed into the back.

And I couldn't believe who was driving.

Chapter Twenty-Eight

"Did you know?" was the first thing I asked Izara, who spun the car out of the parking lot as if we were being chased. Which I thought we weren't, but the fog could hide a lot, especially if a pursuer cut the headlights.

"That Rory was alive?" She glanced in the rearview mirror at me but stayed focused on the narrow road, which ran along the shore. The sea was barely a suggestion through the swirling mist in the gloomy twilight. "Not immediately but soon after. He sent me a text."

"Where?" Neil asked. "How?"

Rory twisted so he could see both of us. "I fell farther than Pepper did but in almost the same place. Or rather, I was pushed."

I gasped even though I'd thought so all along. "Who did it?"

"I don't know." His voice held regret and a touch of anger. "But since I found myself alive, I reckoned my best move might be to stay dead, so to speak. So I used voice to text and told Izara I was all right and to hold up the ruse." He turned to her. "I'm vexed I put you in that position."

"You know I'd do anything to keep you safe." She turned a smile to him, and he planted a quick kiss on her lips.

Whoa. That was not a friendly "you're the marketing person for my best friend" kiss.

"So, you two ...?" I asked.

"Yes." Rory swiveled back to us as Izara turned onto a wider road. "We've been keeping it quiet, thinking it was better for our privacy."

"And your show," Izara said wryly.

"We've seen how obsessed the fans get," he said. "I don't want them anywhere near Izara. When I leave the show, we'll go public."

"You're leaving the show?" I almost shouted.

"Not yet. But I'm thinking about it," Rory said. "There are —reasons."

"I still don't get why you thought being dead might be a good idea, or rather pretending to be dead," Neil said. "And what happened after you went over the edge?"

"I realize the idea might seem oot the blue, but Izara and I had already discussed our concerns about the letters Arch has been getting. I believed some of those threats were directed more at me than him, probably from fans who thought I posed some sort of danger to Arch."

"Especially after the Paintball Piper," I agreed. "That wasn't your doing?"

"No, and I don't believe it was Arch's either. Very strange. But when this happened, I figured my sudden disappearance would clear the way and make the big promotional event safe for Arch."

"When your name gets out as the person who fell and you show up alive, you're going to be in a fearful pot of trouble," Izara said.

"What will they do, fine me?" Rory didn't seem worried. "I'll have a good story to tell, about finding my way out and ending up at the cottage and not hearing about the search ..."

"Slow down," I said. "Tell us everything."

"Let's do it inside." Izara pulled into a short, grass-and-stone driveway blocked by a metal gate.

A low, rustic stone wall ran along one side of the drive leading to a cottage, while a post-and-wire fence lined the other side. A few sheep grazed beyond it. I eyed them warily, wondering if this was the beginning of a sheep phobia.

"I'll get the gate." Neil hopped out of the car.

I felt like I was coming out of a dream. I'd been aware of Izara making a couple of turns but had been so focused on Rory, I had no idea where I was. Even though the fog was thinner here, I could see no other houses nearby.

Neil waved us through, and Izara pulled up to the cottage. It had tan, pebbled walls, a chimney at either end of the roof and a small glassed-in sunroom sticking out the front—what we'd call a Florida room back home. What looked like an addition stuck out of the back of the house.

Neil secured the gate and joined us as we got out of the car.

"Is this where you've been hiding?" I asked Rory.

"Aye."

"Seamus's veterinarian lives here." Izara skipped the sunroom entrance and led us to the back, where a door took us into the kitchen. "I've taken his dog here a few times. The man's retired, but he knows Seamus and was willing to help. He was the first person I thought of to call since he lives close to Birsay. And no, Seamus doesn't know about Rory either."

Did that mean she suspected Seamus of wishing harm to Rory?

"Dr. Mutch?" Izara called. When there was no answer, she set about starting up the teakettle. "He said he might go out."

By the time we'd all used the facilities and settled into a cozy wood-paneled sitting room that bordered the sunroom—more like the mist room at the moment—she'd brought a tea tray out to us. She sat on the couch with Rory, while Neil took a comfy chair and I ended up on a spindly wooden thing with a worn-out cushion. The room was stuffed with bric-a-brac and books, framed paintings filled the walls, afghans draped the careworn furniture, and an unlit fireplace looked sooty and well-used.

A fluffy tortoiseshell cat with white socks and green eyes tiptoed in, leaped onto Neil's chair and curled into his lap. Neil gave me a helpless look, and I laughed.

Izara presented me with a mug of steaming black tea. The scent was pure comfort. "Thank you." I didn't hold back on the sugar. The others doctored theirs; only Neil took his straight. The hot, sweet brew was just what I needed. That and answers. "How did you get from there to here?" I demanded of Rory.

He chuckled. "I'm an adept climber, though I'll admit, I had a few skeerie moments after I texted Izara that I was all right. I'm not an eejit. Usually I climb with thoroughly tested gear. I was very lucky I slid to a ledge where I had good hand-holds and didn't just plummet."

"Wait—did you yell again after he texted you?" I asked Izara, thinking of the children screaming at the palace and not knowing if they were playing or dying.

She looked slightly embarrassed. "Yes. I might have. I would have anyway, if I'd lost him. I didn't have to fake being upset. I was still terrified he might fall on his way back up. Thank God he didn't."

"It was a near thing," Rory said. "I'd hurt myself on the way down; Dr. Mutch says it's just a sprained wrist, but it made hanging on difficult."

He lifted his wrist. A bandage showed beneath the cuff of his sweatshirt.

"The vet treated your arm?" I asked.

"He was more than qualified. At any rate, after I texted Izara, I shuffled sideways for a bit on the cliff face until I found a place where I could hold and wait until most of you had gone, and then I climbed up to the top and moved away from Izara and Magnus." He turned to her. "Again, I'm sorry."

"Stop apologizing. I still think you're mad," she said, "but if we can keep you and Arch safe while we figure out who did this, it'll be worth it."

He nodded and resumed his story. "I thought of hiding out in one of the caves at first. There's a handful. I paused at the mouth of Walter Reid's Hole, but I'd attempted the climb down as a younger man, and it was harrowing. And staying overnight on the island wasn't appealing—it was awfy dreich with the fog and chill—and not practical if rescue crews were out and I wanted to stay hidden. But then I remembered I'd seen a dinghy someone had brought to the shore of the brough. Daft to take it out in the fog like that, but there it was —a way for me to get off the island. I found my way back to where they'd stowed it near the geo."

"Is that what I keep calling the crevasse?" I asked.

He nodded. "Probably. I took the dinghy—"

"Stole it, you mean." Izara softened her scold with a smile.

"The tide took it, obviously." Rory raised his eyebrows and sipped his tea.

"Go on." Neil stroked the cat, who purred loudly. Lucky cat. "Where'd you go from there?"

"I got to the shore, nowhere near the car park, I might add, and waited for Izara. I waited a very long time."

"I had to get my car," she said. "It was a long night."

"When she arrived, I destroyed my cell phone and threw it into the sea. Izara gave me a prepaid mobile. And she brought me here." Rory nodded at our surroundings. "Dr. Mutch checked me out and bandaged the wrist. And I felt like I needed another ally I trusted to help us determine what happened, which is why I went to meet you at the Earl's Palace. Dr. Mutch gave me a ride."

"Where'd you get the cloak?" I asked.

Rory smiled. "He happened to have the costume. He has quite a collection. He's in the same amateur drama troupe I used to perform with when I was a boy."

"Why didn't you tell us Rory was alive at our meeting this morning, Izara?" I asked her.

"I wasn't sure I wanted Seamus to know just yet. He wouldn't approve of the ruse. And I had no idea about the palace. Rory didn't tell me he wanted you in his confidence until he asked for a ride this evening out to Birsay. By then, he said, you were already on your way. And I didn't feel safe texting you or calling with that sort of information when you had so many people around you."

Curious. "Why all the secrecy?" I asked Rory.

"I figured the fewer lies Izara had to juggle, the better for her," he said. "She's not an actor. I am."

"And you wanted to exercise your predilection for theatrics." She rolled her eyes at him.

Or ... Rory suspected Izara? No, that couldn't be. She was right here, helping him out.

"You really haven't slept at all, have you?" I said to her. "You need to rest tonight so you're fresh tomorrow."

She snorted. "So do you. You have a big job to do for Seamus."

"We'll be ready." Neil sounded confident. "But I don't like that we have a would-be killer out there."

Which we finally knew for sure, thanks to Rory. I tried to recall the sequence of events the evening before, but I was tired and my mind was fuzzy. "We need to think about all the people who were on the island."

"That we know of," Rory said. "We had your friends and the Archies and Mixy and his people, plus tourists. And someone else might've been sneaking around, given the fog."

"Maybe I'll have Millie do a quick background check on Mr. Mixy's crew, if that works for you," I said to Neil. "I doubt Stephan would push Rory or Arch, not when he thinks they're his new best buds."

Rory chuckled.

Neil lifted a shoulder in a half shrug. "I have no problem with Millie doing the work, but do you even know all their names?"

"That's the kind of thing she can find out." Millie, our Girl Friday and organizer back home, was a whiz at online research. "Maybe she can do a search on the Archies we know were there, the Kents, along with Elsie Firth and Freya Dearness."

"Freya?" Rory seemed surprised, even as Izara narrowed her eyes at him. "Was she there?"

"Yes, and her whole crew as well." I told him how she'd popped up in the fog. "Tracking them all down might be a lot for Millie."

"Maybe Mark can get their names by asking his old friend Callum. Say he's considering doing a video promotion or something." Neil pulled out his phone and began tapping. "I'll text him. Maybe one of the video people is working for Callum in a more sinister capacity, though I don't think he has a grudge against Rory. Just Seamus and, by extension, Arch."

"Did you all hear anything from the Edinburgh police?" I asked Izara.

She shook her head. "Nothing of consequence. Paintball guns aren't legally considered to be firearms, and they didn't feel they had the resources or the need to track down the shooter, given no one was seriously hurt."

"Could someone on the Brough of Birsay have been the Paintball Piper?" Neil asked.

I gave it some thought. "There were the two young men who people saw. One of them could have been—oh! That's whose dinghy you stole!" I said to Rory.

"A fisherman's dinghy, actually," Izara said. "Those were the university students who ended up being taken off the island with me and Magnus, and they'd hired it. I spoke with them at length on the boat. They'd been traveling around the islands for a week. Not the best travel companions, I don't think, because they bickered constantly, blaming each other for losing the boat. But I don't think they were lying. They wouldn't have been in Edinburgh."

"Well, the dinghy 'washed ashore' and will get back to its rightful owner, I'm sure." How Rory managed to maintain his sense of mischief after almost being murdered amazed me.

"Maybe those young guys are who we heard shouting before Rory's fall," I said. "So who else might have done it?"

"Lark seemed really excited that Arch wasn't the one who'd gone over," Izara said.

"Does that mean she pushed Rory, though? The problem is that no one could see anything in the fog. Anyone could have done it with no one the wiser." I turned to Rory. "I think you might be right that you're better off dead. I mean, playing dead. When are you going to reveal yourself?"

"I can't drag this out." He sipped his tea. "As Izara said, I'm already going to be in trouble, even if I can pass off my disappearance as inadvertent, and I feel guilty about putting the emergency services at risk. My parents are traveling on a cruise, so with luck they won't hear that I'm missing until I'm back on the radar."

"I'd prefer not to pass this off as another Arch and Rory joke," Izara added. "It wouldn't be right."

"Of course." Rory gave her an understanding smile. "I want to wait until the official video shoot is done tomorrow so Arch can do his thing without any distractions. So perhaps I'll appear during the party that follows. By then, we may have more answers."

"That's very optimistic." Izara looked from him to Neil and me. "I don't want Rory in danger again. You're only here for a couple more days. We're running out of time."

Chapter Twenty-Nine

I'd been scared in the fog a lot in the past couple of days, and I felt really lost, even with Neil sheltering me in the warm bed as I slept. Izara had given us a ride to the hotel and headed to her flat to keep up appearances, just in case anyone was paying attention.

So I supposed it made sense that I dreamt of fog. And men in kilts. Actually, everyone in kilts. All my friends, all the people we'd met on this trip, and random strangers besides. And they wore funny little hats and marched to the tune of bagpipes with their backs to me, so I couldn't tell who they were.

The bagpipes were an odd touch, given I hadn't heard a single bagpipe since we'd arrived in Orkney, whose history seemed to be as much Viking as it was Scottish, or maybe Neolithic. As I dreamed, I got the sense I was in an episode of *Sleekit Sim,* where a big battle was about to happen at the Ring of Brodgar, and if I touched the right stone, I would be transported to my backyard in Bohemia Beach, where my aunt and Astra sunned themselves on a lounge chair. Or if I touched the wrong stone, I'd end up in the tomb at Maeshowe, trapped forever. Another stone might bring me to the killer, but did I want to go? My dream character counted on Arch and Rory rescuing me, only Arch was drunk and Rory danced a waltz through the stones with Freya Dearness, who wore a floral circlet on her head and a long, flowing, white robe, unlike all the people in kilts. Blair appeared behind one of the stones, wearing white overalls, until she spotted Callum Cotter (in a kilt, of course) and ran away into the fog. The fog suddenly thickened, and my friends who'd been carousing in the circle vanished into the vapor, one by one, as Elsie tried to tell them the history of the ditch around the Ring of Brodgar. I heard Neil calling for me, but I couldn't see him. A hairy coo emerged from the fog and charged at Rory and Freya, who ran screaming past me. And just before the coo could collide with me, I woke up.

"Pepper," Neil grunted, gently pushing at me. "You're in boa constrictor mode."

"Sorry." I loosened my arms. "Nightmare. I'm glad you're not lost in the fog."

"Same." He kissed my hair.

Light peeked around the blackout shades, but it was only 6 a.m., according to my phone, which was charging on the night table. So I rolled over and went back to sleep, and to my relief, Neil laid a protective arm over me and snoozed as well.

By the time my phone alarm played "Rum and Coca-Cola," it was 10 a.m. Neil was gone. We had to be at the hall by one to make sure we were fully prepared for the shoot at three. Which meant I had time for a meal and primping. I'd taken a truly hot shower last night (when there was low demand on the hot water heater), or should I say early this morning, given my bedraggled state after my cliffhanging experience. But I could use another one, along with some TLC for my nails and hair. And I still hadn't talked to Melody about whatever outfits she was plotting for today.

"Where are you?" I texted Neil.

There was only a moment's delay. "Breakfast, then Melody is getting us guys together for costumes." He added an eye-roll emoji, and I giggled.

"OK. Getting ready now."

"Look out. She's coming for you!"

I snickered again and, on impulse, ordered breakfast delivered to the room so I could eat as I was getting ready. It arrived just after I got out of the shower and, bundled up in one of the hotel's comfy white robes, I nibbled as I dried my hair and pinned it up with rhinestone clips. I added a little makeup, including sparkly eyeshadow that brought out my gray-green eyes, and dug out my rhinestone-tipped black cat's-eye glasses to replace the plain ones that had fallen to their doom. I made sure I trimmed the rough spots from my nails and touched up the silver polish. And I put on my good-luck bracelet, thanking it for being there for me. The rest of the jewelry would wait until I got into my outfit, whatever it was.

My dream had made me miss home. I sat on the bed to check in with Aunt Celestine. She rose earlier than I did, but I texted first to see if she was awake. Otherwise her notifications would be off.

An instant later, my phone buzzed with an incoming video call.

"You're awake!" I exclaimed.

"Of course I'm awake. I had a terrible dream about you." My aunt sat at the table just inside the sliding glass doors in her half of the duplex. She often worked on her books there, where she could look out at our shared pool and her fabulous tropical garden. "Are you OK?"

"I'm OK now." I hated to worry her.

"What happened?"

"Just a slip and fall. Neil and Ro— Neil got me out of it."

Her eyes narrowed. "Neil and who?"

"It's a long story and kind of a secret. Hopefully I can tell you tomorrow. Why aren't you outside?"

"It's horribly hot already. But I went swimming." Her curly red hair, streaked with silver, was still wet. "You look pretty."

I smiled. "So do you. Any … developments?"

She raised her eyebrows. "No incursions. The fortress is secure." Her dry tone masked the worry we both had after our recent adventure in New Orleans, but no news was good news. And we had a great security system. A little wrinkle formed in her brow. "Have you anything to report in that department?"

"No, thank Dionysus."

A bark sounded through the connection, and Aunt Celestine bent down offscreen and sat up with a fuzzy Astra in her arms. The Cavapoo leaned in and licked my aunt's phone, her nose huge in the lens. She barked again.

I chuckled. "Hello, Astra! I'll be home soon, sweetie. Your friend Victoria is here!"

Astra let out a whine of excitement.

"I know," I told her. "Maybe she and Uncle Mark will visit soon."

Aunt Celestine smirked. "Uncle Mark?" She set the dog down, offscreen. "Not hot Mark Fairman?"

"He's still hot, but I have Neil now." I grinned, then sobered, thinking of yesterday. "Unless I scare him off."

"You're not getting into trouble, are you?"

"Only a little bit. We're trying to figure out who's stalking Arch Halliday and not having much luck."

"I'd stalk him if I were there."

I laughed. "You'd love Orkney. Lots of mystical landscapes and stone circles."

"You're right. I would. I have a drum circle tonight. I'll have to make do." She blew me a kiss. "Stay in touch."

"Will do. Love you."

We ended the call, and I felt a little more grounded. And even more motivated to track down the enemy before they actually succeeded in killing someone. I checked my email.

Millie had come through with a lot of details, considering she probably got my request around 10 p.m. Florida time. But there wasn't much new information, and I saw no obvious links between Arch and Rory, the distillers, and the various players who'd been on the island. She even had information on the crew working with Freya, since Callum had directed Mark to the small production firm's website, which Neil had passed on to her. Nothing exciting there so far. Mr. Mixy's crew seemed clean. Elsie ran a consulting firm and was a well-known expert on Orkney history, with no criminal record. And what Millie had discovered about Wren and Lark was on par with what Wren had told us, including the fact the sisters had a troublesome brother, Jay Kent, who'd served a short prison sentence for burglary and still lived in Ohio. It seemed unlikely he'd be gallivanting around Scotland, especially since Wren said the sisters came here partly to get away from him.

I dug out my iPad and set it up against a pillow, pulled up *Sleekit Sim* on the streaming service and started an episode while I finished my breakfast. Hmm, Arch and Rory on my bed. The idea might have given me palpitations before, but I didn't feel quite the same abstract lust now. They were too real to be infatuations. But I still loved the show.

I'd seen almost all of the episodes at least once. I recognized this one, but I hadn't watched it in a long time. It was one of the more serious stories, in which a dastardly duke kidnapped the virginal daughter of a small-town publican—

which I knew from my historical romance reading habit meant the owner of a pub—and Sim tried to rustle the duke's cattle to keep him distracted while eventually staging a rescue. We were still in the first scene, though, when Arch and Rory, as Sim and Kenzie, drank a pint and met the innocent, rosy-cheeked lass while crossing paths with the lascivious duke in the pub.

I got so into it, a knock at the door made me jump.

"It's Melody!" came my friend's voice, singsong with the anticipation of playing dress-up. For really special gigs, Neil had almost completely ceded control of our outfits to her, but she'd been unusually secretive this time. Usually I got a hint in advance or had some say. And now that I suspected she'd been talking with director Alan Woodsy, I was a little nervous about what to expect. Would it be *frou* and *frou* and *frou*?

I opened the door, and Melody waltzed in carrying multiple bags, including two garment bags. Wearing a pink tracksuit, she obviously hadn't dressed yet, but her blond hair was piled high, her makeup was layered and impeccable, and she had a twinkle in her eye.

"Finally, I get to see what I'm wearing." I examined her parcels curiously as she hung the garment bags on a wall hook. "Have you been talking to Alan Woodsy?"

"Maybe a little. I wanted to give the right direction to Penelope."

My eyebrows rose. "You got Penelope involved?" Penelope was our costume-designer friend in Bohemia who was getting bigger and bigger jobs. I was surprised she had time for us.

"She was between plays, and Seamus had a big budget. She was thrilled. Ooo!" Melody nodded toward the iPad. "*Sleekit Sim*! Somehow the guys are not exactly what I pictured. I mean, they're hot, but they're not ... you know."

"Not Sim and Kenzie," I said.

"Right! Probably just as well. I don't think my hormones could endure being in the constant company of Sim and Kenzie." Her smile faded. "There's gossip online that the person who fell at the Brough of Birsay was Rory."

"Oh, crap. I was hoping it wouldn't come out before—" I paused.

She looked at me closely. "Before what?"

I bit my lip, debating what to tell her. But Rory said he'd reappear again today. And I trusted Melody as much as any of my friends. Even if they let slip to Mr. Mixy where I was last night. "I know you can keep a secret. Right?"

She nodded, looking eager.

"Don't tell Luke or Barclay either. They'll know soon enough."

"Oh my God. You're getting married!"

"What?" I laughed in shock. "No! No, it's bigger than that." Or at least more immediate.

"Then what?"

"Rory is still alive."

She put a hand over her mouth, then dropped it and sat on the bed. "Is he OK? How do you know?"

"Long story, but I saw him last night. He says he won't stay undercover for long, but he also says he was pushed. He's hoping to take the heat off Arch by staying 'disappeared' through today's video shoot."

"Holy crap."

We paused to look at the scene playing on the iPad. Sim and Kenzie were in one of their hideouts, talking earnestly by a blazing fire, as Sim—Arch—dashed off a letter to his enemy, the duke. "Let him judge from this just how serious I am," Sim told Kenzie.

Rory's character put a foot up on the hearth, showing off a well-turned leg under his kilt, and scoffed. "Nobody ever takes you seriously, Sim, because you don't ever take yourself seriously."

"I expect you'll find some redcoats who disagree." Arch scribbled with a quill pen, demanding the return of the fair lass, his passion completely captivating.

"Pepper?"

"Hmm?" I looked up. "Oh. Sorry. Arch is so distracting." I grinned. "And I can't tell you how happy I am that Rory is OK." And that he helped get me off the cliff.

"I know! I'm so relieved. Thank you for telling me. And I won't tell the boys, as long as I don't have to keep the secret too long," she joked. "Neil knows?"

"Yes. He was there." I nodded at the garment bags. "Speaking of which, how did it go with the boys' outfits?"

"I think it went well." She quirked her mouth. "I'm not sure Neil is entirely pleased."

"Uh-oh."

"I explained that the client was totally on board. That got him."

"What is he wearing?"

"You'll see." Her lips curved in a mischievous smile.

"Oh my God, I can't stand it. All right. Let's see what's in these bags."

Chapter Thirty

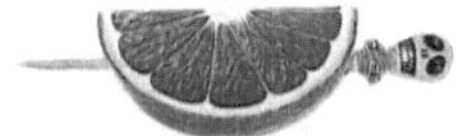

I knew I wasn't a beautiful woman. Melody was. But I could pull off "hot geek" with the right ingredients.

All that said, the dress Melody slipped over my head made me feel almost glamorous. And sort of terrified.

"This thing is transparent!" I exclaimed.

"Only parts of it. That's why you have the bodysuit to wear under it."

The short dress wasn't exactly transparent. But the only things between me and the outside world (other than the low-cut bodysuit, which was the color of my skin, underscoring the naked look) were discs about the size of a quarter, mostly a mirrored silver, linked by tiny jump rings. No fabric. They comprised the entire dress. Some of the discs were black, their crisscrossing lines forming a wide grid of diamond shapes filled in by the mirror discs. The hemline zigzagged along the grid formed by the black discs, which meant a diamond point aimed down atop each thigh. The same thing happened over my butt, and the back dipped scandalously low. The hemline rose in the center in front and barely covered my hoo-ha.

A single column of black discs formed each strap and disguised the spaghetti straps of the supportive bodysuit. I had cleavage for days.

"Do you like it?" she asked as I examined the look in the full-length mirror on the closet door.

"It's a good way to practice before I try that nude beach north of the Cape."

Melody laughed. "You are *not* nude."

I spun slowly in front of the mirror. "It has a certain trampy appeal, as long as I don't fall out of it. What about jewelry?"

She hooked me up with dangly earrings, faux diamonds dripping down to tiny mirror balls. "And do you have to wear that?" She pointed to my good-luck bracelet.

"Yes, I do." I wore it yesterday when I survived falling off a cliff. There was no way I was taking it off today.

She sighed. "All right. But you will not wear a necklace. This dress is all about skin."

Skin and turning me into a human disco ball. I wondered what Neil would think of this dress. He liked the way I looked. I knew that much. But I didn't usually look like I was about to meet a client for a night on the town in Las Vegas. "Given my clothes are usually half as revealing as yours, what are you wearing?"

Melody beamed. And a few minutes later, she stood next to me in a floor-length strapless dress of mirrored pieces, reflecting the colors of the tropical flowers and musical notes tattooed on her arms. The mirror tiles were cut irregularly but fit together like a jigsaw puzzle, providing more coverage than my discs.

But that didn't mean her dress wasn't revealing. The pointed sweetheart neckline perched precariously on her boobs, and a slit up one side went almost to her hip, showing off one long leg.

Her silver platform heels were similar to the black ones she'd brought for me. At least I was taller than usual.

"We look amazing," she declared. "I might take home a movie star tonight."

Would she, though? I wondered if she was still on the prowl, given that moment she had with Luke. Besides, Rory had a secret sweetheart.

And I had more to wonder about when Albert, who'd already delivered the guys, dropped us at the town hall venue and we ran into Luke in the multistory foyer. He wore slim black trousers that emphasized his slender physique, a skinny black tie, a white shirt and a dazzling reflective jacket that perfectly matched Melody's puzzle-piece mirror-ball dress.

"Ladies." It was all he needed to say. I was pretty sure it was all he *could* say after he popped his eyes back in their sockets. He swallowed hard and skedaddled to the restroom.

Melody must've caught my intrigued expression as I watched him go. "The jacket fit his figure best," she said, trying to explain the matchy-matchy. "Wait till you see Barclay and Neil."

We entered the main hall, and I stopped to take it all in. Mirror balls of varying sizes dangled from the two large arches. The cocktail-shaped tables were scattered around the space. The hall's bubble chandeliers were still on, but given the scaffolds full of lights positioned everywhere, I had a feeling the director would get his sparkle when the party started.

Neil and Barclay stood behind the bar in the back, squeezing juices, I thought. Maybe the caterers had kicked them out of the kitchen. It took a moment before they noticed us heading toward them. Their outfits didn't look that wild, from the waist up, anyway. Neil looked nice in a silvery shirt in a subtle paisley print, accented with a black leather bow tie. The bow tie was on point for Neil, but the leather was an unusual choice. Barclay wore a black silk shirt.

"Barclay has the build for that shirt. It flows like water on him," Melody whispered in my ear. I thought she was still explaining why she and Luke were dressed like a couple. I wondered if she doth protest too much.

Neil and Barclay glanced up as we approached and froze. We stopped in front of the bar and let them ogle us. My tummy did the samba under the daring dress. Would Neil hate it?

He opened his mouth and closed it again.

Barclay grinned. "You ladies look *fiiiine.*" At least *he* wasn't speechless.

"You don't look too bad yourself." I smiled and turned back to Neil.

He opened his mouth again, then shook his head before he was able to eke out, "Jesus."

I laughed, and Melody giggled.

"Even Neil doesn't have a quote handy," Barclay joked.

"I think this kilt has fried my brain cells," Neil said. "You're —you're absolutely beautiful."

Heat flushed through me from my toes to all of the parts that were barely covered while I processed what he'd said. "You're wearing a KILT? Show me. Show me right now."

Neil put down the manual squeezer he'd been using and slowly stepped out from behind the bar.

He wore a kilt, all right. But it wasn't the tartan variety. It was black leather, with a chunky belt lined with silver studs and an embossed leather sporran in front. Tall lace-up boots completed the outfit.

I gaped. "Holy—you look like some kind of Scottish dom."

Melody let out a peal of laughter. "He does not! Well, sort of. But he's sexy, right?"

"He is. Of course he is," I said as Neil looked like he wanted to crawl into a cave and never come out. "It's very—becoming." And then I started giggling too.

"Stop it." He looked mortified.

"Come here." I held out my arms and stepped closer to him, about to wrap him in a big hug.

"NO CRUSHING THE DRESS!" Melody screeched. "Do you want all those little discs to fall off?"

"Yes?" Barclay said as Luke returned, his eyes bright with humor.

Now we all started laughing. Neil was the last to join in. "I'm going to have to insist on approving the outfits from here on out. At least mine."

I pouted. "Does this mean this is the last time we'll see you in a kilt?"

"*This* kilt, definitely," he said. "And you haven't even seen Barclay's pants."

Melody beckoned with one finger, and Barclay emerged from behind the bar, holding both hands up in a game show ta-da pose. His trousers were clingy in all the right places and as silver as a roll of aluminum foil.

"They're going to recruit you for the next space station mission if you wear those back home," I said, and we all started giggling again.

Melody took the ribbing well, especially when Alan Woodsy crowed over our ensembles. "You'll look fabulous on camera. Fabulous!"

From that point, prep moved quickly. Melody and I borrowed cotton aprons from the kitchen to protect our glitz and made Luke remove his jacket during prep. I was just grateful to add another layer of clothes.

The cocktails were ambitious. We squeezed lime juice for a scotch variation on a Mai Tai that would feature the Tropical Timeless Reserve, with simple syrup, orgeat, and orange curacao, shaken with ice and served in a rocks glass with mint and a disco-ball-topped swizzle stick. Luke had managed to get those delivered at the last minute. Neil called it the Koa Kilt.

We'd also have a Silky Selkie, with the twelve-year-old scotch, cold espresso, a honey-ginger syrup with notes of cinnamon and vanilla, and chocolate bitters, served in a coupe glass with a sprinkle of cinnamon on top.

Finally, we had the Tartan Goose, featuring gooseberry jam, fresh-squeezed lemon juice, honey and Teapot Bitters along with the scotch, served in a crystal-style jam jar and garnished with fresh Scottish gooseberries on the Aramach sword picks. The berries were a lovely deep pink with subtle pale stripes. The drink was tasty, too, layered and gently jammy, its subtle sweetness balanced by the bright lemon, with a hint of smoke on the back end.

For the sake of the cameras, Barclay was all set up to carve ice cubes. They'd go into straight pours of the whisky. And Neil had procured a glass cloche for smoking a scotch just so Alan could film it.

The film crew had covered the side windows so they could control the lighting. Finally, they shut off the overheads and turned on the atmospheric LEDs and spotlights, with rainbow dazzle everywhere thanks to the mirror balls. Our bar and the cocktail tables glowed, as did the stained glass windows set high in the wall behind us. Disco Devan had set up in a corner across the hall from us and warmed us up with a slinky beat.

The hall began to fill with the early guests and a handful of glamorous ringers, actors Alan had hired. They funneled through one door and vetted by two beefy security guards and Izara. Seamus arrived and hovered in a dark corner, watching the scene unfold. Alan Woodsy ran around as if his colorful graffiti coat were on fire, making the guests wait for his cue to drink.

I stowed my apron and tidied up the garnish tray, then scanned the crowd. Mark and Diana had arrived with Victoria in a flashy rhinestone collar. He wore an exquisite black tux. Diana's romper in a light brown suede stopped just above her knees, and a skinny brown leather belt wrapped around her waist at least three times. Alastair was chic in a creamy three-piece suit that complemented his fair hair.

And there was Mr. Mixy, without his crew—exploiting his minor celebrity status, no doubt. He wore a silver kilt and a shirt that was half silver, half black. He looked like a court jester with Saturday night fever. At least he'd gotten off the island last night.

Another couple caught my eye and waved, he pale in a dark purple suit, she in a pink glitter dress that complemented her brown skin, her hair impressively fluffy.

"Oh, look, Nigel and Lottie are here!"

"Excellent." Neil joined me in waving at our favorite cocktail bloggers from London. "They should add some sparkle."

I giggled. "I'd say we've met the minimum sparkle requirements."

"I think you and Melody put us over the top." He gave me a sidelong glance, scanning the dress. "Do you get to keep that?"

"Why, do you want me to wear it at home?"

"Just so long as I'm there." He grinned.

"Done." I raised an eyebrow. "But you have to wear the leather kilt."

He snorted. "I think it's pleather."

Alan Woodsy called to the room for quiet.

"Ladies and gentlemen, we're about to begin. Please feel free to relax and enjoy yourselves." He paused and assumed a more serious tone. "You may have heard rumors today of a lost friend." Wow, he was referencing the stories about Rory. Which made sense, since Rory and Arch were so close. "I want you to take heart. Have hope. And drink in his honor.

"As the releases you signed indicate, anything we film may be used in promotional materials for Aramach." His face brightened. "We are looking for light and life and love and, of course, sparkle! Lift up those cocktails to the light and the cameras! Laugh if the spirit moves you. Flirt. Dance. And please respond to my direction. We won't use the sound here, so don't worry about that, all right? Get your drinks, and in a few moments, we'll bring in our star. Greet him like he's an old friend as we track him through the room on his way to the bar. We'll shoot for about an hour, and then we'll open up the party to the rest of the guests. We'll still be shooting, but we won't tell you what to do then, and we'll even feed you." Alan smiled as laughter rippled through the crowd. "Everyone ready? PARTY! Action!"

He pointed to DJ Devan, who cranked up a dance tune with a thumping beat, and the horde rushed the bar.

Holy galloping garnishes. "Incoming!" Neil called to the team, and we launched into mixing and shaking.

Alan's crew filmed us working, grabbed stylish closeups of the cocktails, and captured Barclay carving ice. They turned to Neil, who lit up the wood chips in the smoking gun and piped smoke into the glass dome of the cloche, which enclosed a glass of scotch. He ceremoniously lifted the dome, and the cloud of aromatic smoke expanded lazily, its color changing in the lights, its wisps thinning to reveal the glittering glass of whisky. Everyone nearby applauded, me included. Then the crew worked the crowd.

Finally, the doors opened to reveal Arch, the man of the hour, and the crew rushed over to document his procession through the room.

"Stay out of the shot!" the director screamed at Magnus, who shadowed the star. Poor Magnus. He looked haggard as he obediently stepped backward and clung to the wall in the dark near Seamus, eyes following Arch's every movement.

Arch eventually crossed the room three times with the crew filming him from all angles, tracking his entry as he greeted everyone. He even stopped to scratch behind the ears of a very happy Victoria as the pup rested in a bonnie lass's arms. He looked fantastic in a dark blue, subtly shiny suit accented by a silver satin pocket square, his blond hair artfully tousled, wearing his classic mischievous grin. But did I detect a hint of weariness around his eyes?

Rory hadn't told him he'd survived the fall. Why not? Rory hadn't confided in Arch, his best friend. He'd also been cagey with Izara, his girlfriend. Rory was paranoid. But could I blame him? Someone had pushed him off a cliff.

Arch made it to the bar and ordered the Koa Kilt, which looked great with its garnish of mint and a disco ball swizzle stick. I handed it to him with a big smile. "How you doing?" I asked him.

"Fabulous as always, darling." His smile was beautiful and yet unreal. He took a sip of the drink, and that brittleness about him softened. "Ah, this is wonderful. Thank you. Thank you all." He held up the drink in a toast and moved around to mingle, trailed by the cameras. He really was a good actor, I thought, in spite of what Freya suggested.

Alan paused the party multiple times to set up special moments with Arch and the prettiest people in the crowd, at one point firing a cloud of confetti into the air with a portable air cannon whose loud *bang!* had Magnus leaping into the fray until Alan ordered him again to back off.

Finally, the director declared the primary shoot over. "Take a break, everyone, and let our bartenders have a break, too. They have a real party to serve in fifteen minutes." He gave a throat-cutting motion. The house lights came up about half-way, and even the DJ's beats clunked to a halt, replaced by soft lounge music.

"This is so weird," Luke said. "Parties don't have breaks."

"Fake parties do," Barclay replied, stowing his freshly cut ice cubes in a freezer under the bar. Using gloves, he picked up the tray holding what was left of the melting ice block and carried it back to the kitchen.

We hit the restrooms, then made sure the bar was ready for round two. Arch signed autographs and greeted fans. As I watched him scribbling, I thought back to the *Sleekit Sim* episode I'd been streaming in the hotel room. I'd stopped the stream before it was over, and now I had a hankering to see the end. Sure, I'd seen it before, but every episode was so satis-fying. So while we stood around, I snuck my phone out of my bag and tried to find where I'd left off in the streaming app. The stupid scroll bar was so tiny, I couldn't quite get to the right place, so I rewatched the scene where Arch scrawls the letter to his enemy.

The letter. There was something familiar about the letter.

Chapter Thirty-One

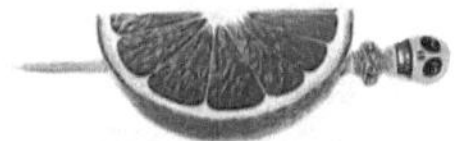

I switched to my phone's photo gallery and found the picture of the letter I'd discovered on Arch's hotel room floor. Then switched back to the episode of *Sleekit Sim* and a closeup of Arch writing with the quill pen. Then the letter from the hotel room again. Then the letter Izara had shared from the Flying Heart.

Was I hallucinating? Could the handwriting on the letter I found and Arch's *Sleekit Sim* letter be the same? I was no handwriting expert, but I'd seen enough *Law & Order* to know certain figures made handwriting distinctive, like the loops in his lowercase t's and the way he connected one letter to another.

And yet the note Izara gave us, the one with the same wording as the letter on Arch's floor, appeared to be in a different script.

But—why? Why would there be a letter in Arch's handwriting that threatened Rory and maybe Arch, too—a copy of a letter they'd received from the Flying Heart? I hadn't thought about the handwriting before. Arch didn't say much about it when we found the letter in his room, but then again, he was drunk and miserable.

I looked up. Arch wasn't signing autographs now. In fact, he was nowhere in sight, but more invited party guests were arriving, from local officials to friends and employees of the distillery. A few media entered, too, including Mr. Mixy's crew. I spotted master distiller Blair Rendall among the new arrivals, in a simple, flattering black dress. But no Arch.

"Where's Arch?" I asked.

Neil caught my urgent tone. "You could ask Magnus."

"I don't see him either." I scanned the milling crowd, half of which seemed to have stepped out.

Then Magnus entered the front doors, stopped for a hurried few words with the door guards and Izara, and made a beeline for us as one of the guards dashed into the lobby. "Have you seen Arch?"

A cold feeling crept over all my amply exposed skin. "No. Is he missing?"

"I don't know. He said he was going to the toilet. I went in there, too, given the opportunity. When I came out of the stall, he was gone." Magnus's voice cracked, and sweat beaded his brow.

"I think we would have seen him if he'd come through here," Neil said.

Just then, there was a commotion at the door. And, smartly tailored in a forest-green tartan suit, Rory Redland strolled in.

To say the crowd went nuts would be an understatement. After a moment of stunned gawking, the partygoers exploded in excitement. "Rory! Rory!" His name was on everyone's lips, and they surged around him, trying to hug him, clamoring for details. The few media people who'd arrived snapped photos and stuck video cameras in his face. Izara appeared next to him and tried to make some air for him, not-so-gently pushing away his admirers and telling the press to back off.

Mr. Mixy stepped up and waved at the pack, and they

descended on him instead as Izara pulled Rory away. Mr. Mixy was that famous now?

"Rory is alive?" Luke exclaimed.

"So it seems." Barclay looked at Neil and me and Melody, who hadn't said anything. "You knew, didn't you?"

Neil raised his eyebrows at me. "You told Melody?"

"It just came up this morning." I hoped he wasn't mad. I hoped Barclay and Luke weren't either. I turned to them. "Sorry we didn't tell you, but Rory wanted it secret. We only found out last night. There's more to the story, but right now, I want to know where Arch is."

"As do I," Magnus growled. "Maybe Rory knows." He got Izara's attention and beckoned her. She tugged on Rory's arm and brought him over to us, then shooed away others in the crowd.

"I think I could use a drink," Rory said with a grin.

"So you're alive then." Magnus didn't look as happy as he should have. Maybe because losing Rory had put him through hell. "Have you seen Arch?"

Rory blinked and accepted a Tartan Goose from Luke. "No. Isn't he here?"

"He was here. And then he wasn't." Magnus looked up as the guard who'd dashed out reentered, looked at him and shook his head. "And he's not in the building."

"He wouldn't just leave in the middle of Aramach's big event. Calling him now." Izara already had her phone to her ear.

Magnus pulled a buzzing phone from his pocket. "That won't do any good. I found his mobile on the sink in the washroom."

We all stared in shock at Magnus holding Arch's vibrating phone.

Izara ended the futile call. "This isn't good. Can you see if there are any messages or calls on it?"

Magnus tried in vain to access the passcode-protected phone. "No."

"Where's Seamus?" Neil asked. "Could they be together?"

Just then, Seamus strolled into the room like nothing was wrong, saw us clustered around the bar and walked over. He staggered for a second when he saw Rory. "Dear God, man, where have you been?"

"Here and there." Rory still seemed stunned himself. He took a gulp of his drink. "The question of the moment seems to be, where's Arch?"

Seamus turned on Magnus. "You lost Arch?"

A new disturbance at the door had us swiveling that way, where the two guards were trying to stop two women from entering. Two screaming women.

"Rory!" Wren called from the doorway. "Rory!"

"We need to talk to him!" Lark yelled. "Please!"

A cascade of emotions shifted across Izara's face. "Not now."

Neil stood up straighter. "Maybe they know something."

"Or maybe they took him," Magnus said.

"If they grabbed Arch, would they be hanging around here?" I asked.

Melody snickered. "They'd probably be off having their way with him." We all looked at her, and she threw her hands up. "What? It's true."

"Bring them in," Seamus ordered, and Magnus hustled to the door.

Izara turned to Rory. "Get behind the bar."

"What?" he said on a puff of laughter.

"Get behind the bar so they don't have direct access to you." Wow, she was going all Mama Bear. Or Girlfriend Bear?

"Yeah, we'll protect you," Luke half-joked, and he and Barclay made room so Rory stood between them. A handsome trio, my easily distracted mind noted, even if the lights flashing off Luke's mirrored jacket were kind of blinding. I supposed I didn't have room to talk.

I turned to watch Magnus escorting Wren and Lark over to us, both of them in little black dresses. Angling for an invitation, perhaps?

"I'm so glad you're OK!" Wren gushed to Rory.

"Thank God!" Lark said. "I was so worried about you!"

Call me a cynic, but I eyed them both suspiciously. We all did.

"Thanks," Rory said after a moment. "But the topic of the moment is Arch. Have you seen him?"

The women exchanged a glance, then Lark spoke. "He just left. We were hanging out across the street by the cathedral just, um, keeping an eye on things."

Stalking. The word is *stalking*.

Mark and Diana, holding Victoria, wandered up to our group, with Mark giving Rory a big smile. "Glad to see you, my friend."

"Thanks," the star said. "But it appears I'm not the only one who's disappeared."

Magnus shot them an impatient look, then turned to the Archies. "What do you mean, Arch left? Where'd he go?"

"I don't know." Lark pouted. "I called out to him, and he ignored me. He jumped into a car and took off."

"Who was driving?" I asked.

"I couldn't tell." Wren looked at her sister.

"Me either. I thought it was an Uber or something. It was a small car with writing on the side."

"What writing?" Neil might've sounded patient, but I heard the hint of frustration in his voice.

"The big type looked like that writing we saw in the tomb at—what's it called?" Lark looked confused.

"Maeshowe," Wren said. "The runes."

The runes? A spark fired in my brain.

"Too bad I didn't see it," Luke said. "I could probably translate."

"What?" A corner of Barclay's mouth lifted. "No way."

Luke shrugged. "I went through a serious heavy-metal phase in high school. Got really into Vikings and stuff."

"Well, we don't have the car, do we?" Izara snipped. She turned to the Archies. "That's all you saw? A car with runes on the side?"

"There was small type, too, in English," Wren said. "I'm not sure what it said."

"Consulting something-or-other," Lark put in.

"So a consultant picked up Arch?" Seamus asked. "Why in the hell would he go somewhere in the middle of our event?"

A consultant. Did we know a consultant? Had we met one?

"Not Rada Consulting?" Mark asked. "That's Elsie Firth's company."

Elsie? The historian? Our tour guide?

"That sounds like it might be right," Lark said uncertainly.

"What on earth?" Izara looked at Mark. "Do you have her number?"

"Of course." Mark dug out his phone and called. After a minute, he left an innocuous message asking for a call back about where to send his donation. "That should get her to respond."

"Maybe she's not answering on purpose," I said. "Or maybe Arch asked her for a ride." But I didn't believe it, not really. Unless Arch wanted to run away for some reason. Maybe ... guilt? That would imply he'd pushed Rory. Unthinkable! But what was the deal with that copied letter?

"Arch got in the car willingly, you say?" Neil asked the Archies.

"More than," Wren replied. "He ran out of the building and jumped in."

Elsie didn't seem like someone Arch would run away with romantically. She was the schoolmarm type, and he was the naughty schoolboy. She seemed pretty disgusted with his and Rory's hijinks during our tour. But maybe it was more than disgust.

The runes. "Oh my God." I lifted my phone and navigated to the stalker letters—specifically, the scariest one Izara had sent me signed by PI.

"I hope Arch isn't mad at me," Lark whined, drawing the attention of the group.

"Why would he be mad at you, darlin'?" Rory laced his inquiry with charm, but I heard the chilly note.

"I—" She looked at Rory with wide eyes. "I'd rather not say."

"Look at this." I held up the phone and the letter signed by PI. "This signature—I don't think it's letters. I think it's runes."

$$\text{Þ|}$$

"Is that one of the letters to Arch?" Izara asked.

"Yes." I looked it over. "The one that says *your fate becomes more grave.*"

"Let me see it." Luke eased next to me and looked at the signature on the letter. "I think you're right. This first one that looks like a P? It can mean giant or a troll like you see in Old Norse stories. Sometimes you see it associated with a thorn or danger."

"Like maybe this is a warning?" I asked.

"What about the I?" Neil asked.

"Ice," Luke said. "And destruction."

Seamus put a hand to his head. "What is happening? Is this really happening?" Izara rubbed his arm, and Barclay handed him a pour of whisky. Over hand-carved ice, of course.

"So this PI or whoever is basically warning of danger and destruction," I said as Seamus knocked back his scotch.

"Or identifying with being a troll or a thorn in your side," Luke suggested.

"The question is, did Elsie write that letter?" Izara said.

"Even if she didn't, she's got Arch, hasn't she?" Rory pointed out.

"But he went willingly." Magnus sounded hopeful. "Maybe he's all right."

"I don't like this," I said. "Elsie had some pretty firm views about tourism ruining Orkney. She said bad things about 'attractions.' Your distillery is an attraction. Heck, Arch is an attraction. And he's a total smart-ass about it."

"Is that enough to wish him harm?" Neil asked.

I looked again at the letter and read it aloud. "*With every joke and every dig, your fate becomes more grave. We're not laughing with you, pig. You'll pay when next you rave.*"

"Would you call this a rave?" Barclay gestured to the crowd, the lights, the party.

"Maybe. She knew about the party. Maybe she planned this." I scanned the verse. *With every joke and every dig.* "The joke reference could easily refer to Arch and Rory. This was sent after the Paintball Piper incident."

"Do you have copies of all the letters Arch gets?" Lark asked.

We all looked at her. "Why?" Izara asked.

"No reason," she said meekly.

"Do you know anything about this letter?" I asked her.

Lark shook her head. "No. No, I don't."

"Me either," Wren said.

"I don't like *your fate becomes more grave,*" Neil said. "If Elsie wrote that, there's an implied threat, along with *You'll pay.*"

"We can analyze this all night, but the important thing now is to find Arch and make sure he's all right," Magnus said.

Izara looked at Seamus. "Maybe it's time to call the police."

"What, and tell them he got a ride with a local histori-an?" Seamus shook his head. "With no idea of where he went?"

"They could keep an eye out," Izara said. "I'll give them a quick call." She stepped away.

"Where did Elsie take him?" Neil asked. "We can't start looking unless we have an idea."

"Say she had evil intentions. Say she pushed Rory," I said.

"I wondered when that would occur to you." Rory held out his glass to Barclay, who used tongs to drop in an ice cube, then filled it with scotch.

"So maybe she'd go back to Birsay," Mark suggested.

"But I think it will be high tide soon," I said, "so that won't work."

"You're right." Neil nodded. "Then not Birsay."

"If she wanted to drop him off a cliff, we have plenty to go around." Rory's dark humor almost made me laugh. Almost. "Yesnaby, for instance."

"It's not funny," Magnus said. "There's been more than one tragic death there."

"Maybe she gave us a hint in this letter," I said. "Could she mean a literal grave? Or a dig?"

"Like an archaeological dig?" Neil asked. "Like that one near the Ring of Brodgar?"

Elsie had mentioned digs to me, but I had another thought. A different kind of dig. "Seamus," I asked, "was Elsie ever one of the peat protesters?"

"I don't know. She's not an environmentalist," Seamus said. "Though there was some collieshangie about banning more peat harvesting on the island given how many archaeological sites we have here. Nothing came of it. We work under a license from the Orkney Islands Council. We're even starting restoration work where we've already dug. How much more do they want?"

"Those protesters were at your farm, weren't they?" I asked. "What was the address, Diana?"

Diana rattled it off.

"That's the place," Seamus confirmed.

"That could be where she took Arch," I said.

"Yes." Diana's excitement prompted Victoria to bark. "Some of their signs said 'Save the Past' and that sort of thing. And there was the one that showed Arch with a knife sticking out of him."

"It's a place to start," I said. "We should go."

Chapter Thirty-Two

"We should go?" Neil protested. "Why would you put yourself in danger again?"

"Arch left here of his own volition. He might be perfectly all right. So maybe there's no danger," I argued, not very convincingly.

"I need to go," Magnus said.

"No." Seamus glared at Magnus. "I'm not blaming you, but you're exhausted. You're useless right now. Stay here. I should go."

"Magnus should stay, and so should you. This is your party," declared Izara, who'd returned to the group. "And this could be a wild goose chase. Unfortunately, I just got off the phone with the police, who say they're dealing with a major incident involving drunken cruise ship passengers who started a brawl in a bar. They're of no use to us now and can't spare a body to look for someone who isn't explicitly missing."

Or to look for a body. I hoped not. "We have to go."

"There's that 'we' again," Neil said.

"But you have to make drinks for my party." Seamus looked over at the restless, burgeoning crowd.

"How about this." Rory tipped his glass toward Seamus. His third? "I'll be your celebrity host until Arch gets back. I'm too blootered for swashbuckling, and frankly, I'm not sure I want to face my would-be murderer right now. I already nearly cracked my curple once this week. Neil and Pepper can go. The rest of these fine mixologists can make drinks. You can mingle with your guests."

Seamus seemed more enthused about this plan. "That'll do."

"If Pepper and Neil are going, we're going with them," said the ever intrepid Diana.

Mark gave her a sidelong glance. "Yes, all right. Albert can drive us."

"I guess I'm going, then," Neil said.

"Can we go?" Lark asked.

"No," Magnus said. "In fact, I want you *gone.*"

Izara wore an inscrutable expression. "No. No, I think they should stay. But stay far away from Rory," she told the women. I had a feeling she wanted to keep an eye on them. "Do you understand?"

"Yes!" Wren was ecstatic.

"Yes." Lark was less than ecstatic. Something was up, but what? I didn't have time to figure it out now.

"All right, we're going," I said. "Do we have the address of the peat farm?"

"I know exactly where it is," Diana said. "Let's go."

I grabbed my bag and took a quick look around. Most of the crowd had settled down, and at Seamus's signal, the DJ pumped up the music, though not quite at the levels we'd just heard during Alan Woodsy's shoot. The house lights came down, and the sparkly lights took over. Caterers entered with trays of delicious-looking snacks, and guests drifted toward the bar. Across the room, Blair watched us with concern.

Which made me wonder: Where was Freya Dearness?

THE DARKNESS of the hall had almost tricked my body into thinking evening was falling, but despite the early evening hour, the sun had hours more to play until sunset. Still, this oblique northern light, shining through thin clouds, lent a certain gauzy unreality to the landscape as Albert drove us out of Kirkwall proper and into the countryside. It seemed the sea was always in view as we drove, emphasizing that feeling of living on the wild edge of civilization, at the whim of nature. Or the whim of a madwoman?

"Maybe Arch wanted another historical tour," Mark quipped.

"If that's the case, Elsie probably wouldn't give it. She hates giving tours," I pointed out.

"Unless a donation is involved," Mark said.

"Pepper is quite logical to think she took him to the protest site." Diana called to Albert, "Turn here."

"I'd like to be right about where he is but not right about Elsie." I looked down at myself. "I'd also like to have real clothes on."

"I meant to tell you, Hot Pepper, that's a lovely frock." Mark showed a dimple, then became aware of Neil's stony expression. "And a handsome kilt there, my friend."

"While this is absolutely ridiculous." Diana waved at her romper. "I only wore it because I didn't want to disappoint Melody, who quite insisted. I suppose it's pretty, but I'd never wear this on an expedition."

"It's very pretty, and if you were with me, you wouldn't have to worry about wearing anything at all," Mark teased.

"Spoken like a man who's never really experienced mosquitoes," I said. In Florida, I was at constant risk of being left a bloodless husk.

He ran a hand through his thick, dark red hair. "Ah, but I have experienced the ravages of sunburn. The ginger curse. That's one reason I ration my nudity. That and not wanting to make the ladies faint."

Diana just rolled her eyes, but I thought I saw a hint of a smile.

We'd turned here and there, and now she had Albert slow down and pause as a bank of pink wildflowers came into view. "See where that gravel lane goes off to the left, near the sea pinks? That's where I saw the protesters."

No protesters were there now. A small stone house and a few outbuildings lay about a hundred yards down the lane, in the middle of a gently rising meadow covered with wildflowers. Farther down the slope but well above the rocky beach was a dark pile, a wall of earth.

"That might be where Aramach digs up its peat," Neil said quietly, as if we could be heard.

"Any other cars?" I asked.

"I don't see anything, but they might be parked near the house," he answered. "Maybe we should walk in if we want the element of surprise."

"In these shoes?" I protested.

Mark chuckled and tugged off his bow tie, ready for action.

"Maybe she should hear us coming so she'll think twice about what she's doing," Diana said. "Assuming she's up to no good."

"And driving is faster," I pointed out.

Albert made an executive decision and turned the minibus down the lane, stopping in a small gravel parking area in the center of the buildings. On the other side of the cottage, hidden from the road, was the car the Archies had described, the runes on the door spelling out only Odin knows what. Odin and Luke, maybe. "Rada Consulting" was printed under the runes.

"That's Elsie's car," I said as Albert turned off the engine and opened the door. He joined us in exiting the van.

The drone of a motor greeted us. "What is that?" Neil asked.

"Let's go find out," Mark said.

The good news, I thought, is that the motor might have drowned out the sound of our vehicle. But how stealthy could all of us and a dog be?

"Quiet, Victoria," Mark whispered to the dog. She was off her leash, though she still wore her blingy collar. Her tail wagged at the promise of adventure. And maybe the smell of sheep, which I spotted in a neighboring pasture at least a half mile away. *Not killer sheep, Pepper.*

"The noise is coming from down there." Diana pointed down the slope toward the wall of earth.

"Maybe we should check up here first." I looked to the others.

They nodded agreement. And it took less than two minutes. The cottage was locked, and a peek in the windows suggested it was empty. Victoria showed no special interest.

The outbuildings weren't locked, and they were empty of people, though one shed with a big roll-up door still had an overhead light burning. Maybe Elsie—or someone else—had been in here already.

It might just be someone working the peat, though Seamus hadn't mentioned that possibility. Then again, did he know what all of his employees were up to every minute of the day?

I ruled out that theory when Victoria pounced on something at the edge of the gravel drive. Mark snapped his fingers, and she trotted over to him with something in her mouth. He extracted it after a brief tug-of-war. "Good girl." He rubbed her head and lifted up a bit of fabric.

A silver pocket square.

"Arch's," I whispered, looking around again. That's when I noticed a dark blue jacket, mostly hidden by overgrown wildflowers, thrown over a low stone wall that formed a kind of corral around the buildings. Maybe he took off his jacket and the square fell out.

"Stay here, please, Albert," Mark said. "Make sure no one comes out of the house."

"Yes, sir. Call if you need me."

With new resolve, we headed down the slope toward the motor sound. I tried not to topple in my tall shoes. At least they were platforms, not spikes.

Whatever was happening was hidden behind the wall of earth, but for how long? I waited for a glimpse of someone, something, and finally got one as we angled our approach toward one end of the barrier, which was several yards long and about six feet high, made of square-cut muddy chunks. The peat was chiseled in big, fat bricks three rows deep and stacked neatly on the grass.

A dark green two-person all-terrain vehicle with open sides, a minimal roof and a wide rack on the back idled at the end of the wall. Mixed with the noise of the motor came another sound. Singing?

We halted and exchanged glances. The voice was female and high-pitched, a bit scratchy as it rendered a familiar Celtic air. Was that the *Sleekit Sim* theme song? And who was singing?

Neil gestured us to get lower, and we all crouched. He pointed to Mark and Diana and indicated they should sneak around the far side of the earthen wall. Then he pointed to me and the near side.

We all nodded.

Neil took point in his pleather kilt, crouching as he moved close to the wall. The peat blocks leaned at an angle and looked like giant bites of fudge, but they smelled more like briny earth with hints of grass and heather. When burned, they would impart these scents to the barley and then the scotch.

Beyond the wall of peat, a neatly cut ditch extended—obviously the source of the peat blocks—but Neil and I didn't see its full length until we both poked our heads around the barrier.

The skinny ditch was straight like a canal and filled with water. On its uphill side, a vertical wall several feet deep had been cut into the slope. At our end, the cuts stairstepped down to a low platform of wet earth just above the strip of standing water. Downhill of the ditch, grass-topped squares of sod had been tossed haphazardly.

Standing in the dirt next to the water, in her wellies and jeans and jacket, Elsie Firth finished cutting a chunk of peat and heaved the muddy block with her cutting tool onto a body lying in the skinny canal, singing all the while.

Arch.

I sucked in a breath. Arch lay face up, pale, terribly still, not quite submerged, his eyes closed, his legs already covered by chunks of dirt. Red blossomed on the bottom edge of his untucked white shirt, and a knife stuck out of his thigh.

Oh, this really was not good.

Victoria must have agreed. She erupted into a furious explosion of barks at the other end of the ditch, and Elsie's head snapped up to look. While she was distracted, I instinctively pushed past Neil and jumped down the stairsteps of the peat and plowed into Elsie. She dropped her long, sharp tool and, arms windmilling, fell forward into the mud, just inches above the water.

"Pepper!" Neil leapt down the mud steps after me.

I followed up my push by jumping onto Elsie's prone form. She struggled, and with strength that belied her slight size, she heaved me off her and I rolled—right into the water and on top of Arch Halliday.

Who groaned. He was alive! And probably didn't need the pinup girl of the Cheese of the Month Club (not really, but a girl can dream, can't she?) lying on top of him.

By then, Mark and Neil had jumped into the fray and tried to secure a thrashing Elsie. Diana hopped down the big drop from the meadow's surface to the low mud platform. I wiggled off Arch, and she gave me a hand so I could climb out of the nasty water.

"Thanks," I gasped as I regained the bank. "Arch is alive! We need to get help out here now."

"On it." Diana whipped out her phone to call 999. "See how he's doing." In a moment, she rattled off the details to the dispatcher.

I knelt in the wet dirt and reached down to elevate Arch's head. Something warm touched my fingers. I realized there was blood on the back of his head, too.

"Arch, it's Pepper. Are you OK? Did she stab you?" *Duh. He has a knife sticking out of his leg.*

"Errrnnnh," was all he got out. Then his eyes fluttered open, trying to focus. His gaze landed on the dirty mirror discs of my dress, and he frowned. "It's me. Look at all the *me.*"

"Arch. What happened?"

He looked up at my face. "Pepper?" He took a thready

breath. "She surprised me. She stabbed me, and I reckon I fainted when I saw the blood. My head hurts. I think she must've hit me after that."

If she hit him with that peat-cutting tool, he was lucky he still had a head. But that explained the ATV. She probably knocked him out, got him on the four-wheeler and brought him down here to—what? Bury him?

I examined the knife sticking out of his leg. The handle looked like bone, marked with symbols—was it historic? I'd bumped it, which probably didn't help things, but it was nowhere near his femoral artery. More valuable *Law & Order* knowledge. I didn't think the wound would kill him, though an infection from this muddy water might.

Elsie could have stabbed him in a much more damaging spot. Did she want to kill him or just scare him?

Looking through my spattered glasses at the ditch and the water and the blocks of dirt half-burying Arch, I was pretty sure she intended to kill. She wanted to bury him alive. Or dead. Let him drown in the ditch or suffocate if the strike to the head didn't kill him. Any way you looked at it, a horrible way to go.

"Arch, why did you go with her?"

His voice was hoarse. "She said she knew where Rory was and that he needed my help. I didn't think. I just went."

Neil and Mark had pulled Elsie to her feet. Diana, now off the phone, secured Elsie's hands behind her with her long leather belt. Victoria pranced on the grass above, watching, feathery tail whipping back and forth.

"You tried to kill him. Why?" I asked Elsie.

"He's not dead? That's a pity." Her eyes burned with contempt. "He is destroying this place. And I am the thorn destined to destroy *him*!" The runes, I thought: thorn, danger, destruction. "There he and his little bampots go, digging up history. Luring in more tourists. Mocking our heritage on his terrible television show. I watched every single episode, and not a single one got the facts right!" Wow, talk about hate-watching. Or did she secretly lust after the guys like everyone else? How twisted. "He's the symbol of everything wrong with what's happening here," she ranted. "He deserves to die. And serve as a warning to the others."

The others? I supposed she meant every business that profited off the magical attractions of the islands. And Rory, too. *With every joke and every dig, your fate becomes more grave.* She'd been angry for a long time, watching Seamus dig up the peat and then bring in this shiny celebrity to join the company and help sell his dream.

Arch was shivering.

"He's cold. Do you think we can move him?" I asked my friends.

"I think we have to," Neil said. "We need to get him warm and take him up top so the ambulance can retrieve him."

"We'll just have to be careful of the wound," Diana cautioned. "It doesn't look like the knife went in very deep."

Elsie laughed, a creepy laugh. "Didn't have to. I didn't stab him quite where I meant to, but a little blood and he passed right out. Then I knocked him on the head. I want that knife back, by the way. It's modeled on one found at the Broch of Gurness—"

Diana smacked Elsie on the back of her head, appropriately.

"Ow!" Elsie exclaimed.

"Quiet," Diana told her, then to the guys, "I've got this one if you want to help Pepper."

Mark grinned as Diana yanked Elsie toward the peat steps

and forced her up toward the grassy field. Then he hopped into the ditch. Interestingly, the cut-out dirt at this level looked more gray and charcoal-like than the upper parts. Like fuel. I began to understand how mud could burn.

The water was less than a foot deep, just enough to soak Mark's tailored trousers and ruin his shoes. He tossed the chunks of peat off Arch's lower body. It took only a minute to uncover him.

I got out of the way as Neil stepped into the ditch next to Arch's head and grimaced as the cold water seeped into his fancy boots. Together, he and Mark got a secure hold on the actor.

"Ready?" Neil asked. "On three. One, two, three."

They lifted Arch with a grunt, moving him up to the bank. Then they stepped up and lifted him again.

I got in the middle and lent minor support as they did the bulk of the work, carrying him up the few mud steps to the grass and the ATV. They laid him across the flat rack on the back.

Mark whipped off his tux jacket and draped it over Arch's torso. But the lower half of the star's legs dangled off the side, and Arch screamed as he settled and the knife in his thigh shifted.

"Sorry!" I told him. Poor Arch.

"I deserve it," he groaned.

What?

Chapter Thirty-Three

Diana marched Elsie up the slope as I tried to figure out what Arch meant. He deserved it? He deserved almost dying thanks to a madwoman?

"I'll go with her and make sure our culprit doesn't get away." Mark was already hiking after Diana and her wriggling charge, a happy Victoria running circles around him. "You and Pepper drive Arch up."

"You're all part of the problem!" Elsie screeched. "Disco drunks and stupid tourists!"

"I'm a botanist!" Diana scolded her.

"And we're mixologists!" I called, climbing into the passenger seat so I could turn around and hold on to Arch and make sure he didn't roll off.

I was desperate to ask Arch more questions, but I waited till Neil drove us up to the small gravel parking area. He got out to help Diana and Mark and make sure Elsie was secured as Albert ran after Victoria with the leash.

I focused on Arch. "What did you mean back there? That you deserved it?"

"I wish I could've told Rory I was sorry. I didn't mean for any of this to happen."

"You'll tell him yourself," I assured him.

"In heaven, you mean?" Arch blinked those pretty green eyes at me.

"No, silly. When you get back to Kirkwall."

He stared at me, uncomprehending, just as Elsie screeched again. "Look at that slut, trying to get into his pants when he's dying. You're all the same! Idiots! Animals!"

"*Excuse* me?" I shouted, glancing over to where Neil and Mark had plopped Elsie down on an overturned crate while Diana looked on, her arms crossed. No one called me a slut and got away with it. Unless role-play was involved.

Elsie hollered back, "You're with this dungeon master in the kinky leather kilt, aren't you?"

Neil grunted, obviously torn between protesting and acknowledging that a whip would make his outfit complete.

"What's this?" Mark had pulled something from Elsie's jacket pocket. "A rock?"

Neil took a look. "You'd better save that for the police. I think there's blood on it. It looks like one of those Neolithic stone axes she was talking about."

"Ew." Mark cringed and set it on the gravel.

"That's mine!" Elsie screeched. "I found it!"

"From the Ness of Brodgar?" Neil asked.

Elsie said nothing.

"So you've stolen from an archaeological site, too, have you?" Diana said with disgust.

Elsie scowled at her. "It means more to me than it would to some museum. And I used it to slay the enemy. Or I thought I did." So this was what she used to hit Arch. "At least I killed the other one!" Elsie cackled.

"Does she mean Rory?" Arch croaked at me. "But I thought Lark did it!"

"Why would you think that?" I asked him.

"Because I asked her to harass him, make him think twice about coming back to the show. I was so petty. Such a fool." Tears leaked from Arch's eyes. "My best friend! He was doing so well, getting all these roles and deals. He got more fan mail than I did. Did you know that? I thought it might be better if he moved on. The show is *Sleekit Sim*. Sim! I'm Sim!"

Ugh. Arch was that selfish? "Are you telling me you asked Lark to push him over a cliff?"

"No! Oh God, no. I never intended for that to happen!"

"Rory's alive," Neil told Elsie. "You failed."

"He can't be." Elsie's voice cracked. "I pushed him over the cliff! Nobody could find him!"

Arch grabbed my hand and searched my face. "He's alive?"

"Yes," I said.

"Thank God." He let out a sob, then closed his eyes, breathing heavily, tears streaming down the sides of his face as he lay there.

"The letters." I gripped his hand more tightly, and he winced. "Did you have Lark write letters? The one in your room?"

He opened his eyes, luminous eyes full of regret, and looked at me. "Yes. That one you found, I wrote it out and had her copy it. I meant to throw it away. I had her write more than one, some signed, some not. I shared them with Rory. You know, to rattle him a bit. I—I'm embarrassed. I'm an idiot. How can I face him?"

How indeed? But I needed to be sure about the letters. "Were any of your notes signed with runes?"

"Nae." Arch's brow creased. "Though she used a tidy little heart with wings sometimes, something she drew on letters to me even before we got together. A play on her name, you see."

I thought about the letter I'd found and where I'd found it. "You had Lark in your room?"

His mouth briefly quirked into a smile. "On occasion. She's in love with me. Aren't you?"

I shook my head at him. Once, I was in lust with him, but so were most of the women who watched *Sleekit Sim* and some of the men, too. "No, Arch. But I hope you heal quickly. I want you to tell Rory yourself."

The smile disappeared. "I'm not going to die, then?"

"Probably not." The sound of sirens tickled my ear. Rescue was coming. "What about Wren?"

"Ha. Poor dear. Didn't suspect a thing."

In my opinion, Wren had a narrow escape. "What do you know about the Paintball Piper?"

"Lark told me later she'd hired her brother Jay to pull that stunt. He needed money, and of course I'd already given her money. I didn't know she'd get so creative when I asked her to make Rory uncomfortable. And then when I thought she'd pushed Rory to his death—oh God. I didn't want anything else to do with her. I never thought she'd go so far. But she didn't, did she? Are you sure he's alive?"

"He's definitely alive."

"Good. Good." He closed his eyes again. "I'm so puggled, Pepper."

Flashing lights and the wail of sirens heralded the approach of the police and ambulance, and he didn't say anything else as the professionals swarmed the scene and took over.

I stepped away from him and watched Elsie being stuffed into a police car. A gloved officer dropped the stone axe into an evidence bag. I looked down at my dress. A few of the mirrored discs hung loose, and they and my whole body were a filthy mess. The platform shoes had stayed on, but they were disgusting. And I didn't smell great either.

Neil walked over to me. "You two were having quite the chat. How is he?"

"He's a very, very bad boy," I said.

ON OUR WAY back to Kirkwall in the minibus, after the police questioned us at the scene, I told the others what Arch had told me. Including details I didn't think the police needed to know.

"And now I suppose the party's over," Mark said with a touch of regret.

"Literally or figuratively? I'm sure today's Aramach party is over," said Diana, who sat across the aisle from him, Victoria back in her lap.

Neil sat next to me, behind Mark. "We might get there just as it ends." He looked at his old-school watch, then tapped it in frustration.

"Did it get wet?" I asked.

"It's tough. Hopefully I can get it working again." Neil pulled his phone out of his sporran and looked at the time. "Maybe we'll get there in time for cleanup."

"I'm sure Seamus will want us arriving at his party like this." I pointed to my disintegrating dress.

"I think he'll be pleased to see you since the face of his brand survived the evening," Mark noted.

"Did anyone let him know?" I asked.

"I'll text him." Neil got to tapping on his phone. "I'll tell him they've taken Arch to Balfour Hospital to be checked out."

We rolled up in front of the town hall to see happy party-goers exiting. For Seamus's sake, I hoped they were unaware of the crisis. Surely Rory's surprise appearance had sated their hunger for gossip, at least for now.

We all stepped out, catching a few curious looks from departing guests. Neil and I debated whether we should go in, given our bedraggled state.

Mark turned to Diana, who now had Victoria on a leash. "Want to go back to the hotel?"

"Yes, please. I want to go to my room and throw myself into a hot shower."

Mark showed a dimple but didn't take up the obvious opportunity for one of his terrible jokes. Instead he turned to Neil and me. "Give Albert a shout when you're done here, and he'll give you all a ride as well. Perhaps we can meet for dinner?"

"Sounds good to me," Neil said.

"I'm ravenous," Diana added.

I smiled at her. "I can see why, after everything you did out there. You ever arrest anyone before?"

She chuckled. "No, but I rather liked it."

"You like tying people up." Mark lifted an eyebrow. "Noted."

I laughed. *There* it was. "Thanks for your help, Mark. You're always there when we need you."

"My life would be terribly dull otherwise."

Alastair emerged from the hall, looked us over and sniffed. "Good God. Are there mud baths around here I don't know about?"

"More like a peat bath," I said.

He rolled his eyes and turned to Mark. "May we leave this beastly event now?"

"All aboard." Mark gestured to the minibus, and Alastair climbed right in. Then Mark threw us a salute and followed with Diana and Victoria. Albert waved and pulled away from the curb.

"Pepper?" A weak voice called my name.

I looked around. "Who is that?"

Neil also looked, his eyes stopping at the cathedral across the street. "What in the—"

I looked in the same direction and spotted a bearded figure bound to the stone cross on the cathedral grounds, thanks to what appeared to be several rolls' worth of plastic wrap.

"Pepper, can you get me off here?" Mr. Mixy called.

At this moment, Blair Rendall emerged from the party venue, followed our gaze to the cross, and started laughing.

"Do you know what this is about?" I asked her.

She got control of herself, then pointed. "That's Mr. Mixy, isn't it? It seems he's been subject to a blackening. He doesn't have a fiancée around here, does he?"

"Not to my knowledge." I crossed the street, and Neil and Blair followed. "What's a blackening?"

"Oh, a local tradition," Blair said. "A bride or groom is covered in treacle and flour and eggs and other disgusting things, paraded around town in the back of a truck, and often bound to the market cross or a signpost. Some think the noise wards off the evil spirits. It's usually an entertaining and drunken affair. How did you end up here, Mr. Mixy?"

Mr. Mixy's hair and face and beard were smeared in something sticky and brown, accented by flaky bits and swaths of other colors. Flour? Eggshells? Oats? He smelled sweet and sour, like Chinese food gone bad.

"I was flirting with this woman at the party, and then this guy shows up and gets really mad and says it's his fiancée,"

Stephan said. "He dragged me outside and I was pretty sure he was going to hit me, but his friends turned up in a truck and said it's time for the blackening, so he makes me get into the back of the truck with all of them. His friends got him and his fiancée dirty, and he talked them into dousing me with even more of the gross stuff before we drove around town in the back of the truck, making noise and drinking and blowing whistles. They were singing and everything. It was fun. And then they came back here and tied me to the post. I thought there'd be a party after, but I've been stuck up here for like an hour. My crew got some shots and left." He seemed to notice our appearance for the first time. "Were you in a blackening too? I like that dress." He grinned at me. His teeth were white through all that muck.

I rolled my eyes. "It's a long story."

Blair chuckled. "Rather unusual to tie him up and not the bride or groom."

"That's Mr. Mixy," I said. "Making friends wherever he goes. Should we cut him down?"

She shrugged. "They'll probably come for him eventually."

I cocked my head at her. "May I ask you something?"

"As long as it's not about Arch. You found him, I hear?"

"That's right," Neil said.

"Was he hurt?" Blair asked. "Rory and Izara ran off to see him at the hospital."

I blinked. That was fast. "He'll be OK, I think." And with luck he'd tell Rory everything. I stepped away from Mr. Mixy, and she and Neil followed. "I'm curious about something. Freya told us how upset Callum was with Seamus when Seamus tried to be your childhood sweetheart, but she wasn't clear about why. And Callum has a picture of you and your father on his office wall. He seems to have some kind of special concern for you. I wondered what it was. I feel like maybe you didn't tell us everything the last time we spoke. "

Blair stepped closer, speaking quietly. "You seem like an all right sort," she said. "May I trust to your discretion? Seamus doesn't need to know this."

More discretion. I had to work on that. I nodded, and Neil said, "Of course."

"When my da died, I learned he wasn't my biological father. Callum is."

My mouth dropped open.

She wore the smile of someone who was at peace with who she was. "My parents couldn't have children. Specifically, the father who raised me could not. And Callum and my da were good friends. They came to an arrangement. I found out in a letter from my da that was bundled with his will, along with the legal documents. As part of the arrangement, I was never to have a stake in Cliffstone distillery. Callum wanted that for his son. I think he cares for me in an abstract way, but he couldn't imagine handing Cliffstone over to a girl, even if she was his blood and knew more about making scotch than his son will ever know." She shrugged. "But I'm making whisky anyway, aren't I? And it's damn fine whisky. Ah, here's my ride."

A black Audi pulled up to the curb. Freya Dearness was driving.

"Good evening, bartenders. I see Seamus's party was a success." She laughed at our dishevelment.

"It went well," Blair told her. "Did you get my text about Rory?"

"I did. I'm so relieved," Freya said.

Blair shot us a grin. "Now to consort with the enemy." She climbed into Freya's car, and off they went.

Neil and I exchanged a look and headed back across the street to help our colleagues.

"Pepper?" Mr. Mixy called out. "You're coming back, aren't you?"

Chapter Thirty-Four

After the bartenders stopped laughing, they let Neil and I help with the last of the cleanup—though we were probably dirtier than anything on the bar. Seamus was happy with how things turned out anyway.

Later, showered and dressed anew in jeans and a lichen-green sweater to match my eyes, my glasses rinsed and dried, I was enjoying an excellent pub dinner in Kirkwall with my friends.

I had the fish and chips. Neil was working on something they called Highland Chicken, which was stuffed with haggis and wrapped in bacon, served with mashed potatoes and a whisky sauce.

I had a whisky when we first got a table, but I'd switched to water so I could make it to sunset without falling asleep.

"Do you think we'll actually see the sunset tonight?" I asked no one in particular. It was our last chance to see the sun go down in Orkney.

"The weather is perfect," Diana said over her salmon entree. "I would think so."

Mark had left Victoria snoozing at the hotel. Also at the table were Alastair, Albert, Barclay, Luke, Melody, and Nigel and Lottie Dashwood, who intended to stay a few days and play tourist.

"What do you recommend we see while we're here? I've never been to Orkney," Lottie asked in her crisp English accent.

"Stay away from the cliffs," I said, and there was a flurry of uncomfortable laughter.

"You can look at them. Just don't get too close," Neil suggested.

"Because of Rory?" Nigel asked in his mellow tones. "But he's all right, isn't he?"

"I'm just fine!" came a voice from across the room as Rory and Izara entered.

"How did they know we were here?" I whispered to Neil.

"Uh, they asked and I texted them," he replied.

We made room and added chairs for them. They ended up sitting next to Neil and me, since the end of the table was open by us. They ordered food, and as the chatter continued down the table, I turned to Rory.

"Did you see Arch?" I asked quietly.

"I did." He managed half a smile as he spun a glass of Cliffstone scotch on the table.

I needed to know more. "He talked to you then?"

Rory looked at me. "He did. I can't believe it, really."

"I think I can believe it," Izara said. "But I'm disappointed."

"He told me he was puggled," I said. "What does that mean?"

"Very tired," Rory replied.

Neil was kind as always. "Maybe he's been working too much."

"Are you suggesting exhaustion drove him mad?" Izara looked mad, too—the American definition of mad. "It's no excuse for what he did."

"Either way, I'm leaving the show," Rory said.

"But you're so successful!" It was my turn to be surprised.

"I told you I was thinking about it. I was thinking about it because I had a sense that Arch was uncomfortable and I wanted to preserve the friendship. And I have a lot of other opportunities right now anyway with the book and the film and the travel show and other offers. I'm more sad that our friendship might not survive this."

Izara put a hand on his arm. "He could've really hurt you."

"To be fair, he didn't push me over a cliff." Rory sipped his whisky. "But what a lot of foolishness. I like a good joke as much as the next fellow, but we could've just had a conversation."

"Maybe it's not too late to fix things," Neil said.

Rory shook his head. "I think it's too late for *Sleekit Sim*. I've already talked to my agent and the showrunner. They're going to find a way to write me off after a few episodes next season. I've thrown a spanner in the works, but my contract allows it, and they seemed to understand. I get the feeling this is going to be the last season anyway."

"And then Arch will lose his starring vehicle," I said. And all of his machinations would have earned him nothing but a near-death experience.

"He'll land on his feet," Rory replied. "At least his personal drama has eclipsed mine. The press won't care that I was missing for a couple of days."

A delicious thought occurred to me. "And they'll probably describe Elsie as a crazed fan. She'll hate that!"

"Perfect," he said. "Even if all of this blows over, I'm making a donation to the emergency services for the efforts they made to try to save me."

"How's Arch doing?" Neil asked.

Izara replied. "He'll be all right. They're keeping him overnight and pumping him full of antibiotics, but they didn't even have to do surgery."

"Good," I said. As much trouble as Arch caused, I didn't want him to suffer. He was already suffering, thanks to his tomfoolery.

The chatter at the other end of the table caught my ear. "I'll be there for the opening," Mark was saying. "And I'll bring Diana and Alastair if they want to come."

"Really?" Barclay grinned. "That would be excellent. We still have a ton to do when we get home, though."

"We'll be open in a month," Melody said. "Almost all the inspections and licenses are wrapped up."

"Thank God," Neil said under his breath. He was an investor in the beachside craft cocktail bar that Barclay and Melody were opening together.

Melody had ditched her job at a lame hotel beach bar and Barclay had left his gig as manager and chief bartender at a downtown club. My friends would still work with the Bohemia Bartenders, but they'd teamed up to create their dream bar. I couldn't wait for it to open.

"Maybe we'll come as well," Lottie said. "I love Florida. We could write you up in the blog, add details about the Bohemia bar scene, do some videos."

"Now we're talking!" Barclay lifted his glass to her and Nigel.

Luke, who worked for Neil at The Junction Box, looked anxious. "Will we still be able to hang out?"

"Of course," Barclay said.

"And you'd better come to our bar." Melody gave him what I thought was more than a casual glance.

Luke returned a foxy smile. "If Neil ever lets me off work, I will."

"Hey!" Neil said as the others chuckled.

"Hey, Rory," I said as our friends went off on another tangent.

"Aye, Pepper," he replied, impish.

"I still don't understand why you didn't tell Izara you wanted to loop me in when you were hiding after your fall."

His chin wiggled for a second. Then he looked at her. "Honestly, mo leannan, you weren't yourself. It's true I didn't want you to have to keep lying to people, but I had a moment of doubt. I'm sorry."

Izara's eyes widened. "I—I don't know what you mean. But I did wonder if there was something you wanted to tell me about Freya."

His brow furrowed. "Not Freya Dearness? We grew up together. She's like a sister to me. You weren't jealous, were you?"

"Maybe I was, a little. But I don't see how you could think I'd throw you off a cliff."

"I didn't! I mean, not really. But you did seem a little bit upset with me."

She huffed. "It seems to me you need to follow your own advice and have straightforward conversations with the people close to you, if you want to avoid more complications in your life. All right, I might have been a little, shall we say, ruffled? But if I'm really upset with you, you'll know it."

He reached over and squeezed her hand. "You're too good for me."

"That's why you need me. I'm going to leave Aramach to be your publicist."

"You are?" I exclaimed.

"This thing with Arch was the last straw," Izara said. "I'm fond of Seamus, but I'm ready to move on. And I miss London."

"You're hired." Rory grinned, leaned in and kissed her on the lips.

All conversation stopped at the table for half a second, and then it picked up where it left off. I'd forgotten that Neil and I had been the only ones privy to their relationship.

We finished our dinner and headed out into the golden hour, the few clouds streaks of purple in a blushing sky.

"How long until sunset?" I asked.

"Another half hour, maybe?" Neil said.

"Seriously?" It was almost ten. We'd had a late supper, and it had been a really long day.

Rory walked hand in hand with Izara. "Oh, sunsets last for hours here in summertime. It's glorious."

"Personally, I'd love to see the Northern Lights here," Izara said.

"Maybe we'll come back at Christmas," he suggested. They stopped and looked out over the marina.

Strung out in twos and threes, the rest of our party moved on down the curving road that gave us a perfect view of the west and the lowering sun.

Ferries and sailboats stretched across the vista, masts poking up and mirrored in the bay. The water turned fiery orange like the sky as the sun slid closer to the horizon. In the distance, low, dusky blue hills provided an inviting backdrop.

"I can't believe this is our last night in Scotland," I said.

"We should've stayed longer," Neil agreed. "But we have work. And Barclay and Melody have to get cracking on their bar."

"At least we can get in one more Scottish breakfast."

He chuckled. "And I'll have time in the morning to buy a case of scotch to bring back to my grandfather."

"He'll love that!" I leaned into him. "You still haven't gotten that tattoo."

"I've been too busy rescuing fair maidens from cliffs."

"Ha ha. Your time will come."

I became aware of a filthy creature sitting on a bench on the roadside.

"Hey, Pepper!" the creature said.

I squinted at it. "Oh! Stephan. They untied you, then?"

Mr. Mixy stood, his previously silver kilt and harlequin shirt now a swirl of grime. "A storekeeper took pity on me. They said I was scaring away the customers."

Neil snorted, and a corner of my mouth lifted.

"I've learned a lot from this trip," Mr. Mixy said. "I think I want to be a liquor spokesman just like Arch. But for something more accessible, you know? Something a lot of people drink."

"Vodka," I said dryly.

"Maybe. Maybe something else." He wore a sly smile, at least as much of it as I could see through the dirt. "I'm talking to some people now. And guess what? Production starts on my biopic this fall."

Neil and I stopped walking. "Your biopic?" Neil asked.

"I just got the call. A production company picked up the rights to my memoir, and we're making it into a movie."

"We?" I asked him.

"I'm a co-producer," Mr. Mixy said proudly. He waggled his eyebrows at me. "Stay tuned." Then he walked off into the sunset. Well, not actually into the sunset, because that would've meant he jumped into the harbor. Which would have been just fine with me.

"What did he mean by that?" Neil asked. "Is his movie going to involve you in some way?"

"I don't know. That's what I'm afraid of."

"Well, it can't be scarier than you hanging off a cliff. Now *that* scared me." He turned toward me and wrapped his arms around me, handsome and warm in his blue sweater, his gray eyes earnest.

"I didn't mean to scare you." I slipped my arms around his waist and looked up at him. "Can I make it up to you?"

"You can kiss me while the sun sets."

"But Rory said it'll be sunset for hours!"

"I'm counting on it." Neil gave me a slow, sultry smile. And my heart fluttered like a Small Tortoiseshell butterfly.

What's Next

**Don't miss *Villainy in Violette*,
Book 9 in the Bohemia Bartenders Mysteries, as
Pepper and her friends must solve a murder that hits
way too close to home!**

Want to get notified when the next book comes out?
Subscribe to my fun, occasional newsletter
at LucyLakestone.com/signup —
and get a free Bohemia Bartenders story —
or follow me on BookBub or Goodreads.

I also have a Facebook group where we hang out and chat
about life and books — please join us in Lucy's Lounge
(answer the questions to get in).
And you can always find me at LucyLakestone.com.

Read on for a look behind the scenes in the
acknowledgments and a cocktail recipe!

Acknowledgments

Orkney is a magical place, with layers of history everywhere and absolutely breathtaking landscapes. I skirted along its cliffs at the Brough of Birsay and Yesnaby, stepped around and through stone circles, traipsed amid castle ruins and gaped at St. Magnus Cathedral.

I have striven to be accurate in my depiction of these places, though I might have tweaked reality in the service of the story. I was licked by a hairy coo in the Highlands, for instance, but I really liked the idea of seeing the kye in Orkney as well.

I was fortunate to visit Orkney (as well as Edinburgh) in the summer of 2023 and see many, if not all, of the historic sites. I didn't tour the Ness of Brodgar, one of the Neolithic sites referenced in the novel, which has only very recently been closed after many years of excavation. Reburied, its remaining ruins have a chance to survive for another five thousand years.

South transept of St. Magnus Cathedral in Kirkwall in Scotland's Orkney Islands

The Ness might have been open when the Bohemia Bartenders visited Scotland, but it's best not to think too much about the timeline of these mysteries, which are based on real dates but occur in an alternate reality free of pandemics and other disasters. The moon phases are accurate to my timeline (the crescent moon is mostly invisible in this novel and setting, where there is not much true night in the summer anyway). The tides occur at logical intervals but might not actually match the June of this timeline. Hey, it's a novel.

Approaching the crossing to the Brough of Birsay at low tide

We couldn't have seen what we saw without the hospitality of Magnus and Ingrid Rendall. Magnus drove us and our friends (including their cousin Karen Temme and her husband, Bill) all around the sites, so we often saw stone circles and ruins at interesting hours when they weren't thronged by tourists. Magnus was more than generous and even gave us a fantastic tour of Ortak jewelers, where he uses symbols of

Orkney like the Maeshowe dragon in his designs. The Magnus in the book is not this Magnus, but I did borrow his name.

Karen is my longtime friend, and I always wanted to visit the place she so often visited and talked about, the place where her mother grew up. Once I got there, I found myself having fantasies of living under those big skies. At least, while writing this book, I got to revisit Orkney through fiction.

It's really thanks to Karen that I thought to go to Orkney at all. I owe her for that and for her knowledge of the islands and the lingo. When I had odd questions about caves and such, Karen would run them through her cousins and give me more points of research to pursue. (Thanks again, Ingrid.)

Puffins at the Brough of Birsay

Sometimes the stories we heard on the islands were distant echoes or trans-formations of what the historians say. In a place like Orkney, history has a lot of crossover with myth and legend.

For background on this book, I read literature I picked up in Scotland and documents I found online about geography, history and archaeology. I also dug into a couple of books about scotch, including the excellent *Scotch Whisky: A Liquid History* by Charles MacLean. And I read much of *The New History of Orkney* by William P.L. Thomson. If you want to get deep into the islands' history, this covers it all.

Regarding scotch, there are multiple distilleries in Orkney, including Highland Park, which we very much enjoyed visiting. But none of the distilleries in *Smoked by Scotch* are real. Neither are the bars and restaurants, even if they might share charac-teristics with real ones. The exception is Panda & Sons in Edinburgh, which is real and wonderful.

As for the cocktails, I wanted to feature a fruit that could be found in Scotland in late June. Gooseberries fit the bill for Neil's garnish. There are several varieties. But as they aren't so easy to get, especially in Florida, my recipe uses jam and not fresh berries.

Some crazy things happen in this book, but I tried to make them exist within the realm of possibility. There really are fogs that thick, for instance.

I am grateful to my friend and fellow storm chaser George Kourounis, who climbs into volcanoes for fun, for his tips on rock climbing in a crisis. Any inaccuracies are mine.

A shout-out to The Office and BFA: Thank you. I really need your dose of daily sanity in an insane world. Speaking of which, I am grateful for the positive thinking of my writing and storm chasing buddy Alethea Kontis when I have trouble dredging up the sparkle. And to Naomi: Our chats over coffee are priceless.

Thanks again to Karen for an early read of the book and scanning my Scottish slang, and to Maria Geraci for her generous and helpful read of the manuscript.

As always, I'm hugely grateful to editor Holly Martin for caring about the words so much and pointing out where I careen off the road.

To my travel companion, house mixologist and fellow cocktailian George Jenkins, I offer all the thanks for all the things. Especially since he prefers a boat to planes, trains and automobiles.

And thank you, dear reader, for sticking with this series and for the notes and comments that tell me you enjoy hanging out with the bartenders as much as I do. Cheers.

Cocktail Recipe

THE TARTAN GOOSE

I wanted the Bohemia Bartenders' signature cocktail in *Smoked by Scotch* to have a touch of Scotland other than, obviously, the scotch whisky. I drilled down to gooseberries, which are grown in Scotland and available in June. They might not be the easiest fruits to find, but hey, this bar team can make it happen! While Neil skewers fresh berries for a garnish, the cocktail itself uses more readily available gooseberry jam. You can always garnish your drink with a lemon twist, as I did.

In keeping with the setting of the book, I used Orkney's Highland Park Single Malt 12. Its subtle smokiness provides a counterpoint to the mellow sweetness of the jam and honey, with the lemon juice adding a bright note.

The gooseberry jam (at least the one I used, Tiptree Green Gooseberry Preserve, which is not green) is chunky, and the more aggressive you are about incorporating it before the shake, the jammier your drink. I found a lighter hand made for a very pleasing, balanced cocktail. Experiment to see what works for you.

Why Teapot Bitters? The flavor works well with the cocktail, and if my characters aren't drinking gin or scotch in this book, they're drinking tea! I suggest measuring the drops into a bar spoon first so you don't overpour.

2 1/2 ounces gently smoky scotch whisky
2 tablespoons gooseberry jam
1/2 ounce lemon juice
1/2 tablespoon honey
2 drops Dr. Adam Elmegirab's Teapot Bitters
Garnish: lemon twist, unless fresh gooseberries are available

Measure scotch, jam, lemon juice, honey and bitters into a cocktail tin. Stir first to incorporate the more viscous ingredients, but don't go crazy trying to smooth out all the jam chunks. Add ice and shake well till chilled.

Using a Hawthorne strainer, strain into a small rocks glass or a pretty jam jar. This will filter out unwanted chunks of jam. Garnish with a lemon twist unless you have fresh gooseberries on hand.

The **BOHEMIA BEACH** Series

Award-winning hot contemporary romance

In a beautiful small city on Florida's east coast, artists meet, create, laugh and love. Where restless hearts are fueled by secrets and imagination, romance is impossible to resist. Welcome to the seductive tropical escape that's home to drama, humor and lots of heat – Bohemia Beach.

BOHEMIA BEACH

BOHEMIA LIGHT

BOHEMIA BLUES

BOHEMIA HEAT

BOHEMIA NIGHTS

BACK TO BOHEMIA - *story free to subscribers*

BOHEMIA BELLS

BOHEMIA CHILLS

Bohemia Beach Series Boxed Sets:

Books 1-3 | Books 4-7

The **STORM SEEKERS SERIES**

Writing as Chris Kridler

FUNNEL VISION

TORNADO PINBALL

ZAP BANG

Storm Seekers Series Boxed Set: Books 1-3

About the Author

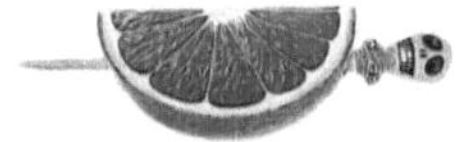

Lucy Lakestone writes books that offer fun escapes, whether they're humorous mysteries, hot romances or storm-chasing adventures (as Chris Kridler). She loves sipping a classic cocktail and chasing tornadoes, but not at the same time. An award-winning author and photographer, she's also told stories as a journalist and video producer. She lives on Florida's Space Coast, which inspires many of the colorful settings in her books.

Learn more at LucyLakestone.com

facebook.com/lucylakestone

instagram.com/mslucylakestone

amazon.com/Lucy-Lakestone

bookbub.com/authors/lucy-lakestone

goodreads.com/lucylakestone

bsky.app/profile/lucylakestone.bsky.social

pinterest.com/lucylakestone

threads.net/@mslucylakestone

youtube.com/@lucylakestone